A SUMMER WEDDING AT THE COTSWOLDS CANDY STORE

HANNAH LYNN

First published in Great Britain in 2024 by Boldwood Books Ltd.

Cover Design by Alexandra Allden

Cover photography: Shutterstock

A CIP catalogue record for this book is available from the British Library.

Paperback ISBN 978-1-83603-167-3

Harback ISBN 978-1-83603-166-6

Ebook ISBN 978-1-83603-168-0

Kindle ISBN 978-1-83603-169-7

Digital audio download ISBN 978-1-83603-165-9

Boldwood Books Ltd
23 Bowerdean Street
London SW6 3TN
www.boldwoodbooks.com

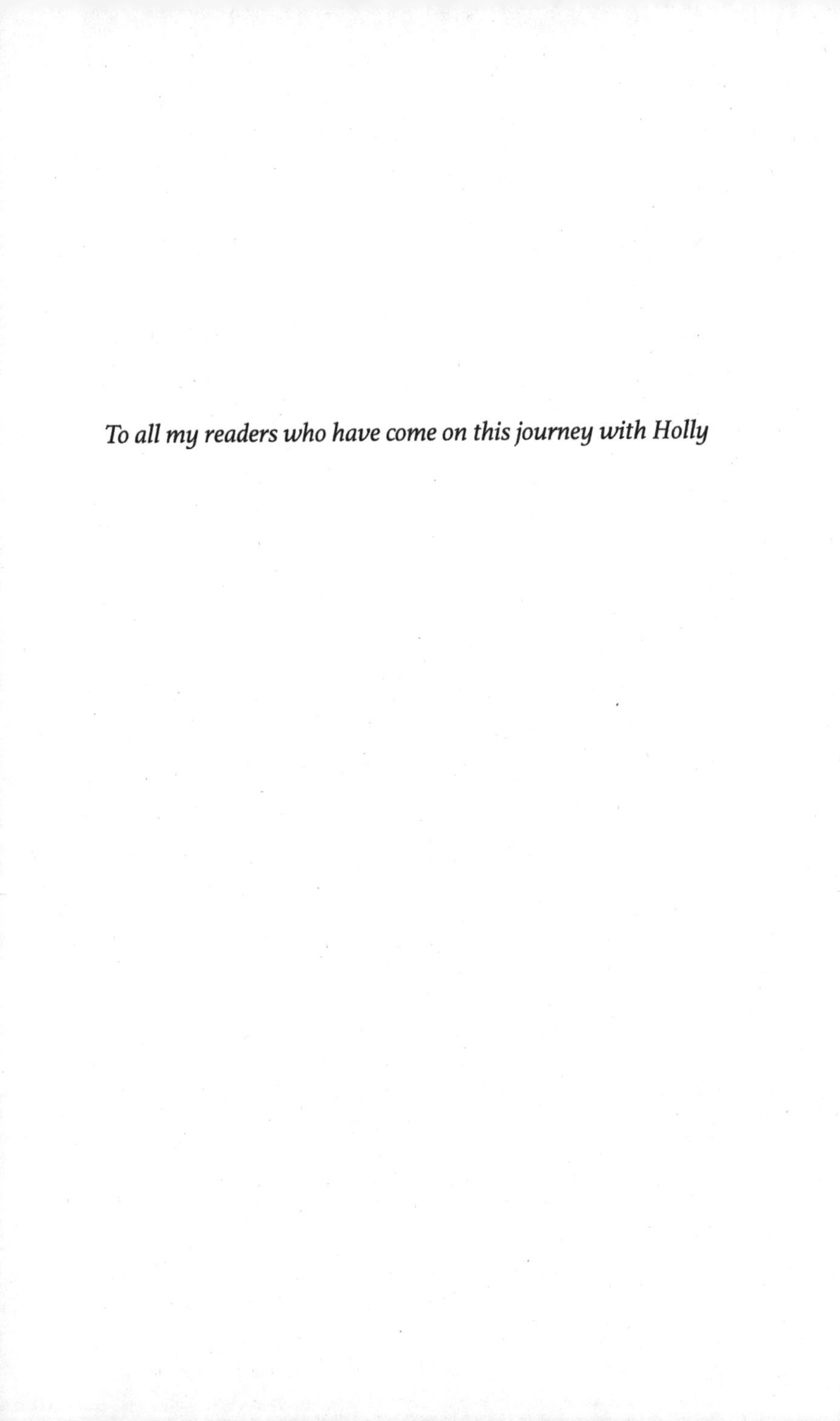

To all my readers who have come on this journey with Holly

1

Holly took a step back and looked at the sweet platter in front of her. It was certainly impressive, with a whole host of customer favourites from peppermint patties to sherbet lemons and coconut mushrooms, all laid out meticulously on the silver tray. It looked good. But good wasn't what she was after. She wanted perfection. With a slight groan, she picked up a handful of jellybeans before letting out a deep sigh.

'I want to get all her favourites in,' she said to Caroline, who was standing beside her weighing out a bag of cherry lips for one of their regulars. 'But I feel like there needs to be a colour theme, right? It's a wedding. There has to be a theme. But how can there be when she likes things like rosy apples, rhubarb and custard and coconut teacakes? It all looks so muddled.'

'Can muddled be the colour theme?' Caroline suggested, but Holly didn't reply; after all, there was no sensible answer she could give. Besides, her mouth was currently full of jellybeans.

In just over two weeks, one of her best friends, Jamie was going to be tying the knot with Fin. Everything was arranged, with a beautiful venue in the Cotswolds that sorted everything, from the food to the music and even the accommodation to ensure the entire day was as stress-free as possible. But there was one little extra that Jamie wanted. One that only Holly could provide. Sweets. Platters on all the tables.

Holly must have done at least a hundred sweet party platters since she took over Just One More, the picture-perfect sweet shop in the heart of the Cotswolds. But this one was different. This one had to be 100 per cent perfect. But with no directions from Jamie other than, 'I trust you to do something awesome,' Holly was panicking. She had tried three set-ups already, but none of them looked right. As the till opened and closed, and the customer trundled off chewing their cherry lips, Caroline sidled up next to Holly and studied the platter.

'Do you know how many tables there are to be at the wedding?' she asked.

Holly thought about it. Jamie and Fin had been talking about the wedding non-stop since they'd arrived back from France three weeks before, which wasn't surprising, given how much there was to arrange. While the venue dealt with most of the stress, Fin and Jamie still had plenty to busy themselves with. Over a dozen members of Fin's family were flying in from America, and another ten or so of his friends were coming in from various other places in the world. The entire wedding would host nearly a hundred people, so while Holly wasn't exactly sure how many tables there were, it was going to be quite a few.

'Probably about fifteen,' she said, going back to the shelves and staring at the glass jars.

'Well, why not make different themed ones then?' Caroline said. 'You can have a red table, a green table, a chocolate table, a fudge table.'

Holly thought about it. 'But what about if people don't like the sweets that are on their table? What if someone who hates chocolate is on the chocolate table?'

'Well, for starters, if they don't like chocolate, they're insane and I'm not sure why Jamie would have invited them to her wedding in the first place,' Caroline said unhelpfully. 'But really, it's not like anyone is going to be sitting in the same place the entire night. This is Jamie and Fin's wedding, remember? Everyone is going to be up, moving around, dancing, socialising. Having different sweets in different places might be good. I mean, ask Jamie, but I think it's a great idea.'

Holly pondered the suggestion a little longer. It would definitely be easier to make the trays look attractive like that. She could do a couple of rainbow ones too, using the different colours of bonbons. They were always a hit at children's birthday parties, and there were several children attending.

'You're right. That'll work. I'll put some ideas together and run them past Jamie as soon as I get a chance. Though it might have to wait for a day or two.'

'Oh really,' Caroline said, a smirk twisting on her lips as she looked at Holly. 'Why's that? Do you have something important going on?'

She was winding her up, of course. Caroline was fully aware why Holly was going to be occupied for the next twenty-four hours and Holly couldn't help but feel embarrassed. It was obviously a sign she'd talked about it way too much. She opened her mouth, ready to give Caroline a sarcastic reply, but before she could respond, her phone rang. She frowned at the unknown number before answering.

'Now?' she said down the line. 'Yes, no, that's fine, I'll just be five minutes, is that okay?'

A second later, she hung up and looked at Caroline.

'I'm really sorry, I've got to head home.'

Caroline was back across the shop, straightening the jars.

'It's fine, I thought you'd have left by now anyway. Don't you have stuff to sort out for tonight?'

A series of butterflies took hold inside of Holly. 'Probably,' she said. 'But by the sounds of it, I've got something else to deal with first.'

2

Back at home, Holly was struggling. So far, she'd tried moving her armchair, Hope's playpen and the dining room table and chairs, but there was just not enough room in her tiny little cottage. She'd known when she'd moved into her and Hope's first home on their own that it would be small. Bourton-on-the-Water in the Cotswolds may have had some lovely big manor houses, but they were a long way out of her budget. To be fair, the only reason she could afford the cottage was because the landlord seemed oblivious to modern-day rental rates and massively undercharged her. Still, the size of her home had never been that much of an issue. Until now.

She stepped back and looked from her mantlepiece to the dining-room table and then to the kitchen counter before she finally let out a sigh of defeat. With a sad groan, she called Jamie.

'Do you want a bunch of flowers?' she said the moment she picked up.

The phone call at the shop had been from a delivery company, saying they had a bunch of flowers waiting for her at the cottage and she needed to sign for them. A couple of weeks ago, Holly would never have expected to receive bunches of flowers delivered to her door, and certainly not the type that were so large, they dominated her entire home, but recently it had become a familiar occurrence.

'A really big bunch of flowers,' she added.

A slight pause followed the question. 'That's not an offer I normally get at the start of a phone call, but sure,' Jamie said.

'Great, then can you come and get them? Now.'

'Holly? Is everything okay? You sound stressed.'

Rather than replying, Holly took a deep breath in, hoping the silence would be enough of an answer for Jamie to come over and get the flowers pronto.

Holly was stressed, but in her defence, she had a lot of things to be stressed about. In two hours, she was going to see her boyfriend Evan, who she hadn't seen since she left the south of France over three weeks ago, the holiday where they'd first met. It was safe to say this was going to be a flying visit. In less than twenty-four hours, he'd be gone again. Back to London to prepare for another trip abroad. But it wasn't seeing Evan that was worrying her. No, she was looking forward to that. What was worrying her was the fact that they were meeting at her dad's sixtieth birthday party.

Taking another deep breath in, she tried to quench the torrent of nerves that had been plaguing her for days.

It wasn't that she didn't want Evan to meet her family. She did. Especially Hope. But she had wanted to do it gradually. Not to mention getting a little time to see him on her own first.

Now, Evan's first visit was going to involve meeting Hope, Holly's parents, her parents' neighbours, and their friends, not to mention every long-lost relative that showed up. The thought of it all was what was stressing her out, although not half as much as the flowers were.

'Hol? You still there? I asked how big this bunch of flowers is?'

The sound of Jamie's voice reminded Holly she was still on the phone.

'This one's too big for the house. I mean, the other two were big, but this one's enormous. I had to put it in the bath overnight, but Hope was grabbing handfuls of petals and shoving them down the toilet. It's a miracle she didn't block it, though I'm pretty sure she ate some too. Honestly, I can't cope with this.'

An unsympathetic chuckle travelled down the line.

'It must be so difficult to have a boyfriend who sends you enormous bunches of flowers,' Jamie said sarcastically. 'I can't imagine how terrible that is for you. So, are you looking forward to seeing him?'

Holly groaned, a full belly groan that made her heart ache.

'So much. I can't believe it's only been three weeks. Feels like it's been forever.'

'And the fact you've only actually spent four days together. I can't believe how smitten you two are.'

'Me neither,' Holly admitted.

It was ridiculous, Holly knew that. The last time she'd seen Evan was at the airport in London. While she had got a train back to the Cotswolds, he had hopped straight back on another plane, first class over to America, where he had been working ever since. Every day, they had talked on the telephone, or messaged if they couldn't manage that. But the time difference made it tricky. It felt like every time they'd tried to speak, one of them had been busy – Evan with meetings or business dinners and Holly with the shop or trying to clean up smashed avocado out of Hope's hair. To say she was excited about having him there in person was an understatement.

'So, what time is he getting here?' Jamie said, clearly keen to get as much information about Evan's imminent arrival as possible.

'He messaged about an hour ago to say he was through immigration, but apparently there's been some trouble with the luggage, so he's going to meet me at Mum and Dad's.'

'Well, good luck. Your parents will love him, you know they will.'

'I know, of course they will. Sorry, Jamie, I'd better go. I can hear Ben and Hope coming now. But you won't forget to come and get the flowers, will you?'

'No, I'll use my spare key if you're not in.'

'Thank you. Love you loads.'

'Love you too.'

There was a time in her life when Holly would have thought it ridiculous to tell her friends that she loved them. That, she thought, was the type of thing reserved for American teen dramas, or overly emotional, middle-class women who called everyone darling, with an extra-long 'a' sound. But the truth was, she loved her friends. They weren't like the friends she'd had in London, who she sent a message to when she needed someone to go for a drink or to visit a new exhibition with. Caroline and Jamie had been with her through thick and thin. Her friends here in Bourton were her family. And with Ben being Hope's father, he really was.

Having already heard them coming up the driveway, Holly swung open the door before they reached it, which resulted in a whoop of delight from Hope.

'Hey there, my little girl,' Holly said, as Hope stretched out her arms from her pram. After unbuckling the straps, Holly scooped Hope up into her arms and squeezed her tightly. 'Have you been a good girl for Daddy? Did you have fun?'

'Oh, we had lots of fun,' Ben said, with a dry tone that implied his afternoon had been anything but.

'What happened?' A flood of concern filled Holly. Schedule wise, she should really have had Hope, but Ben had been away in London earlier in the week and wanted a little more time with her.

'Oh, it was entirely my fault,' Ben said with a roll of his eyes. 'I thought that soft play would be calm, and she'd be content in the baby pit. Nope. Every time I glanced at my phone, or tried to strike up a conversation with a dad next to me, she'd bolt off into the grown-up kids' part. Do you know how quickly our child can crawl?'

'Oh, I know,' Holly said. She had only turned her back on her for thirty seconds to grab a clean top that morning when Hope had raced off to the bathroom to shove the flowers down the toilet bowl.

'And climb?' Ben continued. 'She climbed up a set of steps into a trampoline. A trampoline! Do you know how hard it is to get a small child off a trampoline? Every time I took a step towards her, she bounced into the air. Of course, she found it hysterical.'

Holly had to laugh. She wouldn't have done if it had been her in the situation, but Hope had come back in one piece with no noticeable bumps and bruises, and that was what mattered.

'I don't know if it's going to be better or worse when she's walking,' Ben said, as he pulled a changing bag off his shoulder and dropped it in the doorway.

'Worse, definitely worse,' Holly said with certainty. 'That's when she can fall over and really hurt herself. Nope, I'm happy with fast crawling.' Switching Hope onto one side so that she could sit on her hip, Holly leaned down and picked up the changing bag. 'Well, I'm glad Hope had a good time. And I'm sure she's going to get lots of fuss this evening. Talking of which, I'd better get her ready for Grandad's birthday party. Mum wanted me to be there early to help get things ready.'

Ben smiled.

'Sure. Well, I won't keep you. And let me know if you need me to bring anything. Drinks or nibbles or anything. Georgia and I are really looking forward to it.'

Holly tipped her head to the side, not sure she had heard him properly.

'You and Georgia?' she repeated. 'You're coming to Dad's party?'

It was Ben's turn to look confused as a frown line appeared between his brows. 'I thought your mum would have mentioned it. She invited us to come. You know, as part of the family.'

3

Holly didn't know why she was surprised. Of course this was something her mother would do. Not maliciously. No, Wendy didn't have a malicious bone in her body, but Holly and Ben still got on well, and co-parented Hope with such ease that Wendy had obviously decided that Holly wanted him invited to all family events. And now Ben and Georgia were a thing, the invitations clearly extended to her too. Maybe it wouldn't have been so bad now and then, but this was a family event – and Evan was attending. Suddenly, Holly's stress reached a whole new level.

'You didn't know?' Ben said apologetically. 'It's fine. We don't need to come. It's not a problem.'

'Of course you need to,' Holly said. 'Mum will never forgive me if you don't. And there's nothing to apologise for. It's not your fault. No, you have to come. It'll be nice. It'll be nice for me to see Georgina again.'

'Georgia,' Ben corrected.

'Yes, sorry. I know. I know that. It will be lovely to see Georgia again. That's what I meant.'

Holly tried to sound as genuine as she could. She really didn't have a problem with Ben dating Georgia, but there was something about having another woman in Hope's life. That was where the jealousy struck. It was ridiculous and Holly knew it. Hope was her baby girl and nothing would change that. But some days, Holly couldn't help but feel that with the perfect Georgia on the scene, she would be scarily easy to replace.

Swallowing back her paranoia, she forced herself to smile. 'This will be good. It'll be a chance for me to get to know Georgia more,' she said, trying to convince herself as much as Ben.

'Honestly, Holly—'

'No, you have to come. That's the end of it. It'll be nice.' Her throat tightened as she debated whether to say the next words. But she had to. After all, Ben was going to find out sooner or later. 'I guess it'll be nice for you to meet Evan too.'

'Evan is going to be there?'

It was the same level of surprise that Holly had shown only moments before, but now it had shifted to Ben. Given how Evan was only staying for one night – and that Holly had planned on warming Evan up to her life in the Cotswolds before she introduced him to the father of her child – she hadn't mentioned his whistlestop visit to Ben. Thankfully, Ben seemed to accept the news far quicker than Holly had Georgia's invitation.

'Well, that'll be great then,' he said, his smile a fraction too broad. 'I get to meet Evan. Evan and Georgia. It all sounds perfect.'

The pair looked at each other, a mirror image with both their lips pressed tightly together into straight lines. Holly wondered what she was supposed to say next when Ben broke the silence.

'I promise we won't stay long. Just long enough for your mum and dad to know we came.'

Holly let out a loud sigh of relief.

'That would be perfect. Thank you.'

Ben laughed. 'No problem. Now, Hope, give Daddy a kiss goodbye. And I'll see you later, okay? Bye bye.'

Ben offered Hope an exaggerated wave before turning to leave.

'Ben! Look!' Holly shouted. As Ben turned back, his eyes fell on his daughter. Hope was still in Holly's arms, her hand swinging up and down as she imitated Ben's wave. 'She's doing it, she's doing it!' Holly said, jumping up and down with such vigour that Hope immediately stopped waving again.

'Did you wave, Hope?' Ben rushed back over. 'Did you wave to Daddy? Can you do that again?'

* * *

Holly was running late. After the excitement of Hope's first definitive waves, Ben had come inside for a cup of tea, solely so that he could keep walking out the house and saying goodbye repeatedly so that Hope would laugh and wave again. When he finally left, Jamie arrived to collect the flowers.

'You weren't joking when you said they were massive,' she said, as she went to move the bouquet. 'I've seen florists with fewer flowers in.'

'I know.' Holly sighed.

The last time a man had bought her flowers, it had been Ben, and those had been flours, as in almond, spelt, wholegrain and a whole heap of other one-kilogram bags. It would have been a rather random gift if she hadn't loved baking so much. As for the fresh, garden variety, she could probably count on one hand the number of times she'd been bought those in her life and three times were in the last three weeks.

'I don't think I should take the entire bunch,' Jamie said, having picked them up only to put them back down again. 'I mean, what if

Evan notices? He's coming here, after all. And he must know what he sent you?'

It was a good point, which Holly pondered for a moment before she spoke.

'You're right. There's a measuring jug above the sink. Can you grab it? We'll put a bunch in it for me to keep, and then you can take the rest with you.'

'A measuring jug? Do you not have a vase?'

Holly pointed to where a vase on the windowsill contained half of the first bouquet Evan had sent her when she'd arrived back in the UK. There was another on her bedroom windowsill and the bathroom, too.

'Yes, but I've run out,' she said. 'Now, are you going to get me that jug or not?'

4

When Jamie left, Holly finally had Hope to herself. Unfortunately, all the delays meant that there wasn't time to sit and play. Instead, she had to try to force her daughter into one of the beautiful – if wholly impractical – dress and bloomer sets her mother had bought only a few weeks ago. Once it was on, Holly ensured she had several much more comfortable shorts and baby grow options packed in her bag. As long as her mother saw Hope wearing the outfit, it would be fine. They would get a couple of nice photos with her dad to remember the day, and then she could get her changed into something far more suitable for crawling around the garden.

According to her mother, they were expecting around thirty people to attend the party. Thirty people felt like a reasonable number for such an event. What Holly couldn't work out was how they were going to fit them all in her parents' back garden. The answer, she discovered shortly after arriving at their house, was that they weren't.

'Here you are. I'd started to wonder what had happened to you,' her mother said, as she opened the door and swept Hope out of

Holly's arms. 'Now you leave her here with me. I need you to go out and help your dad. He's still struggling with the fence.'

'The fence?' Holly asked, confused. 'What are you doing to the fence?'

'Removing it. How else did you think we were going to fit that many people in the garden?'

Realising that it was easier just to head outside and help her dad, rather than try to get any coherent answer from her mother – who was now cooing over Hope's outfit – Holly kissed Hope before heading through the kitchen and into the garden.

The small patio opened onto a reasonably sized lawn area at the back of which was a small, wooden arbour seat surrounded by a succulent-filled rock garden. The seat and succulents were both recent editions to the outdoor space. After her father's heart attack, the doctor had suggested he needed to slow down, and tending to succulents was something he had been keen to try for many years. Apparently, it offered him a way to be outside while taking it easy – though at that moment, he was doing anything but. Instead, he was red-faced, holding the entire weight of a fence panel while their neighbour June stood by, shouting such helpful comments as, 'Mind my begonias!'

'Dad. Hold on for a second. Let me help you with that.' Holly sidled up beside him and placed a hand under the end of the panel to take some of the weight. Her father sighed audibly at her help.

'Thanks, love. We just need to move it to the side a bit. Prop it up against that other part of the fence. Yes, that's it. Slowly does it.'

Within a couple of minutes, the removed fence panel was securely placed further down the garden and her father was wiping the sweat from his brow with the back of his hand.

'Thanks for that, love,' he said. 'Was trickier than I'd expected.'

'You should have waited. You shouldn't be moving things on your own like that. What would the doctor say?'

Whatever her father did or didn't think the doctor would say, he clearly had no intention of telling Holly, as rather than responding to her, he ambled over to the hole in the fence where the neighbour was standing. Judging by the relieved smile on her face, all the begonias had survived.

'Thanks for that, June, love. I'll put it back tonight, when everyone goes.'

'Oh, there's no rush,' June replied. 'Besides, my Lenny will be back from work then. He'll be able to give you a hand.'

'That would be grand. Thank you. Well, I'd better have a shower. Don't want all the guests turning up and me looking like this, do I?' he said. He looked at Holly as if he expected her to make her excuses and come into the house with him, too. But there was something she wanted to do first.

'I'll just be a minute, Dad,' she said. 'Oh and say "bye" to Hope when you go upstairs. You might be in for a surprise.'

As her dad left, Holly approached the gap in the fence. June and Lenny were at least ten years younger than her parents, yet they'd always had the air of much older people. June's hair, which was dyed a brassy blonde, was often held back with metal clips and Holly was sure the only type of shoes she owned were plastic gardening ones. Still, she was a friendly neighbour and a good person. Not to mention someone that Holly owed a lot to.

'June, do you have a minute?' she asked.

'Of course, deary. How can I help?' June replied. Even the way she spoke sounded older than her years, but Holly found it endearing.

'I know it's been a while, but I realised I've never thanked you for telling Mum about the cottage in Bourton.'

'The cottage?' June frowned.

'If you hadn't told Mum about it straight away and given her the keys so we could look around, I'm sure someone would have snapped it up. And it's been so perfect for me and Hope.'

Although Holly had finished saying what she needed, the frown still hadn't left June's expression. If anything, it had grown deeper.

'Sorry, Holly, dear, I'm not sure what you mean?'

Holly smiled patiently. Apparently, June's elderly characteristics stretched as far as having variable memory skills. 'You're friends with the landlord? You gave Mum the keys to look around it.'

At this, June shook her head.

'No, not me, love. Your mum's told me about the cottage, of course, but it was nothing to do with me. You've got the wrong person, I'm afraid.'

'Oh,' Holly said. 'Perhaps it was Lenny then. She just said a neighbour, so I assumed—'

'Lenny? Know a landlord in Bourton? No, love, you're definitely barking up the wrong tree here, but I'm pleased you're happy.'

Holly wasn't sure how else she was supposed to reply, but there was no doubt that June didn't know what she was talking about. And it felt unlikely that she would be mistaken about Lenny, either. Before she could think of a reply, June was speaking again.

'I'd love to stop and chat, dear, but I've got a potato salad to make. You won't mind if I excuse myself, will you? I'll see you out here in about an hour, right? We can catch up then?'

'Sorry, what?' Holly shook herself back to the moment, with June's words taking just a second longer to sink in. 'Yes. Yes... the party,' she said. 'I'll see you then.'

5

Back in the house, Holly's mother was spooning mouthfuls of mashed banana into Hope, making aeroplane noises as she went. There was no point in Holly explaining she was trying to get Hope on a relatively strict feeding schedule. Firstly, as separated parents, both she and Ben had formed routines that suited them best as individuals, and no matter how much they tried to unify them, something always seemed to get in the way. Besides, her mother looked after Hope for more weekdays than Holly did, and the last thing she wanted to do was say anything to rock the boat. Still, as she entered the kitchen, she couldn't help but shake the feeling of perplexity from her conversation outside.

'Thanks for helping your dad with that, love,' her mother said.

'It was no problem,' Holly replied, as she took a seat next to Hope. 'Hey, Mum, I spoke to June. Thanked her for putting you in touch with her landlord friend who owned the cottage. But she didn't seem to know what I was talking about.'

'Did she not?' Her mother continued feeding Hope as she spoke. While Holly couldn't be certain, it seemed like she was avoiding her gaze. 'Oh, well, no, of course she wouldn't. She wasn't the one who gave me the landlord's information.'

'But I thought you said it was your neighbour.'

'I know what I said,' she replied, with the slightest of huffs.

'Well then, which neighbour was it?'

Her parents lived in a semi-detached house, with June and Lenny sharing the adjoining walls. On the other side of them was a bungalow, with an old man who only ever appeared to snap at passers-by walking with dogs to tell them to stop barking, even when they weren't. Considering her mother had never had a pleasant word to say about the man, it seemed unlikely he was the neighbour she was talking about.

Holly fixed her gaze on her and waited for a reply. None came.

'If they're going to be here tonight, then I'd really like to say thank you,' Holly pressed. 'I should have sent them something before now.'

Her mother let out an irritated sigh. 'Really Holly, do you have to go on about it now? I can't remember who it was at the minute. There's a lot going on today, in case you haven't noticed. And it was quite a while ago. Maybe I saw an advert in the newsagent's. Yes, come to think about it, I'm sure that's how I heard about the place. Someone local placing an ad in the newsagent's.'

Holly pressed her lips together tightly as her mother turned her back to her and began washing up the banana bowl. There was no denying it – Wendy was definitely avoiding looking at her.

Checking that Hope was firmly strapped into the highchair, Holly stood up and moved across to the sink by her mother.

'No, you definitely said it was a neighbour, I'm sure of it. Besides, they gave you the keys, remember? They wouldn't have been able to do that if it was an advert in the newsagent's.'

'Well, if you're that sure of it, then that must have been what I said. Now, are you going to help me or not? Your father's still in the shower, and outside isn't ready. He hasn't sorted the barbecue and I haven't even made enough bread rolls. So if you'd like, you can make yourself useful and give me a hand and make a bread dough. Otherwise, I'm not entirely sure why you came early at all, unless it was just to pester me?'

Holly bit down on her lip. Snapping wasn't something her mother did ever, really. Even when she was under stress. And it wasn't like she hadn't organised parties before this. Bigger ones too, for which she had done all the catering. Whatever the situation was with the landlord and the neighbour, the last thing Holly wanted was to upset her mother before her father's big party. As such, she was about to apologise when Wendy let out a deep sigh.

'I'm sorry, love. I'm just on edge, that's all.'

'I can tell. What is it? Is there anything I can do?'

Her mother took a long inhale, throwing a glance at Hope before looking back at Holly. 'It's your father's present, you know,' she said quietly. 'I'm starting to worry that we've made a mistake.'

6

The joint present had been Holly's idea. Together, she and her mother had clubbed together to get Arthur and Wendy a last-minute city break to Brussels. Like Holly, her parents had experienced very little in the way of travelling. But when she came back from the south of France, unable to stop talking about all her escapades with Evan and the girls, she couldn't help but feel how much her parents had missed out on that side of life. Then, by chance, as she was browsing the internet one evening while Hope was at Ben's, a last-minute deal for Eurostar tickets to Brussels serendipitously pinged up on her phone. The next day, she mentioned it to her mum.

'I don't know if he'll like it. You know he's funny about things he doesn't know.' Her mother's initial response had been less than enthusiastic.

'But this is Brussels. Brussels as in Belgium. As in Belgian chocolate!' Holly emphasised the word chocolate with large gesticulations. 'He'll love it. Besides, I always thought it was flying that made him anxious? There's no flying on this. You'll be on the train the entire way there. And he does love trains.'

She watched as her mother mulled the idea over.

'Well, we both have our passports. We got them done five years ago when his cousin Emily decided she was going to get married in Italy. What a whole kerfuffle that was. Thankfully, the only thing we lost was the money on getting our passports renewed. I'm not sure we'll do that again,' she said rather sadly.

'Then don't you see this is the perfect reason?' Holly continued to press. 'Otherwise, your passports would've been renewed for nothing. I think you should do it. I've already rung them up, and there's only six places left on this deal, so we'll need to book it fast. And I can split the costs. Or pay two-thirds if that helps.'

Her muscles clenched as she'd said those words. Holly had lots of happiness and love in her life. She had found joy in so many things she had never expected, from Hope to the girls and the shop. What she didn't have was lots of money. She'd come back from Jamie's hen do expecting to have dug a substantial chunk out of her savings, but instead everything had been paid for by Fin or Evan. Even when she had tried to make Jamie take some of the money to put towards her honeymoon or wedding, she'd outright refused. At least this, giving the money to her mum for a trip, would help ease some of the guilt she felt still having that money in her account.

'Fine.' An apprehensive grin flitted across her mother's face as she spoke. 'You're sure he'll like it, though?'

'There's a chocolate-making course he can do, Mum. He'll love it.'

Finally, her mother allowed herself a more fully formed smile.

'Okay. Let's do it. Let's book it.'

Forty minutes later, and her parents had been booked on the Eurostar, with three nights in Brussels, and her father was none the wiser. That was two weeks ago now, and Holly and Wendy had been keeping it a secret ever since. Now, they finally had to tell him. But Holly understood her mother's nerves. She knew it might take a bit of time for her dad to let the idea sink in, and if that was the case, there was no saying how he might react in the moment. So, they had agreed to wait until the end of the night.

Holly was still going through the reactions he might give to the surprise when her mum spoke again.

'Right, I think it's time we both got changed,' she said.

'Changed? Why do I need to get changed?'

When her mum scanned her up and down and didn't speak, she pursed her lips in a manner that meant no words were necessary.

'What's wrong with this?' Holly was wearing a newish pair of jeans, paired with a top that had no baby milk or sick-up stains on it at all. As far as current clothing went, it was as good as it was going to get. 'Dad's not going to care.'

'It's not about your dad,' her mother said, straightening her back. 'What about Evan? It's the first time he's seen you in England. The first time we've met him. You don't want him to turn up and... and...' She struggled to find the words to finish her sentence, so Holly stepped in for her.

'Regret his decision to go out with me?' she said, raising her eyebrows.

'I'm not saying he would do that. It's just, you do want to look nice for him, don't you?'

'Mother, listen to me very carefully. If Evan arrives and decides he doesn't want to date me because I'm not wearing some girly dress or strappy sandals, then I'm fine with that. I'd rather not date him, either.'

Her mother's pursed lips tightened.

'Fine, but I'm going to go upstairs and get dressed nicely.' She bent down and picked up Hope from her highchair. 'Come on, Hope, you can help choose a pretty dress for Grandma, can't you?'

With one last look at Holly, Wendy disappeared out of the kitchen. It was only when the footsteps rattled on the stairs that

Holly remembered she had something else she wanted to say to her mother.

'Oh, and don't think I've let you off the hook about inviting Ben and Georgia either! We're going to talk about this when you get back down here. You need to be taught boundaries. Do you hear me? Boundaries!'

7

Unsurprisingly, the first people to arrive were those local to Northleach, all on foot, and all with a bottle of wine and cans of beer to fill up the fridge and the cool box outside by the barbecue. Given how her parents hadn't moved to the village until after Holly had left home, she spent the majority of the time introducing herself and Hope and trying to remember the stream of names she was confronted with.

Shortly after, people from further afield began to arrive, including some of her parents' oldest friends whom Holly knew from her time growing up in Bourton. There was Lyn and Ernie, who lived two doors down and had babysat Holly frequently when she was a child. Not to mention old Mrs Forester, who everyone had referred to as old Mrs Forester even when Holly was in school. Holly couldn't fathom exactly how old the grey-haired ex-doctor was, but she was still walking happily with the aid of a stick, and her red lipstick was applied with far better precision than Holly could manage.

Most of the Bourton residents had seen Holly since she moved back from London. Either they had deliberately come to see her in the shop, because they'd heard she'd taken it over, or else had stumbled in for their bag of Liquorice Allsorts, only to find her behind the counter.

But now, it was nice to chat to them without the pressure of a queue forming, although people seemed far less interested in Holly and how she was doing than they were in Hope.

'She's such a good girl, isn't she?' One woman squeezed Hope's legs, while another pulled faces at her.

'Beautiful eyes.'

'Very focused, isn't she?'

Holly smiled and lapped up the compliments. She knew that for some babies, the attention could get too much, and what started as a lovely, innocuous cuddle could end up in a screaming fit which only her favourite snuggling teddy and a cuddle with Mummy or Daddy could solve. But Hope wasn't like that. Hope would giggle away, delighted with all the fuss. No doubt at some point in the evening, every person who wanted a cuddle would get one. Still, it didn't matter how many people arrived. Holly couldn't hide the fact that there was only one person she wanted to see that night, and every minute waiting for him made her more and more anxious.

Wendy had just taken Hope from Holly yet again – this time carrying her through the gap in June and Lenny's fence to introduce her to some people having a drink over there – when Holly's phone buzzed. As quick as she could, she snatched it out of her pocket and read the message on the screen. Her stomach triple somersaulted.

I think I'm outside x

Holly's heart leapt, only to sink again as, for a split second, she worried about what her mother had said. Should she have put on something a bit nicer to wear? The thought formed only for her to dismiss it again. Evan had fallen for her while she was travel sick on a plane, and later with a swollen ankle, not to mention wearing less-than-fashionable water shoes on the boat. He would just be happy to see her, the same way she was with him. Slipping her phone into her pocket, she raced into the next garden and tapped her mother on the shoulder.

'You're all right with Hope, aren't you?' she said. 'I just need to go inside. I'll be two minutes. Maybe a bit longer.'

Normally, her mother would never miss out on a chance to show off Hope to her friends, but rather than immediately agreeing, her eyes lit up.

'Is he here?' she said, near breathless with excitement. 'Shall I come with you? Invite him in? I should probably come with you. After all, it is our house.'

'I think you've got plenty of people here to host, don't you?' Holly said with just a hint of firmness. 'Besides, you're looking after Hope. Don't worry, he's not going anywhere. I hope.'

Before her mother could say anything more, Holly pecked her on the cheek and headed into the house.

It felt impossible that her cheeks could smile as much as they were. Her jaw was already aching, and it felt as though all the skin had been stretched so tightly, she couldn't have frowned had she wanted to. She was going to see Evan again. She was going to see her boyfriend, in real life, away from the luxury of a holiday.

With one last look in the mirror, and a quick adjustment to her hair, she swung open the front door.

8

Holly couldn't move and nor did she want to. For a second, she just wanted to stand there and stare. Evan looked better than she remembered. Just as handsome, just as sun-kissed, and yet even better, because now he was hers. He was hers, and he was standing in the Cotswolds.

'Hey there.'

His American drawl was all it took to melt her insides. Without even bothering to reciprocate the greeting, Holly stepped forwards, reached up on her tiptoes, interlocked her fingers around the back of his neck and kissed him.

It was, without doubt, the most she had ever needed a kiss in her life. Three weeks? How had she managed without him for three weeks? Only as she held him did Holly realise that part of her hadn't believed this was real. Even with all the phone calls and messages and all the goddamn flowers, part of her had still found it impossible to believe that what had happened between them was really as magical and romantic as she'd let herself believe. But the moment their lips touched, all that worry and anxiety washed away, and instead, the memories of their time in France flooded back. It was impossible to believe it had only been four days they had spent together or that he could feel as intensely for her as she did for him after such a short time. But when she broke away, a grin matching hers was plastered on his face.

'Well, it seems like I've picked an awkward time to show up,' another voice said.

Holly pushed herself onto tiptoes to glance past Evan. There, standing on her parents' path, was Caroline, with her hands on her hips and an eyebrow arched.

'Oh, no, please don't let me interrupt. I could stand here all day.'

'Caroline.' Evan twisted around and pulled her in for a tight squeeze. 'How have you been?'

'Good, but we can catch up later. You've got far more important people to talk to than me.'

With a wink and a quick peck on the cheek for Holly, Caroline squeezed through the doorway and into the house. Given that Caroline was a guest, Holly suspected she probably should have shown her the way through the house and into the garden where the party was happening. But that would mean leaving Evan or taking him with her and sharing him. And that simply wasn't something she was ready to do just yet.

'I can't believe you're here,' she said, finally finding her voice.

'I can't either, but it's good, right?'

'Very good.'

He tilted his head down and kissed her again. Perhaps, Holly thought, they could just slip off. Or maybe go for a quick walk around the village before she took him to meet everyone, just so they got a little time to themselves? After all, he was leaving again tomorrow. Unfortunately, Holly knew it wasn't possible. As she broke away, a heavy sigh filled her lungs. If she didn't take him to meet everyone soon, her mother would come looking for them, and that would be even more embarrassing.

'Are you ready for this?' she said. Her tone was apologetic and yet she still couldn't stop grinning.

'I guess I'd better be. Is it wrong that I'm quite worried about meeting your family? Especially Hope.'

'Hope will love you, trust me.'

'I thought you said she threw up over Ben's new girlfriend the first time she met her.'

Holly couldn't help but feel a slightly wicked internal grin at that memory.

'She did, but I think that was more because of loyalty to me than anything else.'

Evan chuckled lightly. The pair shared the same sense of humour. All the conversations on the phone had confirmed that. But this was so different to talking into a screen. Here, she could touch him. Hold him. Smell him. And good God, he smelt delicious.

'Why don't you leave your bags here?' she said, snapping herself out of her daydream. Thinking about how good Evan smelt when she was at her dad's birthday seemed less than appropriate. Besides, the sooner they met everyone, the sooner they could hopefully slip off.

'I bought this for the party,' Evan said, handing Holly a bag of duty-free champagne while he tucked his suitcase next to the stairs.

'You didn't have to do that, but thank you. And you can leave that bag upstairs too, if you want.' She gestured to the manly leather satchel that crossed his body, no doubt containing important things like his phone and wallet and passport. Possibly a laptop too. Whatever was in it, it was full. Unlike the stereotypical slim man-bag, this satchel bulged outwards, as if it had been stuffed to the brim. Perhaps that was the reason he only took one suitcase on his travels – he packed his hand luggage as full as possible. She couldn't remember him doing that before, though, on the trip to France.

'I'll keep this one with me, if that's okay?' he said, patting the stretched fabric.

'Of course. Come on,' she said, offering him the quickest kiss on the lips. 'Time to go face the music.'

As he looked at her, his brow crinkled and he formed the biggest puppy-dog eyes she'd ever seen on a grown man.

'You know what? I think I've changed my mind. I think I'm going to hide in here with you just a bit longer?'

Holly stepped back and folded her arms across her chest.

'No way. You can't back out on me now. Do you need reminding of my first introduction to your mother?'

Even now, Holly wanted to curl up with embarrassment at the memory. After he had asked several times to go on a date with her, Holly had finally agreed, only to find half a dozen photos of different women in his wallet. Obviously, she had confronted him about it, and the result had been Holly on a video call to Evan's mother, learning about all his sisters. It was fair to say she trusted his word a little more after that.

'Fine then, show me the way,' he said with a mock sulkiness.

Holly felt like she was in some kind of parade as she walked through the kitchen and out into the garden. All eyes turned on them, and from the way the volume dropped, it made it seem like this was the first man she had ever brought home. Either that, or they had all suddenly grown an extra head. And Holly wasn't the only one who felt it.

'They're all staring at me, right?' Evan whispered into her ear as they made their way up to the patio.

'You're a new person in a small Cotswold village. That's going to happen a lot, believe me.' She squeezed his hand tightly. Partly to offer reassurance, partly to keep reminding herself that he was really there.

Still, they were barely on the patio when her mother raced forwards, arms wide.

'Evan, it's so lovely to meet you.'

Before Holly even had time to drop Evan's hand, her mother was in there, kissing him on both cheeks. 'I've heard so much about you. Now come, what can I get you to drink? We've got Prosecco. Or wine. And some nice lagers that were on offer at the Co-op. Do you drink lager in America?'

'Of course they drink lager!' Holly said, a flood of colour rushing to her cheeks. Her mother also shared Holly's trait of babbling when nervous and right now, she was definitely nervous.

'We do, yes, but I'm actually fine with a soft drink right now, Wendy,' Evan said, in his ineffably calm voice. 'Flying always dehydrates me. But I brought a couple of bottles of bubbly that I've put in the kitchen.'

'Isn't that lovely of you? Well, there are some cans of pop in the cool box. Now come on in, come on in, you've got so many people to meet.'

9

As Holly watched her mother make her way through her guests, Holly was left in no doubt that her babbling matched her own. She was firing off a dozen questions a minute and giving Evan exactly zero seconds to answer them.

'Was the flight okay? Was it direct? I'm not sure Holly said where you flew into, was it Bristol?'

'Mum, please give him a chance to breathe,' Holly said, trying not to glare too obviously. Thankfully, Wendy listened and took a quick breath in before she spoke again.

'Sorry, of course. Now, come meet Holly's dad. Arthur's been talking about meeting you non-stop since he knew you were coming to his party.'

This, Holly knew, was an outright lie. When she mentioned that Evan would be attending her father's sixtieth birthday and checked that it was all right during a shift at the shop one afternoon, her father had grunted, showing his complete indifference to the idea. Her mother was the one who had rung her that night, needing to chat for forty minutes.

'Arthur, Arthur, come here, love. Giles has just turned up.'

The name flew so effortlessly off her mother's tongue that for a moment, Holly didn't realise why it sounded so wrong. The moment she did was the same moment the realisation struck her mother. Wendy's jaw dropped, and a crimson flush coloured her cheeks.

'Evan. I'm so sorry. I'm terrible with names.'

Evan smiled. 'Well, if you're going to mistake me for someone, I'm glad it's the guy with a yacht.'

With her face still bright red, her mother chuckled awkwardly. The laugh was tight and overly fast, and Holly squirmed with both sympathy and horror. Wendy clearly wanted the world to swallow her up, but Holly wasn't that far behind. She'd never known her mother get a name wrong before, and she couldn't have picked a worse time.

'I... I...' She continued to stutter, though before she could apologise again, Holly's father was standing beside them, his hand stretched out.

'Evan.' He paused slightly after saying his name, making it clear there were no mistakes there. 'Glad you could make it. Help yourself to a drink. Wendy, dear, why don't you come and help me get the cutlery sorted?'

Offering Holly a slight and secretive smile, her dad took her mum by the hand and led her back towards the house. A fraction of the tension lessened in Holly's shoulders.

'Now that we've got that over and done with,' Holly said, as she slipped her arm around Evan's waist, 'there's someone even more important than my parents you need to meet. And fingers crossed, this introduction goes a little better.'

At that moment, Hope was in Caroline's arms. No doubt her friend had come straight into the party and swept Hope away from whoever was holding her previously. Probably her mother. But Hope was perfectly content with her aunt Caroline, giggling up and down as she bounced around on her lap. Only when she saw Holly did she stretch out her arms for her mum.

'Hey, baby girl.' Holly lifted her straight up into the air and kissed her belly before lowering her back down. 'Guess what? Mummy's got somebody she'd like you to meet. Hope, this is Evan. Evan, meet Hope.' Holly angled her daughter, so that she was looking straight at Evan. But rather than looking at Hope, as Holly had expected him to be doing, Evan was opening up his bag. It took less than a minute to realise why.

'Hey, Hope, look what I found at the airport.'

From out of his bulging satchel, Evan pulled the softest, cuddliest bunny Holly had ever seen. Hope's eyes lit up at the sight of the little brown toy, as she immediately reached out to grab it.

'You didn't have to do that,' Holly said, kissing him lightly on the lips. When she broke away, his smile twisted slightly.

'Actually, I had a bit of a problem at the airport.'

'You did?'

'Well, I wanted to get Hope something, but the problem was, I couldn't decide which colour bunny was the cutest.' He reached back into his bag and pulled out an identical-sized bunny rabbit with the same adorably floppy ears. Only this one was blue.

'Evan...'

Holly could feel herself using a warning tone, but there was no point.

'I liked this blue one too, but then there was the yellow one...' Evan proceeded to pull the next bunny out of his bag. 'But then I thought, Hope's a girl, so obviously I've got to get her a pink bunny.' The pink rabbit was the next one to come out. 'But then I worried about the whole gender-neutral thing and stereotyping her before she was ready.' A green one quickly followed.

'Evan?' There was no hiding the hint of sharpness in Holly's voice then. 'Exactly how many bunnies did you buy for Hope?'

He looked at her bashfully, a slight smirk twisting on his face.

'Seven, I think.'

'Seven?'

Holly took one of the bunnies out of Hope's arms, and though she tried to protest, it was pretty difficult, given how many she was still holding. Holly had seen this type of teddy before. They sold them at the florist in the village, and the garden centre in Burford too, and while she didn't know the exact price of them, she knew they weren't cheap. Her stomach somersaulted with the fact that Hope was probably holding a hundred pounds of soft cuddly bunnies in her arms.

'Evan. This is way too generous. Way, way too generous.'

'It's fine. It's bunnies. It's not like she's going to grow out of them. Besides, first impressions matter.'

'I don't think that's true with a nine-month-old.'

'It's especially true with a nine-month-old.'

Holly wanted to be cross. She really did, but the way Evan's eyes were glinting at her made it impossible.

'Face it – I win, right?' he said, his smirk growing wider. 'In terms of first impressions, this is much better than being vomited on.'

Holly's lips twitched, finally breaking into a smile.

'Yes, fine. You win. She didn't vomit on you.'

'Speaking of Hope's vomit...' Caroline infiltrated herself back into the conversation. 'Ben's here, so I guess that must be...' Caroline's words drifted into the ether, and Holly knew exactly why. Feeling like she wished she'd taken her mother's advice and put something slightly nicer on, Holly tried to fight back the sinking feeling in her gut.

'Yup, that's Georgia.'

10

'Wow. She is gorgeous,' Caroline said, as she crouched to pick up one of the bunnies Hope had dropped while continuing to stare unsubtly at Georgia.

'I know.' Holly sighed.

'I thought you were exaggerating,' Caroline continued.

'Nope. No exaggeration there. And she's really smart. And nice.'

Like Caroline, Holly found her attention fixed solely on Georgia, until Evan unexpectedly dropped his head onto her shoulder.

'Too dressy for me,' he said. 'My kind of gorgeous is standing right here.'

Even with Holly holding Hope in her arms, Evan somehow squeezed around the baby and planted a soft, lingering kiss on Holly's lips.

'Oh, if this is what I'm going to have to put up with, I'm going to need more drink,' Caroline said, before reaching out to take Hope. 'She doesn't need to witness that yet, either. Besides, we need to think of some names for these bunnies, don't we?'

Offering Holly a quick grin, Caroline took Hope off towards the back of the garden, already suggesting names for the new cuddly toys.

It would have been lovely if Caroline's disappearance had genuinely left Holly and Evan on their own, but there were still two dozen people mingling around, and Holly knew her mother well enough to know she wouldn't be forgiven if she spent the entire party huddled close to Evan, no matter how much she wanted to. Besides, she still had to sort out the cake and candles, not to mention say hello to Georgia, though Holly was confident Ben knew his way around her family well enough to make his girlfriend feel comfortable.

'I need to do a quick loop and see if Mum needs any help,' she said, still holding on to Evan's hands. 'You should probably stay out here and mingle. It'll make you look good.'

Evan flickered his eyes at her. 'I can mingle. No problem.'

'Oh, I know you can.' Holly pushed herself up onto tiptoes, ready to kiss him again, only to drop back onto her heels. If they carried on like this, her father would never get a cake. Not trusting herself, she took a step back.

'Good, okay. Safe people to talk to are my dad, my mum, June, and Lenny next door. Avoid Aunt May.' She pointed to a woman with bright-red hair, in a floral summer dress, who was throwing her head back in laughter.

'Why do I need to avoid her? She looks nice.'

'Oh, she is nice. Only she's on her second gin and tonic right there, which means she'll start getting silly and pinching your bum the minute she's within arm's reach.'

'I shall avoid her at all costs. Anyone else I need to worry about?'

'I wouldn't start talking to Jonathan over there, in the chinos, unless you want to get embroiled in a forty-five-minute conversation about kit cars,' Holly said, gesturing to one of her father's old work colleagues.

'That doesn't sound too terrible.'

'Okay, why don't you go over there and tell me how you feel in forty-five minutes?' Holly smirked.

Evan's eyes glinted. 'You're right, I'll stick around here, perhaps chat to your mum and dad some more. You know, make them confident in my future son-in-law possibilities. Assuming your mum doesn't still think I'm Giles.'

Holly bit down on her lip. The fact that Evan had mentioned being a future son-in-law should have been enough to set her heart into overdrive, but it was the comment about Mum that she focused on more. It wasn't like her mum to mess things up. And it wasn't like the name was the only thing. That whole weird incident with the neighbour and the landlord was leaving Holly more than a little perturbed. Holly wasn't naïve about the fact that her parents were getting older. That was what parents did, but she never imagined the changes would be so swift. Particularly when her mother seemed so together the rest of the time.

'Right, I'm going to see if Mum wants any help.' She pecked Evan on the cheek yet again. 'Try not to buy Hope any more presents while I'm gone.'

'Is there a shop here?' Evan joked before giving her one more kiss, this one on the lips and lasting far longer.

Holly wasn't sure when she became the type of person who needed half a dozen kisses and soft farewells just to leave her boyfriend so that she could go to the kitchen, and yet, somehow, that was who she had become. Still, she wouldn't feel guilty about it. She had waited long enough to find her Mr Right. And she deserved this.

When she realised it was getting ridiculous, Holly finally tore herself away long enough to head back into the kitchen. Her mother was standing in front of the oven, pulling out the fresh bread rolls, though the second she saw Holly, she ended the task to embrace her daughter.

When she broke away, her face was wrinkled with worry.

'Holly, I'm so sorry,' she said. 'How could I have got his name wrong?'

'It's fine, Mum, it's fine.'

'I don't know what came over me. And he's ever such a nice man. He'll forgive me, won't he?'

Holly couldn't help but laugh. 'You mean for calling him the name of a man who wasn't even my boyfriend? I'm sure he'll get over it.'

Wendy nodded, her eyes glazing with tears.

'Mum, it's fine. Honestly. Evan is fine. You don't have to worry about it. Really.'

She looked her mother squarely in the eye until she finally relented with a nod. Only then did Holly squeeze her in a tight hug. When they broke away for a second time, her mother's worry lines had faded by a fraction.

'Well, your dad seems very happy,' she said. 'He loves a good barbecue. Still, I was thinking we should get the cake ready now.'

'Cake?' Holly said, once again concerned. 'But the barbecue food isn't even ready, is it?'

'No, not yet. But you know what your father is like with barbecues. It'll take him ages. Everyone will be starving, then he'll check the chicken and then everything will need to go back on again for another fifteen minutes. Then your Aunt May will start complaining about how she needs to get home, and how she always misses the cake, and then she'll start whining about how an oven is better than a barbecue. I think it's just easier to get the cake.'

At least now her mother was making sense. Aunt May was never one to complain quietly; if she was grumpy about something, everyone would know.

'Okay,' Holly said, thinking through the logistics. 'Why don't you take those bread rolls out, then check there's room on the table for me to bring the cake? I'll get the candles and bring it out in five.'

'Sounds like a plan,' her mother said, fetching the tray of browning rolls out of the oven, before placing them on a cooling rack, while Holly searched in the drawers for the 'six' and 'zero' candles she had bought weeks in advance and hidden in a paper bag somewhere amongst the kitchen utensils.

'Alright, love. Don't be long,' her mother said, as she headed outside.

A minute later, Holly had found the brown paper bag and some scissors to open the plastic packaging on the candles. She was cutting open the first one when a voice spoke behind her.

'So Evan seems very nice. Even if he is trying to buy my child's affections.'

11

Holly dropped the scissors with a clatter, her heart racing.

'Jeez, Ben! Didn't you ever learn not to startle people when they're holding scissors?'

'Sorry,' he said, as he walked forward and kissed her on either cheek, like they had been old friends that hadn't seen each other for a long time, not a co-parenting pair who had seen each other only a couple of hours before.

'So, the bunnies?' he said again.

'Yeah, Evan can get a little carried away with things,' she said, thinking about all the flowers currently filling her little cottage.

'Well, you two looked happy together. It's nice to see.'

'Same with you. Georgia looks lovely.'

Holly hadn't intended to emphasise the word 'looks' quite so much, but Ben raised an eyebrow in response.

'She likes to dress nicely,' he said. 'Particularly when she doesn't know people. It's a nervous reaction. You know, like people who talk too much when they're under scrutiny?'

'I didn't mean it like that,' Holly replied, ignoring the dig.

'Although I suspect she could wear a bin bag and still look fantastic.'

'I won't deny that,' Ben replied. He paused, studying Holly for a moment. 'So how are all the wedding plans going? I've seen Jamie outside the house a couple of times, but whenever I've gone to speak to her, she's been on the phone. And I haven't wanted to intrude. I'm sure there must be a lot of sorting out to do with Fin's family coming over.'

'Honestly, I think that's the only stressful part of it. They really lucked out on the venue. The place sorts out so much, all Jamie and Fin really have to do is show up. And she'd hardly find you checking up on her an intrusion. You are friends as well as neighbours.'

'I know, you're right.'

'I usually am,' Holly smirked. 'Still, I can't believe how quickly this wedding has come about.'

'I know. Seems like only a couple of months ago Fin was filling the restaurant with paper cranes for her birthday.'

Holly thought back to that night. It was certainly memorable, partially because of all the paper cranes Fin had made, but also because that was the same night she discovered she was pregnant. She was still lost in the chaos on the memory when Ben cleared his throat and spoke again.

'Also,' he said, 'I was thinking, tonight after the party, maybe you want me to take Hope with me. Or you could drop her off, if you'd rather.'

Holly frowned. Ben had already had Hope that morning, and he knew that Holly didn't sleep particularly well when she was away.

'You haven't seen Evan in weeks,' he continued. 'I'm sure both of you would rather not spend the first night that you've seen each other with a nine-month-old to contend with.'

Holly swallowed. Of course, Ben would think of something like that. In Holly's mind, having Hope there with Evan had been part of what she'd been looking forward to. Time for the three of them to get to see how they worked together as a family. But that was before Hope had started her latest sleep regression, waking up in the middle of the night, and not settling unless Holly was cuddled up with her. Evan was a relaxed guy, but perhaps that wasn't what he'd envisioned for his first night seeing his girlfriend in nearly a month.

'Are you sure?' she asked, not wanting to put extra pressure on Ben. Or make it seem like she didn't want the night with her daughter.

'Absolutely, but only if you want. Georgia's got to travel for work tomorrow morning, so she's not going to be staying. So it'll just be Hope and me. Just in case you needed to know that.'

'Oh... I...' Holly wasn't sure how to respond. Since she had found out about Ben and Georgia's relationship, she'd made a concerted effort not to pry. What Ben did wasn't her business. If he thought having Georgia over to stay the night when he also had Hope staying was a sensible thing to do, then she just had to trust him with that. No matter how much it made her feel slightly uneasy to have another woman reading her daughter a bedtime story.

'Yes, okay. That would be nice, thank you. But I won't be able to drop her off until late, as I need to stay until the end to give Dad his present. Is that okay?'

'Of course, the Belgium trip.' Ben's face lit up unexpectedly. It really was sweet how much love he had for her parents. Maybe she would have repaid it, only she never saw Ben's family. Apart from the naming day they'd had for Hope, they'd had about as much presence in her life as the Easter Bunny.

'Mum and I want to do that together. But maybe afterwards? If it's still okay, maybe I can drop Hope over then?'

'That sounds fine.'

'And you've got enough clean pyjamas and everything. You know she needs the thin ones in summer?'

'Holly?'

'Yes?' She paused. 'Sorry.'

The pair locked eyes, and so much passed between them in that moment. The relationship may not have lasted like she had hoped, or ended in a manner which she was proud of, but that didn't change the fact that she felt incredibly fortunate to have Ben in her life.

'Can I hug you?' she said, suddenly overwhelmed.

'Always.'

When she wrapped her arms around him, her head fell softly onto his chest. It was no small blessing to have people she felt as comfortable with as she did with Ben.

'Anything I can help with in here?' Ben said after they broke apart.

Holly shook her head. 'Keep an eye on our daughter. I don't actually know where she is.'

'She's out in the garden with her favourite aunt, her grandparents, and two other adults vying to be step-parents. I think she'll be fine, don't you?'

'You're right. Of course you're right.'

With Ben continuing to linger, Holly finally remembered the cake. After checking she had not only the candles but a lighter too, she opened the fridge, ready to pull it out when her mother came rushing in, breathless.

'Stop! Stop what you're doing!' she said.

With her hands frozen in position, Holly turned around.

'Are you alright, Mum? Is everything okay?'

'We don't want the cake now. We do not want the cake now.'

Ben and Holly exchanged a look that involved suppressed

smirks. Panicked Wendy was a whole different kettle of fish to deal with.

'Okay, is there a reason?'

'I just heard your dad saying to Lenny how he hates it when I rush things and bring out dessert before he's had a chance to do the barbecue properly.'

'So we're not doing the cake yet?'

'No. Not until he's done the meat. And put these away, will you,' she said, grabbing the candles and shoving them back in the drawer, before she turned around and rushed back out of the house, leaving Ben and Holly still smirking at one another.

'I guess it's back to mingling,' he said.

'You really should. I just realised you left Georgia on her own out there. Does she even know anyone?'

A crease formed on Ben's brow.

'She knows Hope.'

'You need to rescue her,' Holly said. 'And I should probably see how Evan is getting on.'

Having left the kitchen as empty-handed as she came, Holly headed back outside, close on Ben's heels.

'Apparently, they are clubbing together,' Ben said when they reached the patio.

It took Holly a moment to see what he was talking about. Over by her mother's rosebushes, Georgia and Evan were chatting away. A knot tightened in Holly's stomach. There was no way around it. Georgia looked like a much better match than she ever did for Evan. They were similar heights, both athletic, and they were both, undeniably, beautiful.

She shook her head to clear those thoughts from her mind. She would not be paranoid about things like that. Evan loved her as she was.

'You two seem to be getting on well?' she said when they reached them.

Georgia turned to her and flashed a brilliant white smile.

'We really are. Holly, it's so nice to see you again.'

'You too.'

'Everything okay?' Holly said, looking up at Evan, who flashed an equally brilliant smile as Georgia.

'Absolutely.'

'In fact,' Georgia said, slipping her arms into Ben's as she spoke, 'everything's been going so well, Evan and I were just saying the four of us should head out for a double date? What do you think?'

12

Holly didn't know how to reply. Double date? With her ex and his new partner? Was it a joke? Perhaps Georgia just had a really peculiar sense of humour and that was why Ben liked her. That was what Holly hoped at least, but that hope faded rapidly as Georgia carried on speaking.

'Well, I've been saying to Ben for ages that I want to get to know you better. After all, alongside Ben, you're the joint most important person in Hope's life.'

There was something about the way she said *alongside* and *joint* that made Holly's teeth ground together. Trying to disguise the action as best as she could, she stretched her lips out tightly into a smile.

'Yes, yes, absolutely. I'm really sorry, Georgia, but I just need to take Evan here. My Aunt May has been wanting to meet him properly.'

'Your Aunt May? I thought you said—'

'Come on Evan, honey. Ben, Georgia, I'm sure we'll catch you later.' Looping her arm in Evan's, she pulled him across into June and Lenny's garden, only to stop and hiss at him.

'A double date? Really, Evan?'

'Why do I feel I'm in trouble?' he said, his eyes narrowing in confusion. 'I thought it would be nice. You and Ben get on, Georgia seems nice. There's the whole extended family thing, but I guess I misread that. Sorry.'

Holly shook her head and let out a sigh. 'No, no, you didn't misread anything. She is nice, and Ben and I get on great. But that doesn't mean I'm planning on double dating with my ex. At least, not until we have things like school performances, or university graduations, and events that we really can't avoid.'

'Sorry,' Evan said again, his wide eyes back in that puppy-dog manner. 'We can just say I'm too busy. I *am* busy. I'm very busy and very important. I don't even know when I'll have time to see you next.' He laughed. 'I probably don't. Maybe we should just call it quits. No dating for me, of any sort. Not double dating or single dating. Nothing at all.'

Holly slapped him playfully on the shoulder.

'Now you're just being ridiculous. How about this? You keep your arm looped in mine for the rest of the evening, and then you won't have the opportunity to say anything wrong again?'

'That sounds good,' he said, before kissing her long and hard. It was the type of kiss that could have gone on a lot longer had Evan's phone not buzzed in his pocket. Shifting away, he pulled it out and frowned at the screen.

'What time are we planning on heading back to the cottage tonight?' he asked. 'It's already quarter past seven. You said eight thirty, right?'

'That was the plan,' Holly replied. 'I'm not sure. It depends how long people stay, I suppose. I'll need to help Mum tidy up. And we need to give Dad his present, too.'

'Well, that might be a lot later, right?'

Evan's face was surprisingly serious. He fixed his gaze on Holly, awaiting an answer.

'I don't know. Maybe. Why? Is everything okay?'

'Yes, yes, it is.' His expression shifted back into a smile, but it was tighter than it had been earlier. Less easy? Holly tried to read the situation the best she could.

'Are you sure you're okay? I mean, you can slip off earlier. I'm sure Caroline wouldn't mind giving you a lift back to Bourton.'

'No, no, it's fine. It's just the jetlag, you know. Long flight. Baggage delays.' He took a step towards her. 'And as I'm only here for one night, I'm desperate to get you to myself for a bit.'

Holly smiled. She hadn't even thought about him and his jetlag, and that he'd come straight off the plane to her parents' house. She hadn't even offered him a shower or the opportunity to freshen up.

'You know, you can always have a kip upstairs? I don't mind.'

'A kip?' It took him a second. 'You mean a nap? No, no, it's fine. I just want to make a couple of phone calls. That's alright, isn't it? You know, working things.'

'Yes, of course.'

A moment later, Evan was walking back into the house with his phone pressed to his ear, leaving Holly confused.

Holly had never been in any doubt about how much Evan worked. He didn't get a house in London and one in the south of France by spending his evenings watching reruns of American sitcoms on television, but for the next hour, he remained almost entirely glued to his phone. It even rang at the exact time she brought out her dad's birthday cake. Rather than waiting for the song to end and calling the people back later, Evan blushed with embarrassment, headed into the kitchen and immediately answered it. By the time he came back, the candles were all blown out, the cake cut and slices already being dished out.

As Holly tried to keep her cake out of Hope's hands, Evan reappeared and placed his hand around her waist.

'I'm so sorry. Work stuff, you know. But it's all done now, I think.'

Holly nodded. She wouldn't lie. This distracted Evan wasn't what she'd hoped for, and given how he was heading back home to London the very next day, she couldn't help but wonder what was so important it couldn't wait twenty-four hours. Then again, what could she expect after all his travels? It wasn't like he could answer all his messages on the plane.

'It's fine,' she told him, bouncing Hope as she spoke. 'Caroline's going back to Bourton now. You can take my keys, go have a shower. I won't be long at all.'

'No, it's fine. I want to be with you. Besides, you haven't given your dad the rest of his birthday present. And I want to be there, as long as you don't mind? I realise it could be a family thing.'

'No, of course I want you to be there. I want you to be part of the family. If that's what you want?'

He moved his head down to hers, slipping another hand around her, so that Hope was fully trapped between them.

'You know it is. As long as it's not moving too fast for you? If it's moving too fast for you, then I'll back off.'

Holly took his hands in hers and pulled her closer to him.

'No backing off,' she said, although she couldn't help but feel a niggling within her. If this was how much Evan was on the phone when he was supposed to be taking a break, then she hated to imagine what he was like when he was busy. But she wasn't going to think about that now.

13

An hour later and most of the crowd had dispersed. There were a few of the nearest and dearest still hanging around the garden, but they were the type who were going to stay until they were kicked out of the door and her dad didn't look like he was ready to do that anytime soon. But Holly needed to get Hope back to Ben and in bed. Besides, Evan was looking anxiously at his phone again, and something told her he would prefer to get to Bourton sooner rather than later.

'Do you think that it's a good idea to tell him tonight?' her mother said, her nerves about the gift showing again. 'He's had a lot to drink.'

'I think it's the perfect time. Besides, we need to tell him now – you set off tomorrow,' Holly reminded her.

'Yes, of course, of course we need to tell him,' her mother agreed. 'Let's do it now.'

She made a move for the back door, to head out into the garden, only for Holly to catch her by the hand.

'Maybe we should get him to come into the house, though,' she added. 'We should tell him away from all the guests. Just in case he's not too keen.'

Wendy paled further. There was a time when Holly had believed her mother was made of steel. That there was nothing in the entire world that could nerve her up, but the older she got, the less true she saw that was. And since her father's heart attack, it had got a whole lot worse. It was like her mother could see the bad in any situation, often before she saw the good in it.

Holly reached out and squeezed her hand. 'It's going to be fine. Trust me, Mum. He's going to love it.'

While her mum headed outside to fetch her dad, Holly remained with Evan and Hope, who was bouncing away on his knee. It was an energetic bounce, not the soft lulling rock Hope needed to fall asleep at that time of night. But just seeing the pair of them there together, smiling at one another, was enough to make her heart ache. She crossed the kitchen, ready to plant a kiss on both their heads, when her mother returned, this time with her father in tow.

'What's this about?' he said as he came in. 'Lenny was about to get out his sloe gin. You know he only does that when it's a special occasion.'

'I'm sure the sloe gin will still be there when you go back outside, Dad,' Holly said, well aware that Lenny would classify any occasion as special if it meant he got to drink a bit more. 'We wanted to give you your present.'

Having decided earlier that it would be sweet for Hope to hand her grandfather the envelope, explaining the details of his present, they had already given it to her, swapping it out for the yellow bunny she'd been cuddling beforehand. It had been an easier swap than expected but getting her to part with the now crumpled envelope and hand it over to Arthur was another matter.

'Here, Hope. It's Yellow Bunny. Do you want Yellow Bunny?'

Evan waved the stuffed animal in front of Hope, hoping the same exchange tactic would work again. 'Yes, there you go.'

After an intent look at the stuffed animal, Hope pulled it from Evan's grip, then threw it across the room.

'I knew I should have gone for the red one,' Evan said.

After much cajoling with yet more bunnies and no success, Holly finally went for the baby biscuits. A second later, Hope dropped the scrunched and crinkled envelope into Holly's hand.

'Happy birthday, Dad,' Holly said as she handed it over. 'This is from the three of us. Me, Mum and Hope.'

'Well, it feels quite thick...' Her father scrutinised the envelope as he turned it over in his hand, flattening it out as he went. 'And it's in a bigger envelope than a book token would be. Let me guess. A voucher for the garden centre?'

'Close, very close,' Holly lied.

'Well, it better not be a voucher for the sweetshop!' He laughed.

'How about you just open it, Arthur? Then you can stop guessing,' her mother said. Holly could hear the worry still choking in her mum's voice as she swallowed repeatedly, pursing her lips the way she did when she was really nervous.

As instructed, her father opened the envelope and pulled the paper out from within it. Rather than anything fancy, Holly had simply printed off the booking confirmation, meaning there was a lot of jargon on the page, and it would probably take him a little while to realise what the actual present was.

Holly and the others watched fixedly as his eyes scanned down the paper. Even when his eyes stopped moving and lips opened as if he was going to say something, silence swelled around them.

'Well?' her mother said impatiently.

Finally, he lifted his eyes from the page and shook his head slowly.

'You have to be joking?' he said.

14

No one was speaking. Arthur was still staring at the piece of paper in his hand, which trembled ever so slightly. Holly and Wendy were looking at him. And even without turning her head, Holly knew that Evan was looking at her. And Hope? Well, Hope was now trying to get back the yellow bunny that she had thrown across the room only minutes before.

Was the fact that her father had said nothing good or not? Holly couldn't work it out. She knew people could be stunned into a silence when there were happy, but she'd never seen her dad that way before. And the longer the silence went on for, the more the tension wrapped itself around the room.

Finally, Holly swallowed down the lump in her throat and spoke.

'Brussels is meant to be incredible, Dad. You know, there's that massive place where they had the world expo in the fifties, and chocolate, of course, there's chocolate.'

'And I'm going?'

He looked at his wife, then Holly, and only then did she see the glazed sheen in his eyes.

'Yes... Yes, if that's okay. I mean, it's non-refundable, so if you weren't going to go—'

'Why the hell wouldn't I go?' His face was awash with disbelief. 'Brussels? In Belgium? And on a train? You know, I've always loved trains.'

'You have?' Wendy asked.

'Well, yes. Who doesn't love trains? Go to sleep in one country, wake up in another.'

'I'm pretty sure you can do that on planes, too,' Holly said. 'And boats.'

'But on trains, you can see it all. The entire world passing by your window. I can't believe it. I really can't.'

The glaze that had covered his eyes only moments before was gone, but a single tear trickled down the side of his cheek.

'Thank you, love,' he said, holding his wife's face as he planted a long kiss on her lips. 'Thank you for this.'

'It was your globe-hopping daughter's idea,' she said, throwing Holly a teary grin. 'And I suppose we should thank Evan for that, too – putting all this travelling into her head.'

'Well, whoever I should thank, thank you,' he said. 'Thank you very much.'

'It's only three nights,' Holly told him, just in case he hadn't had time to read through all the details yet. 'We thought it was best we start with a short trip, you know, to find out if you enjoy it. Then maybe we can look at finding other deals in the future. Maybe other parts of Europe.'

'Three nights?' he said, his face smiling so wide, it looked close to bursting.

A series of hugs followed, with Holly and her dad, then with her mum, and even Holly and Evan. It didn't really make much sense, but she was grateful for the extra time to hold him.

When the laughter and hugs had finally died down, her dad glanced out of the window.

'Well, I guess we better get rid of all of them lingering outside. We've got to pack.'

'We don't get the train until tomorrow evening,' Wendy told him. 'We've got plenty of time if you want to enjoy one of Lenny's sloe gins.'

'And have a hangover when I need a full day to plan an itinerary and make sure we have the correct clothes for the weather forecast?'

Holly and her mother exchanged a glance.

'Just make sure you take it easy when you're there, Dad,' she said, placing a hand on his shoulder. 'You need to think about your heart.'

'Oh, just let me have a little fun, will you?'

When the hugging finished, Holly and Evan bid her parents farewell. While her father offered Evan only a brief handshake, her mother made a concerted effort to say Evan's name right several times, just to demonstrate that she knew it.

'See you next time you visit, Evan,' she said, as she waved them away from the door.

As they moved down the path away from the house, Hope on Holly's hip, Holly's free hand slipped effortlessly into Evan's and for a second, she couldn't help but wonder if every couple's hands fitted so perfectly together as there's did. It seemed unlikely.

'So, time for me to see this cute little cottage of yours,' Evan said as they climbed into the car. 'I can't wait.'

'You're going to have to wait a few minutes longer, I'm afraid. I'm going to drop Hope off at Ben's first.'

'You are?'

In all the business of the evening and the terror of a potential double date, Holly had forgotten to tell Evan that Hope would be staying at Ben's for the evening. Still, she'd assumed he would be grateful for the alone time. However, if that was the case, his face certainly didn't show it. Instead, it displayed the same hardness he had shown earlier when Holly had mentioned staying later than planned.

'It will only take a couple of minutes,' she assured him. 'It's really not that far. You can walk home from there if you really want?'

Evan took a deep inhale before taking his phone out of his pocket and staring at the screen.

'No, no, it's fine. It should be fine.'

'Should be fine?' Holly didn't mean to sound terse, but this demeanour, unpredictable and slightly controlling, wasn't anything like the man she'd met on holiday. He'd been in the Cotswolds only a few hours, but already this side of him was a serious red flag she hadn't expected. Maybe it was better Hope was out of the cottage tonight. The last thing she wanted was for her daughter to hear Holly calling it quits on a relationship.

15

Dropping Hope off at Ben's house went far quicker than Holly anticipated. Hope had started grizzling when they strapped her into the car, and even Evan sitting next to her making up plays with the bunnies wasn't enough to stop it. By the time they reached Bourton, it was full on wails. Thankfully, Ben was waiting. He had opened the front door before Holly had even got Hope out of the car.

'I should come and check everything is alright,' she said, as she handed a crying Hope to him.

'Don't be silly. She's just over-tired. It's absolutely fine. You go, have fun with Evan.'

'Thank you.' She kissed Hope lightly on the forehead. Given the mood she was in, she wasn't even going to hope for a bye-bye wave. Still, she had just turned to get back into the car when Ben called out to her.

'Oh, Holly?' he said.

'Yes?'

'About that double date?'

She smiled, feeling the heat rise to her cheeks. 'It's absolutely never happening.'

'I thought you'd agree with that.' He grinned back.

Given that this was the first time Holly had been truly alone with Evan since he had turned up at her parents' house, she'd expected the car journey back to be slightly more exciting. Even if they weren't buzzing with conversation, hopefully there would be the buzz of anticipation. Of finally getting to curl up in one another's arms. Instead, Evan remained in the back, where he had been next to Hope, and continued to check his phone. All the while, his foot tapped on the floor with such force that Holly could feel the shake to the car.

'Is everything okay?' she asked.

'Sorry? Yes, just looking forward to seeing the cottage.'

'Well, the wait's over. We're here.' She pulled up in her driveway, only to hear a sharp intake of breath from behind her in the passenger seats.

'Well, you weren't joking when you said it's small,' Evan said. 'This driveway is way tinier than I thought it would be.'

'Well, I only have a small house, and the cottage is plenty big enough for me and Hope.'

Holly didn't know why she was being so short with him, but then, it wasn't like Evan was being his normal self, either. She was feeling like she'd made a mistake. After all, how well did she really know him? Maybe he was far grumpier than he came across on the phone.

'Sorry,' Evan said when she went to unlock the door. He slipped an arm around her waist. 'I guess I'm just still suffering from jetlag.'

Holly turned around and looked at him.

'In that case, do we need to get you upstairs to bed?' There was no denying she had been looking forward to the physical side of the relationship. And she thought he had been too, at least in the conversations they'd had on the phone. But instead, several creases formed on his brow.

'Do you mind if we just have a drink first? A cup of tea, maybe.'

'Of course not.'

Holly opened the door, letting Evan into her and Hope's home.

Given how Holly knew that Evan was visiting that day, she'd attempted to keep the place tidy, but she couldn't help but compare this place to Evan's house in France. His second house.

'Are those the flowers I sent you?' he asked, gesturing to the half bunch that had been decanted into a plastic jug that morning before Jamie took the rest.

'One of the bunches, yes.'

'They look smaller than I thought. I won't use that delivery company again.'

Holly pressed her lips together, momentarily tempted to confess to what she had done, but before she could speak, Evan's phone rang again. Rather than looking disappointed by the interruption of their alone time, he looked elated.

'I just need to go outside to take this,' he said. 'I'll be a couple of minutes. Don't worry about the tea. I've changed my mind.'

The rumble of a truck filtered through from outside. Another spark of annoyance burned in Holly. This time, not at Evan. One of the neighbours had been doing work on their house for several weeks now, and it had been mostly okay, except during Hope's nap times when the hammering seemed to get louder. She'd never known them to have a builder come in this late, though. If it happened again, she might need to have a friendly word. After all, she doubted she was the only neighbour it would annoy.

Deciding it wasn't something she wanted to get into now, she flopped down on the sofa, trying to beat down the nerves that were churning through her stomach. Nerves that she was sure Evan must be feeling, too. After all, why else would he be acting this way? It wasn't like they were strangers, not with all the time they'd spent talking on the phone. Even so, this wasn't what she'd expected. And he was leaving tomorrow. The last thing she wanted was to spend the entire night feeling awkward.

Deciding that even if Evan didn't want a cup of tea, she did, Holly headed back to the kettle and switched it on, only for the front door to swing open.

'Okay, you can come outside now.'

Evan was standing in the doorway, but it wasn't the Evan of the car journey with the nervous foot-tapping and constant phone checking. This was the Evan from France, the one with the beaming smiles. Who had constantly made her laugh. This was the one who had greeted her outside at her parents' house and kissed her so much that she'd never wanted to let go. This was the Evan she had been waiting for, but she wasn't sure what had made him return.

'Come on. This should explain why I've been acting weird,' he said, as if he'd been reading her mind. 'Now, make sure you've got your shoes on, too. I'll pick up your jacket for you.'

'My jacket? I thought we were staying in.'

'Just hurry up, will you?'

Doing as instructed, Holly slipped on her trainers and headed out of the front door, but she was barely one step out when she stopped. Babbling was her go-to nervous reaction, but being stunned to silence wasn't something she could remember having happened to her before. Yet at that moment, her mind was a complete blank. The sight in front of her made no sense. No sense at all. After blinking several times, and discovering the image didn't change, she finally found her voice, although with it came the words her father had said to her only a couple of hours before.

'You have to be joking?'

16

Holly couldn't move. She could see Evan in her peripheral vision, his eyes looking at her, expecting some form of response, but at that moment, she couldn't even think, let alone speak. Her heart was hammering against her ribs. Her throat was dry. So dry, she could barely swallow. Yet she tentatively took a step forward.

'So it turned out the driveway was big enough after all,' Evan said, finally breaking the silence. It was a joke. She knew he was making a joke, but she couldn't work out how to respond. When she still didn't say anything, he spoke again. 'So, are you going to tell me what you think?'

What did she think? This silence was getting ridiculous. It was even worse than at her parents' house, when they'd waited to see what her father thought of his birthday present. Only it wasn't her birthday. And even if it was, she would never have imagined something like this in a million years.

Holly needed to say something. She knew she did, but how? All she could do was stare at the vehicle in front of her. Its perfect, sky-blue paintwork glimmered. It might have been past sunset, but she could still see it perfectly, and there wasn't a single chip or scratch on it. The chrome wing mirrors gleamed while the black leather seat looked as comfortable as her couch.

'Is this for me?' she said eventually.

'If you want it?' Evan stepped towards her. 'I mean, it's in your name, insured in your name and MOT'd. But if there's a problem, I can always take it back.'

'No, no.' For the first time since stepping outside her cottage, Holly moved with a concerted effort, darting towards the brand-new Vespa and wrapping her arms around the handlebars. The metal was cold and yet inviting. And the smell... How was it possible a machine could smell so good?

'So I take it you like it?' Evan said.

Suddenly realising she still hadn't actually said anything properly since seeing the Vespa, Holly pulled herself away and looked at him.

'You bought me a Vespa? You actually bought me a Vespa?' She kept a questioning tone in her voice. After all, it still seemed unbelievable. Yet Evan's lips twisted into a smile.

'You know, the way you're saying that makes it sound like it's a problem. It's not a problem, is it?' His eyes glinted with his smirk, and Holly shook her head.

'It's not a problem, it's... it's insane.' She looked back towards the vehicle, her stomach suddenly cramping with laughter. She couldn't stop.

'You can't do this. You can't buy me a Vespa.'

'I very much can,' Evan said, sweeping in and wrapping his arms around her so that he was leaning into her ear as he spoke. 'The only question I want to know is, do you want it?'

Holly gazed at the vehicle. The only other time she had been on one was in the south of France. Evan had taken her down the winding roads and undulating hills as they made their way to a vineyard. And she had driven on her own too.

Just looking at the vehicle parked there on her driveway brought about that sense of freedom she had felt as the wind blew through her hair, the world at her fingertips. Evan had mentioned at the time how Holly should get one when she got back to England, given how much she had enjoyed it. But she'd told him outright that it wouldn't be possible. She didn't have the money to throw around and buy something so clearly self-indulgent as this.

'I... I love it,' she said, her throat finally loosening enough that she could speak.

'Good, because the tank's full and as we don't have Hope, it seems like the perfect time to go for a spin. So why don't you show me what these cute Cotswold villages are all about?'

17

It was entirely different, driving through the Cotswolds compared to being in the south of France. To start with, Holly had to weave past the various parked cars on her lane to get to the main road. Then there was the added factor that she was driving at night. For those first few minutes, Holly gripped the handlebars so tightly, her knuckles were a stark white. However, as they turned off the Fosseway and onto the quiet, country roads, where her headlights gleamed brightly out in front of her, her muscles began to relax.

Back in France, Evan had referred to her as a natural on bikes, which she'd dismissed, assuming it was nothing but foolish flattery. But now, as she took one corner then the next, laughing to herself as rabbits loitered precariously on the edge of the road, and owls swooped low in the fields, she couldn't help but feel that perhaps he was right. She and this little Vespa were going to have so much fun. She only wished that Hope was big enough to bring along, too. Maybe when she was bigger, she could look into little sidecars. Perhaps that would be a way she and Hope could travel together when she was in her teens. The thought snapped Holly back to reality. It wasn't as if she had the money to buy a sidecar, or anything else. She wasn't even sure she was going to have enough money to put petrol in both this and the car some weeks. Still, she was going to make this full tank last as long as possible. But then, could she really keep it? The excitement gave way to a feeling of uncertainty.

Above them, the first stars of the night were appearing in the sky, as Holly drew up to a small village green. She flicked on her indicators and slowed to a stop. Then she pulled off her helmet and held it in her arm, before turning to speak.

'So?' Evan's smile was probably as wide as her own. 'What do you think?'

'This is amazing. But there's no way I can accept.'

'Why not? Besides, you have to. The minute you drove it, its resale value went down by like 20 per cent. At least. You're stuck with it now.'

He was playing with her, Holly knew it, but she didn't have the heart to laugh back. It wasn't a laughing matter.

'Evan, you know how I feel about you. And I know that you're serious about me. But like I said in France, you and I are from different worlds. If we're going to make this work—'

'We *are* going to make this work.'

'I know we can.' Holly chose her words carefully, trying not to offend. 'Evan, the way we are going to make this work is by meeting halfway. I'm not expecting you to give up your lifestyle that you've worked hard for. That's not what I'm saying. But you can't go spending over a hundred pounds on bunnies because you couldn't decide which one to get. That's a week's worth of shopping for Hope and me. And I like flowers. Actually, I love them, but I don't need a bunch so massive, I have to split it in two and give half away to my friend because they won't fit on my dining table.'

'So that's why the bouquet looked so small,' Evan said, before adding a smirk. 'I'd better not send that letter of complaint after all.'

He was trying to lighten the mood and Holly appreciated it. Though the unease hadn't lessened by much, she managed to reply with a small smile.

'Look, do you want to keep it?' Evan said firmly, offering no room for her to misconstrue the question.

'Yes, of course I want to keep it. But it's—'

'Good, that's settled.'

She took his hand.

'This is too big, Evan. This is too generous.'

'Says the girl who deliberately missed her flight and took a taxi across one country into another to go in search of a guy she barely knew? Trust me, it's going to take a lot of random presents to ever make up for that.'

Holly struggled to think of a reply to that one. Only that she didn't need anything making up for. Being with Evan was enough. Before she could say as much, he was speaking again.

'Holly, I want to spoil you. Trust me, all that money sitting in my account isn't worth a thing if I can't use it to make you smile.'

It was such a sweet comment. Sweeter perhaps than even the Vespa. Still, she paused before she replied.

'How about this as an arrangement,' she said. 'Whenever I'm at yours, you have free rein. If you want to spoil me and take me out to fancy restaurants, then fine. We can do that. But when you're here at mine, then no more massive gestures are allowed. No big cuddly toys for Hope. No extravagant gifts for me. How's that for a deal?'

As she finished talking, she noticed Evan staring at her with an intensity she had never seen before.

'Holly, when are you going to realise I'll do whatever you want? No big gestures, all the big gestures. Whatever, I'll do it. You've got me. Hook, line and sinker.'

With that, Holly leaned forward and planted a kiss on his lips. There were no cars passing, no people on the village green, and it could have been as if they were the only two people in the world. That was certainly how it felt. Like it was just her and Evan. And when they broke apart, he was continuing to look at her with that same intense gaze.

'What?' she asked, mildly perturbed. 'Is there something on my face?'

'No,' Evan said, shaking his head. 'I was just thinking about your cottage.'

'The cottage?'

'There is a room upstairs, right? Well, I'm dying to see it.'

18

Holly rolled over in the bed, only to find herself trapped on her side. Normally, she had an entire bed to spread out in whatever manner she fancied. Sometimes, she would lie diagonally corner to corner, other times adopt a starfish pose, stretching out to take up as much space as physically possible. But that wasn't possible last night. Because last night, she hadn't been alone in bed. Evan had been with her.

'Morning.' She didn't know how he knew she was awake and looking at him. His eyes were still closed as he spoke, though his lips smiled, as if in a dream. 'How did you sleep?'

'Sleep? I'm not sure we managed that, did we?' Holly said, a yawn forcing its way out as she spoke.

'I'm so very sorry.' Evan opened his eyes. 'Had I known, I would've stopped kissing you sooner.'

'I think it's fine,' she replied. 'Remember – my house, my rules.'

She kissed him on the lips, closing her mouth to avoid any of the horrendous morning breath she knew was likely afflicting them both. Any worries that had crept in through the evening at her parents' had disappeared the moment they'd started driving on the

Vespa. The Vespa. The thought caused a hundred butterflies to erupt within her. She had a boyfriend who had bought her a Vespa. She breathed in deeply, refusing to let her thoughts get locked on to all the reasons that it was completely insane. After all, they were in Bourton now, which meant that for the rest of the time he was here, Evan had to stick to her rules.

The flutter of butterflies flickered into a new sense of excitement as she shifted herself up to sitting.

'So, are you ready?' she said, unable to stop the grin on her face. 'You know what you agreed to today?'

The relaxed smile on Evan's face shifted by a fraction. He followed her into a sitting position, only he wasn't grinning. Instead, he looked at her with mild trepidation.

'You know,' he said. 'I'm starting to think I've made a mistake agreeing to this.'

'Quite possibly.' Holly smirked back. 'But it's too late to back out now. Now come on, I want to get to the shop early and make sure we've got an apron that fits you.'

* * *

Given how Holly's father worked as many hours at the shop as Holly did now, his absence while he was in Brussels would not go unnoticed. Although he wasn't going until the evening, her mother had volunteered to look after Hope, meaning he needed to be the one to get everything packed ready to go. Previously, Holly had got support in the form of Drey. Drey, the former Saturday girl whom Holly had once accused of being a shoplifter, had been paramount in helping Holly set up the shop. But now, she was busy with her business administration course, spending more and more time in college, and doing work placements at other businesses, from art galleries and boutiques to factories and plant hire depots. Still, the sweet shop was in her heart, as much as it was in Holly's, and whenever there was a great need, she would always come to the rescue.

Still, that morning, with Ben at work and Caroline having covered the late afternoon shift the day before, Holly had no choice but to head in, even with Evan staying.

'You're not seriously going to make me wear that, are you?' Evan said, as Holly slipped the blue and white striped apron over his head. 'You know this will do nothing for my street cred.'

'I wasn't aware you had any street cred,' Holly responded, before tugging the apron down a little further and moving around the back to tie a bow. 'And yes, I am completely genuine. You are wearing this.'

Never had Holly wished so much that she had a full-length mirror in the shop. However ridiculous Evan thought he looked, she could guarantee it was a hundred times worse. The fabric barely went around his chest and finished above his knees, like some confusing sixties-style mini dress. The ruffles round the hem and neckline looked infinitely more pronounced than they did on Holly or any of the other employees. But there was no chance she was letting him take it off; he had said he was happy to help work in the shop and that meant he was going to wear the uniform the same as the rest of them.

As it happened, the pinstriped apron wasn't the only part of Just One More that Evan struggled with.

'I'm sorry, but this doesn't make any sense,' he said, as he tried to loosen the strap Holly had tied so neatly. 'How do you have so many types of the same sweets? Liquorice Allsorts, liquorice root, liquorice laces, liquorice wheels, liquorice bullets. Why not just sell one type of liquorice?'

'Because people don't want just one type. They all like different things.'

'But how are they all different if they're all liquorice?'

'Well, because that one has coconut with it, and those are covered in sugar, and I'm not getting into it with you now. We'll have customers any minute, and I need to show you how to work the till.'

'The till?' Evan said, raising an eyebrow.

'Yes, I've got some things that need sorting out upstairs, so if we have a quiet spell, I'm going to leave you down here on your own.'

Evan didn't move, but his skin took on a decidedly greenish hue.

'You're joking, aren't you?'

'You run a multi-million-pound business,' Holly said accusingly. 'I'm sure you can deal with a customer or two.'

As she spoke, a familiar face walked in through the door. Hurriedly, Holly pushed Evan round to the back of the counter.

'Oh, this will be perfect.' She grinned.

19

Holly was grateful for all her customers. Without them, she wouldn't have a business. And as important as the tourist trade was, it was the locals who kept Just One More running. The regulars who came out regardless of the weather to get their sweet treats and keep the bills paid. But while she was grateful for them all, there were some that were far nicer to interact with than others.

'Mr Bettinson.' Holly forced herself to smile as the old man limped in. 'What would you like to get the grandchildren today?'

Mr Bettinson, whose weekly habit was purchasing sweets for his grandchildren, was normally only mildly amiable at the best of times. He looked up at Evan and scoffed.

'Bit old to start a Saturday job, isn't he?'

'Evan's just helping me out for today,' Holly said in her sweetest voice possible. 'And maybe a couple of days here and there in the foreseeable future. Evan, this is Mr Bettinson.'

'Pleased to meet you, sir.'

Holly didn't know if it was nervousness, or deliberate, but she had never heard Evan speak with such a deep American drawl. Mr Bettinson's eyes widened.

'Are you from America?'

'Yes indeed I am, Mr Bettinson. Now, what about those sweets for the grandchildren? What kinda thing do they fancy? You know, we have a whole range of liquorice here.'

Whether it was because he was wearing the pinstripe blue pinafore that looked completely ridiculous, the fact that he was definitely not local, or just somehow new, Mr Bettinson continued to eye Evan with distrust.

'Jelly babies.' His answer came in two words. 'Big bag.'

Holly smiled. Thankfully, customers like Mr Bettinson were few and far between, and Holly rarely had to worry about people like him. He was likely the most unpleasant person Evan would have to deal with all day. Still, it didn't hurt for him to see that her days weren't all sunshine and roses.

'Okay, Evan, over to you,' Holly said. 'A large bag is two hundred grams. If you want to grab the jelly babies from the shelf and bring them over here, you can weigh them out.'

'He said he ain't a Saturday boy, but you're sure treating him like one,' Mr Bettinson commented.

Evan smirked as he collected the jar from the shelf.

'You're quite right. She is, isn't she? Now, jelly babies. Good sweets, these. Classic. It's a taste you never forget. My grandmother's from Bath, do you know it? She loves her jelly babies.'

Mr Bettinson's glare lessened by a fraction.

'So you've got some of this country in you, have you? Not totally foreign?'

'Not totally,' Evan said. 'Now, let me weigh those out for you.'

Three minutes later, the jelly babies had been weighed out, bagged and paid for, and Holly and Evan were once again alone in the shop.

'I didn't know you had a grandmother in Bath,' she said. She knew there was still plenty she had to learn about Evan, but she was sure she would have picked up on something like that.

'That's because I don't,' Evan replied. 'But I figured it was the type of thing a little guy like that would like to hear. So I made it up.'

Holly laughed and patted him on the shoulders.

'You just can't do that.'

'Why not?'

'Because they'll remember. People like that remember everything.'

'Fine, I'll try to stick to the truth from now on. Now that was easy. Where is the next customer?'

Evan got his wish as ten minutes later, the shop was full. While Holly stuck to the till, he was running from shelf to shelf, trying to find the sweets that the customers asked for. With most of the regulars, they already knew where their favourites were and were helpful enough to point them out for him. For those that were undecided and wanted to know what Holly had in stock, she had to answer. But it didn't matter. Somehow, they found a rhythm between them.

It was fun.

A lot of fun.

'I can see why you love it,' Evan said, as the busy spell died down and gave them time to talk to one another again. 'It was a weird rush. Being busy like that.'

'So does that mean you're okay if I leave you on your own while I pop upstairs and sort out a few things? The shelves up there are a complete mess.'

Evan looked at her with a hint of fear in his eyes.

'I didn't actually think you were serious about leaving me,' he said.

'Evan, you run countless businesses, substantially larger than this, and fly across the world regularly to help keep them all in order. You can handle taking two-pound sixty for a packet of sweets.'

He nodded his head rapidly, in a manner that was most ridiculous and incredibly endearing.

'Two-pound sixty,' he repeated. 'Sure I can. It's fine. And if I mess up, I'll give you the money.'

'No, no, you won't do that,' Holly said firmly. With Evan's generosity, she could just imagine him letting people have whatever they wanted off the shelf, then covering it out of his own pocket. 'And you won't mess up. Now, I'm just going to be upstairs. Yell if you need anything.'

Holly really did have a fair few jobs that required doing. From unpacking boxes of fudge to looking at her months' invoices. Still, it was hard not to listen in to how Evan was doing.

'Jazzies?' His bewildered voice travelled upstairs, catching her attention. 'That's a type of sweet?'

A second later, he was talking again.

'Wow, I never knew that was what you called these. I guess I just thought of them as sprinkled chocolate drops. It makes sense now. The colours. They are jazzy, right?'

The till pinged open and shut every few minutes, and after ten minutes, when he still hadn't called her in need of help, Holly finally took the plunge and opened up the computer.

There was a time when looking through her invoices would make her stomach churn with dread. Particularly when she'd first taken over the shop and was still desperate to find out if she could even get a mortgage. But those days were gone, and the shop was going from strength to strength. She'd even joked about opening up a second branch, perhaps in Stow or Moreton. Maybe even as far afield as Cirencester, but that was something she wasn't going to think about seriously right now. Managing the staff, Hope, and now a relationship with Evan, was more than enough for her to juggle, without adding anything else to the chaos.

She was still busy, looking at the last month's profits, when a voice came from downstairs in the shop.

'Pontefract cakes. How can you not know what Pontefract cakes are? Little, round, black, gooey, delicious.'

'Well, it's only my first day. Sort of,' she could hear Evan respond. 'I'm not too familiar with all the sweets yet. Give me a minute and I'm sure I'll find them.'

'They should be on the top shelf. And when you find that jar, you need to try one. I mean, what is Holly teaching you young people?'

There was something recognisable about the voice. It was someone frail and old, yet the way she spoke about the sweets was peculiarly familiar.

'And talking of Holly, where is she? I was hoping I'd be able to speak to her.'

That was it. That was the moment it clicked. Shutting her laptop, Holly jumped to her feet and bounded down the stairs.

There, standing next to Evan in all her miniature glory, was Maud.

20

It probably wasn't sensible to squeeze the old lady as hard as Holly did, but she couldn't help herself.

'Evan, this is Maud. Maud, Evan. Maud, Evan is my boyfriend. Evan, Maud is—'

'The old owner of the sweet shop. Of course.' Evan stretched out his hand, which Maud shook without a moment's hesitation. 'Pleasure to meet you. Holly told me so much about you.'

'I hope at least some of it was good?' Maud chuckled.

'Oh, every word of it was good,' Evan said.

'Is that right? Well, jury's out on you.' She looked at Holly as she spoke. 'He's nice to look at and everything, but really Holly, that man needs to learn his sweets if he's going to work here.'

Holly couldn't help but grin.

'Don't worry, he's not going to work here – not full-time, at least. He's just helping me out today. It's a way we get to spend some time together.'

Maud looked at Evan again, though this time, her gaze changed. It was far more wistful. She nodded slowly, turning back to Holly.

'Then, in that case, I approve very much. This is a good place to spend time with your loved ones.'

The silence swelled between them. Holly couldn't remember how much she had told Evan about Agnes and her passing away, but she didn't want him to say anything that might cause Maud distress. So she cleared her throat and spoke as joyfully as she could.

'So, what do you think of the place now? We've got quite a few new lines in.'

Maud let out a slight chuckle before turning in a circle. It was hesitant, slow. A nervousness bubbled through Holly. Even though Maud had let the sweet shop fall into disrepair before she handed it over to Holly, her opinion still mattered greatly.

'I think you've done wonderfully,' Maud said, causing a sigh of relief to flood from Holly. 'You know, I stood outside for a bit earlier. I didn't want to come in. I saw you here, the pair of you, and you had some big queues to deal with. It was like we used to be, back in the day. Me and Agnes and you all together.'

With Agnes having been mentioned again – this time directly – it didn't seem right for Holly to ignore it.

'I hope she would be proud of what I've done with the place,' Holly said quietly.

'Oh, she would, my love. She would be so proud of you. Her legacy carried on by a person she loved most in the world. How could she not feel proud of that?'

Tears pricked the back of Holly's eyes, but she hurriedly sniffed them back. Back in the day, Agnes and Maud had had a rule that you never let your sadness show on the sweet shop floor. And the last thing she wanted to do was break that rule with Maud standing right beside her.

'So, what are you doing here?' Holly said, deliberately making her tone more jovial. 'Why didn't you tell me you were back?'

'Oh, you know, life. Lots of things going on. Not that I want to bore you with them now. Not when you're at work with your man.'

'Then why don't you go for a coffee or lunch together?' Evan's voice cut into the conversation. For a second, Holly had almost forgotten he was there. 'It looks like there are plenty of cafés here in the village. I can call you if I need any help.'

Rather than being grateful for the offer, Maud grimaced.

'She hasn't just spent the last two years building this business back up again for you to ruin it,' she said. 'If you think I'm trusting you to look after this place while she crosses the road, you'd be mistaken. What are Pontefract cakes, good lord.'

Holly laughed. 'I am sure he would be completely fine for half an hour,' she said.

'No, no,' Maud continued. 'I won't disturb you now and I'm meeting some friends for lunch, anyway. But I'm going to be around for a few days. Perhaps we could do dinner one night?'

Holly leapt at the opportunity. There was so much about the business she wanted to tell Maud. Yes, she could see from the shelves and the customers how it had grown. But there was so much more to it than that. There were the party platters, Drey's idea, that they were doing for birthday parties and businesses. There were the sweets they gave out each year as part of the Christmas carols to the children and their donations to the care homes, bringing a taste of nostalgia back to the residents there. There was so much to talk about.

'Well, Evan has to leave this afternoon. He's heading back home to London for a couple of days before he goes to America again.'

'So would tonight be okay?' Maud suggested. 'Or do you already have other plans?'

'Tonight would be perfect.' Holly smiled. 'You can meet Hope.'

'Hope?'

Holly shook her head. It was ridiculous to think that Maud

hadn't even learned about Hope, but then, when would she have done? They hadn't kept in great contact.

'Hope is my daughter,' Holly said, unable to contain her smile. The look of glee transferred to Maud, whose eyes welled up with tears.

'Oh, congratulations!' She grabbed Holly's hands and squeezed them tightly. 'I'm so proud.'

She moved to Evan to take his hands in the same way, only he quickly moved them out of her reach.

'Actually, Hope isn't mine.'

Maud looked back at Holly, her eyebrows arched.

'Like I said, there's been a lot to talk about.'

Maud's face relaxed into a smile. The type of smile Holly had almost forgotten she was capable of.

'Well, dinner tonight sounds perfect, but if this fella is off in a bit, I should let you spend all the time you can together.'

21

Maud's visit left Holly with a feeling of elation that only increased when Drey walked through the shop door an hour later. As was often the case, Drey was sporting a brand new look, that included a platinum-blonde bob and silvery eye makeup. Holly couldn't remember the last time Drey had worked in the shop, and for a solid minute, the pair squeezed each other tightly and bounced up and down on the spot like they were both a pair of teenagers, despite the fact that Drey was now officially an adult.

'Thank you. Thank you so much for helping,' Holly said.

'Are you serious? After all you've done for me? I'm fine to put in a few extra shifts.'

Holly released her friend and employee, and turned to Evan. 'Evan, this is Drey. Drey, Evan.'

'The incredibly attractive, overly generous, rich, American boyfriend with the villa in the south of France?' Drey questioned, before turning to Holly. 'You know I chat to Caroline, right?'

'I will happily claim all of those titles, Drey.' Evan grinned. 'But just to check, you're the bossy teenager who was practically running this place before Holly, right?'

'Well, I'm no longer a teenager,' Drey said. 'But I did get myself arrested once and needed to call Holly for help.'

'Sounds like an employee of the year, there.'

Drey turned to Holly, satisfied by the amount of banter she had put Evan through. 'I like him,' she said.

'So do I,' Holly replied. 'Okay, Caroline is in the village if you need help. I'm just going to drive Evan to the train station. But if there're any disasters—'

'I'll pretend there weren't, cover it all up and won't let you know,' Drey replied.

'Perfect.'

With that, Holly and Evan left hand-in-hand.

'So that's it: Drey, Caroline, my dad, and Maud. You've met every single person involved in the sweet shop.'

'And it's so special. I can see why you'd never want to give it up. Never want to live anywhere else.'

There was something held in the silence at the end of his words. This was only the second time they had met, but she had fallen headfirst. Though what neither of them had thought about addressing was how long could a long-distance relationship last? It was impossible to know without trying, but even now, she was taking him to the station after only one evening together. It was enough to turn her stomach.

'You want to tell me what you're thinking,' he said, as they climbed into the car.

Holly shut her door, turned the key in the ignition, and let out a deep sigh. No, she didn't really want to tell him, but by the look of him, he knew that.

'Look.' Evan reached across and took her hands. 'I know you're worried about how this is going to work, but I need you to be honest with me the whole time. Whether it's about buying too many bunnies, or sticking my nose in where it shouldn't go. That's the only way this is going to work. And while we are talking about being honest, I want you to know that I'm happy doing the travelling, Holly. You don't have to feel like you need to come up and see me. I don't need you to fix your life around me. That's not how a relationship works. We do what's best for both of us. And right now, I'm the one who is able to travel more. Who gets more free time. So it only makes sense that I'm the one who comes down here. Besides, property prices in the Cotswolds are a sure investment.'

Holly looked at him, not sure whether to smile or shout.

'There is no way you are buying a property in the Cotswolds. Not yet. Not until we've been together for at least six months.'

'Four months?'

'You're ridiculous, you know that?'

'Ridiculously in love, yes.'

The pair leaned together simultaneously, resulting in a long and lingering kiss.

The rest of the drive, they barely spoke, but it wasn't an uncomfortable silence. It was warm and contented with Evan's fingers slotted perfectly into hers as she gripped the gearstick of the car. This was so easy. If this was her life, seeing Evan when she could, running the sweet shop, surrounded by her friends, then she could deal with that. For now, at least. She was living in the present and the present was good.

After dropping Evan back at the station, there was no need to go back to the shop. After all, Drey was more than capable of taking care of it. So instead, Holly drove straight to her parents'. She needed to pick up Hope, but she also wanted to know what her mother's opinion of Evan was.

22

After Holly showered her daughter with hundreds of kisses, the way she normally did when she saw Hope in the afternoon, her daughter then gave her the task of kissing every single bunny. One by one, Hope picked them up and pushed them against Holly's lips.

In the last twelve hours, Hope had formed an unbreakable bond with the stuffed toys. Ideally, she would carry them all, all the time, while she crawled along the carpet, but that was easier said than done. When Holly arrived, she was carrying four, two in each hand, which her mother informed her was the minimum. All were held by their ears. It didn't make crawling very easy, but anything that slowed her down was a good thing.

With all the bunnies kissed and Hope happily playing with them back on the carpet, Holly braved the question.

'So, what did you think?'

'About?'

'About Evan? What do you think about Evan?'

A sly smile curled on her mother's lips, showing she knew exactly what Holly had been talking about.

'Oh, he's very tall and good-looking,' she started. 'And very American.'

'I believe that happens when you come from America,' Holly said sarcastically, before pressing for a slightly deeper answer. 'But he's nice, right? You liked him? I mean, how could you not?'

'Well, I didn't see much of him, but he seemed nice enough,' her mother agreed. 'Although all those teddy bears he bought Hope was a bit over the top, but you know how some Americans can be.'

'I think you'll find that's stereotyping, Mum,' Holly said, not quite sure whether her mother was joking or not. 'You are right, though. He's very generous. But he has a lot of money and he likes spoiling the people he cares about. I think there are a lot worse character traits than that in a person.'

For a split second, Holly considered telling her mother about the Vespa. After all, it wasn't like she could keep it a secret forever. Her parents would see the vehicle when they came to the house. Besides, if she didn't tell them about it, someone else in the village likely would.

But something made Holly hesitate. If she told now, her mother would get all worried and start questioning Holly about whether it was safe or not. Then she would start giving her lectures and pulling out old horror stories from her childhood, and people who had had terrible accidents, and that just wasn't something Holly wanted to hear. So, deciding to gloss over the subject for now, she carried on talking.

'Don't worry, I have now put him in his place about extravagant gifts, so hopefully he'll be slightly more mindful with presents for the both of us from now on. I've already got enough flowers to last me until Christmas.'

Her mother looked at her, and Holly expected another line, about a man buying extravagant gifts, or how she ought to be careful not to get her heart broken again, but instead, a light glimmered in her eyes.

'Well, I think it's lovely you've finally got someone to spoil you the way you deserve, darling,' she said.

A moment formed between the two of them, and Holly found herself wanting to say something, perhaps thank her mother – and her father – for the role models they'd been for her, and through that, helping her to pick out a life partner. But before she said anything, another thought struck.

'Oh, Mum, I forgot to tell you. Guess who came into the shop today?'

'Barack Obama,' her mother said without missing a beat.

'Why would Barack Obama have come to the shop?' Holly frowned.

'I don't know. But you said guess, and you sounded excited, so I thought someone exciting might have come in. And I think Barack Obama's exciting.'

'No, Mum. It wasn't Barack Obama. It was Maud.'

'Maud?'

'Yes, do you know Maud? Maud as in Agnes and Maud.'

'I know who you meant, I only thought that...' Her sentence faded into the ether, before she looked directly at Holly. 'Did you get to talk to her much?'

Holly shook her head. 'Not really. Evan was still in the shop, but we're going to meet up for dinner tonight. I'm going to take Hope to meet her too. Can you believe she hasn't even met Hope yet?'

She expected her mother to add some comment about how Maud would love her, and how nice an evening they were likely to have, but instead her eyes had a faraway look in them.

'Why don't you leave Hope with me tonight,' she said after a pause, glancing down at her granddaughter. 'She's perfectly settled here, and that way you and Maud can have a proper conversation.'

It was Holly's turn to frown. 'I can't leave Hope with you because you're getting a train tonight, Mum. Remember? To Brussels?'

Her mother shook her head, and a broad, tight smile rose on her cheeks.

'Of course I remember. Ignore me. A silly slip. Too much excitement going on. I'm all over the place. I'd lose my head if it wasn't screwed on. Yes, of course, of course I'm going to Brussels.'

Holly pressed her lips together. Before yesterday, she had never been worried about her mother. Her father, yes. Her dad's heart attack had made her constantly nervous that he was doing too much, or too little. A tangible reminder that they were getting older. But she'd seen none of these signs in her mum until yesterday, and yet now they were coming thick and fast. Had she just been oblivious to it before? Whatever was going on, if her mother was still behaving oddly when she got back from Belgium, Holly knew she'd need to mention it to her father. Not that she wanted to worry him, but it was important to keep on top of these things.

'Do you have everything packed?' Holly asked, moving the conversation back towards the holiday. 'You've got your passport, your tickets?'

'Everything packed, double checked, and I made a list and ticked it off, too.'

Holly didn't doubt it for a second. That sounded much more like her mother.

'And Arthur has picked out a couple of places he wants to visit. Did you know there is a miniature Europe just outside the town? Like our model village.'

'I did not,' Holly responded. 'You'll have to make sure you send me some pictures.'

'Oh, we will. Well, we can video call you. I've checked with the phone company and I've got all the internet and telephone calls I need so we can keep in touch. I'll ring you the moment I get to the hotel.'

'Good,' Holly said. She wanted to know that they'd arrived safely, although from the way her mother mentioned the unlimited internet, Holly had a feeling she might receive a voice call every time they saw something remotely interesting.

'Well, now that you've reminded me, we'd better get a wriggle on. We need to get to the station.'

'Are you sure you don't want me to give you a lift?'

'There's no need, love. Lenny already offered.'

Her mother stood up, and Holly squeezed her tightly.

'I should probably say goodbye to Dad, too. Where is he?'

'Oh, he's gone to get snacks for the train. Do you know he doesn't want to get ripped off by their expensive prices?'

Holly smiled. They may be starting to travel the world, but they were still the parents she knew and loved.

Holly grabbed her bag, picked up her daughter and moved towards the door.

'I hope everything goes okay with Maud tonight,' her mother said, that same wistful look on her face.

'I'm sure it will. I'll send you a text.'

And with one more kiss on the cheek, Holly left.

23

Back in Bourton, Holly tried to get hold of Jamie. She wanted to discuss the idea of the different themed platters for the wedding and fill her in on some of the details from her and Evan's evening, but after the call went to voicemail twice, she decided to head into the village and try again later instead.

After checking up on Drey and the shop, Holly took Hope over to the green to have a crawl on the grass and a splash in the water. The plan was only to stay there for half an hour, but as the pair of them sat on the grass, watching the world go by, Holly found herself with no desire to leave. The bus tours and day visitors were slowing, making their ways back home, and with a bag packed with snacks for Hope, there was no rush to go anywhere.

Around half five, Drey came out to tell her she had locked up and was heading home, and Holly thought about heading back too, but it seemed a shame to take Hope back to the cottage when she was having such a nice calm time. So, they went and got a takeaway coffee from one of the restaurants and it was only another hour later, after Hope pulled off her second pair of socks and threw them in the river, that Holly finally decided it was time to head back and give Hope a bath before meeting Maud.

Hope loved baths. She could splash about in the water, kicking her little rubber ducks, and giggling with joy as Holly poured water on to her belly, or spinning the little contraption that was fixed to the wall, to her heart's content. She also found joy in lots of other aspects of the bathroom. Recently, she had learnt to flush the toilet. She'd pull herself to stand with her head above the bowl as the water spiralled down and then begin to refill. Holly's weighing scales also gave her great delight as she pressed her hands on them and watched the dials go up and down. Not to mention the wash basket, which she was always desperate to climb inside, although Holly knew she was partly to blame for that one, having put her in it once about a month ago, pretending it was a boat.

Yes, normally the bathroom was a happy place for Hope. But that evening, Hope did not want a bath for one very simple reason. The bunny rabbits.

Prising them out of Hope's hand so Holly could get her into the bath was proving almost impossible. The moment Holly freed one of the animals from Hope's fist and dropped it onto the floor, her daughter picked another one up.

'Look, we can put them on the edge of the bath, so they can watch you?' she tried gently, and for a second, she thought Hope was about to release one of them. But then she grabbed it again and pulled it back to her. Holly's voice grew firmer. 'Okay, but the bunny is going to get wet. Are you ready for that? Because that's the only option, Hope. Bunnies stay out of the bath or they get wet.'

Hope's eyes widened, as if she'd actually understood what Holly had just said. Then, a second later, her face turned bright red and she began to cry. But if Holly had thought her daughter being upset would offer an opportunity to separate a bunny from her, she was mistaken; Hope's grip on the animals only tightened.

'Fine, then, it's a shower.'

The shower wasn't much easier. Holly had to hook one arm around Hope to hold her steady while using the showerhead with the other hand, all while trying to ensure the spray didn't reach the rabbits. It was not going to be a hair wash day.

When Hope was finally clean, Holly took her out of the bath and placed her on the mat before wrapping her up in the cute, hooded bath towel her mother had embroidered for her. Hope always looked adorable in those. Like she belonged on some whimsical television advert. And she had to admit, she looked even sweeter with the bunnies. That said, when Hope went to sleep that night, she decided she'd probably to hide one or two of them. That way there would be spares if she lost any too.

With Hope sitting on the bathmat, Holly allowed herself the luxury of attempting to clean her teeth. It was times like this, evenings like this, that she thought about other single parents. How tough it must be for them. After all, Hope was a good baby, and Holly had Ben and her parents to support her. People who raised children on their own, with no network around them, really were superheroes.

She had just turned on the electric toothbrush when Hope crawled beside her.

'Bubba. Baba.'

Nothing like 'Mumma' was coming out of Hope's mouth yet, though every new sound felt like an achievement, and Holly wasn't entirely unconvinced that Hope wasn't trying to say bunny. What was more surprising, though, was how quickly she stood up. One second, Hope had been sitting there on the mat, all four bunnies in her hands; the next second, she had pulled herself up on the toilet seat.

'Don't do that,' Holly said through a mouthful of toothpaste foam. 'It's dirty. Do you hear me? Dirty.' She tried to angle herself to pick Hope up, only for toothpaste to spill from her mouth. Standing back up, she decided it was probably just easier to wash Hope's hands afterwards.

With Holly focusing back on her teeth, Hope cruised along, holding on to the edge of the toilet, and Holly thought she was going to take steps to move towards her. Instead, Hope did one of her favourite tricks and pushed down on the toilet handle.

'Did you hear me? Dirty.'

Holly stopped her toothbrush with her teeth only half done and placed it on the edge of the sink.

'No, darling. What did I say about dirty? You know I told you...'

Holly never got as far as finishing her sentence. The words caught in her throat as she looked into the toilet bowl. There, swirling down into the pipes, was the yellow bunny.

Lunging into action, Holly picked Hope up, swept her to the side, and plunged her hand into the bowl. But she was too late. She looked around, aware that there were now only two bunnies on the floor by Hope's feet, meaning that at least one more had disappeared down the toilet bowl and was trapped somewhere in the pipes.

A circling feeling of dread settled in Holly's stomach.

'Great, just great,' she said.

24

Holly lifted Hope up onto her hip, while watching the ever-increasing height of the water in the bowl.

'Hope? What have you done? What are we meant to do now?'

Whatever babbling response Hope gave, Holly paid it no mind. Instead, she was rooted to the spot, watching the water rise simultaneously with the feeling of dread in her stomach. It seemed unlikely there was anything she could actually do. She had already shoved her hand into the bowl and not been able to grab any of the bunnies. There would be no chance she could do that now.

Fortunately, the rate at which the water was filling started to slow. Finally, just a few centimetres below the rim of the seat, the water stopped rising altogether.

'Okay, that's good, Hopey. That's good.' Holly let out a sigh of relief as she continued to speak her thoughts aloud. 'We just need to work out what we should do now.'

They might not have flooded the house just yet, but they only had one toilet, which was now out of action. And it wasn't like she even had a neighbour she was on good enough terms with to use their facilities. As much as she wished it could wait, this was a problem that needed to be dealt with immediately.

With Hope still wrapped in her hooded towel and resting on Holly's hip, she headed downstairs and picked up her phone. As frustrating as it was, there was one person who she needed to call, and they answered on the first ring.

'Holly, darling, I was just about to call you. We're en route to departures. Your dad was going to get an overpriced croissant, but I stopped him. I mean, why would you buy a croissant here when we're going to Belgium? And why would you get a croissant in the evening?'

Holly wasn't sure why Belgium would be an ideal place to buy a croissant from, but she decided not to say as much to her mother.

'Mum, I need the landlord's number.'

'The landlord?' Her mother's voice tightened. 'What do you need his number for?'

'Because there's been an incident.'

'An incident? What type of incident? Do you need us to come back?'

'No, no. Of course I don't. I just need the landlord's number so I can get a plumber to come out. Preferably this evening.' A short pause followed. When it became obvious that her mother wasn't going to say anything, Holly tried again. 'There was a plumber the landlord used to refit the bathroom, remember? And he came out with the sink issue too. I'm positive he was local, and it's obviously someone the landlord trusts, so I wanted to try them first.'

'It's difficult to get plumbers to come out in the evening, love,' Wendy said. 'What happened?'

Holly gritted her teeth. What should've been a two-minute conversation was already spiralling out of control. Still, Holly knew that she wouldn't get anywhere unless she gave her mother at least some of the details.

'Hope flushed two of her bunnies down the toilet.'

'Hope flushed her bunnies down the toilet?' Her mother's voice was aghast, but also at a volume which implied she was relaying this information to her father on the other end of the line. 'Why would she do that?'

'She didn't mean to do anything. Obviously, it was an accident. But I need a plumber. And I need to speak to the landlord so I can get that plumber's number, because I've got to go meet Maud in half an hour. Please, would you just tell me what it is?'

Another pause formed at the end of the line, and Holly could feel her frustration boiling inside. Why her mother was being so secretive, she had no idea. But it was another sign that things weren't quite right with her. When they got back from the trip, Holly was going to be talking to her father about it. And probably a doctor too.

'You don't need to call him, Mum. You can just give me his number.'

'I don't want to do that, darling. He can be quite a funny chap. It's best he continues dealing with me. That's what he's used to.'

Holly's teeth were grinding together, and Hope was looking at her, eyes watery, left hand forlornly open, as if she just realised that the two rabbits were no longer in it.

'Don't worry, love, I'll let him know about the incident. I'm sure you'll be able to sort something out. He is very accommodating, you know.'

'If he's so accommodating, could you just give me his—'

There was no point in Holly continuing. The line was already dead.

With her mother insisting she remain in charge of the situation, Holly knew there was very little she could do. It was now only thirty minutes before she was due to meet with Maud and she still hadn't got Hope dressed or cleaned her teeth properly. She needed to get a wiggle on.

25

They were meeting at The Little Lodge. The establishment wasn't one of Holly's local haunts – not that she really had a local since Hope had been born – but it had a fabulous reputation for food and it was also the place where Maud was staying.

For a minute, Holly considered driving down there. The whole disaster with the bunnies meant she was running late, and the restaurant was at the other end of the village. But driving meant putting Hope in the car seat, and after the bath escapade, she just didn't know how she would cope with that. By contrast, Hope was always happy in the baby carrier, strapped to Holly. So, with only one bunny now grasped in her daughter's fist, Holly locked the front door and began the walk.

The warm evenings and long daylight hours meant that the outside courtyard of The Little Lodge was packed. All the tables in the al fresco area were full of families and couples enjoying themselves, but a quick glance told Holly that Maud was not among them. With Hope still in her baby carrier, she headed inside to look into the various rooms and nooks of the restaurant, only to spot Maud was sitting just on the other side of the door where Holly had walked in, her frame so slight, she was almost lost amongst the shadows.

Holly took a moment, watching her friend. It was impossible not to be shocked at how much she had changed. How she had shrunk in on herself. Growing up, Maud and Agnes had been such sources of light and laughter. Their personalities were bigger than any other people she had even met. But here, if Holly hadn't known who she was looking at, she would think it was just another frail old woman. Not the incredible owner of Just One More. The wonderful wife of the beloved Agnes. Holly's heart dropped a little as she thought of her own mother. How long would it be till people saw her as nothing but an old, frail woman too?

'Holly, there you are. I was thinking I'd got the wrong night.' Maud chuckled. She pressed her hands against the table, as if she were pushing herself up to stand, but Holly hurriedly rushed over to her.

'Stay seated, stay seated. It's fine. I'm so sorry I'm late. We had a bit of an incident.'

'Nothing too serious, I hope?'

Holly grimaced. 'Hopefully nothing a plumber can't sort out. Preferably tonight.'

Maud, Holly realised, wasn't actually listening. Instead, she was looking at the little head protruding from the top of the baby carrier.

'Oh, my word, she is just perfect.'

Holly beamed. She knew that was what people said about babies. It was a line that you had to say. And yet she couldn't help but feel the truth in it about the hype. She really was perfect.

Maud's gaze remained on Hope a moment longer, before she lifted it to Holly, and by some impossibility her smile broadened further.

'Do you know, I think motherhood suits you. Well, I can tell it does. You look wonderful.' Maud reached up her hand, which Hope promptly grabbed hold of. 'Look at you. Aren't you a happy thing?'

It was true. Hope was back to her normal, joyous self, not the terror that Holly had been faced with in the bath. But she was glad it was this way round. She was glad Maud got to see the very best side of her daughter.

'So it seems like quite a lot has changed since I've been gone,' Maud said. 'I'm thrilled to see you're keeping up the sweet shop's reputation of giving the villagers something to talk about. Having a baby without a ring on your finger. Agnes would have laughed, that's for sure.'

'Yes, well, it's not the way I would've planned things,' Holly admitted. 'But honestly, I couldn't imagine it any other way now. Hope's dad is perfect for her. He balances me out nicely. You might know him, actually. He used to be the bank manager in the village, though he's taken another role since you left.'

'A bank manager? That sounds like the type of person I would've avoided.'

Holly laughed. 'He was one of the good ones, trust me. I'm sure you'd recognise him if you met him. He certainly remembers you. His name is Ben Thornbury. He's the one who made it possible for me to get the shop. Well, made it possible for me to get a mortgage at least.'

'It sounds to me like you're lucky to still have him in your life,' Maud said.

'I am. I am.'

Holly took a moment to ruminate on the point. She often told people how lucky she was to have Ben as Hope's father. She hoped he said the same about her.

'So, what about that handsome young man who had zero knowledge of sweets this morning?' Maud continued. 'Where did you meet him?'

'Would you believe we met in the south of France? We were staying in his villa there.'

Maud's eyes twinkled.

'Well, that sounds like a story I need to know all the details of. And don't miss out on any of the juicy bits, either; it's what us old people live for, you know.'

26

It may have only been four weeks since they had met and started dating, but Holly was happy to tell the story of how she and Evan got together to anyone who asked. She never forgot to include how she tried to swap seats on their first flight over to France so that she didn't have to sit next to him. Or how she had been ill on said flight. Or how she thought he was a complete player, but then had a video call to his mother before they'd even shared their first kiss. But as she opened her mouth, ready to begin, something about Maud made Holly stop. It was the way she was sitting there, gazing at Hope so wistfully. It was like she wasn't really paying attention to what Holly was going to say at all. She just wanted to listen to her talk and drift off into her own little world.

Holly reached across the table and placed her hand on her friend's.

'I've already told you plenty about me,' she said. 'I want to know about you. How was Austria? Why are you back? Why are you in Bourton and how long have we got you here for? I'm sure Hope would love to see more of you.'

Hope, who had now been transferred to a highchair, giggled

obligingly, causing a slight smile to rise at the corners of Maud's lips. However, when her old friend turned to face Holly, the smile didn't quite meet her eyes.

'Actually, there are a few things that have happened. Things I wanted to catch people up on.'

'Well, I can't wait to hear them,' Holly replied genuinely.

Maud and Agnes's stories were one of the things she remembered most about when she had first worked at the sweet shop. Their ability to infuse humour into all their escapades. While Holly waited, Maud took a sip of her drink – a large red wine that was already half drunk. Before she could put it down and start talking, a loud ringing cut through the conversation.

'Sorry,' Holly said.

Hastily diving into her bag, she grabbed her phone from one of the pockets, only to see Jamie's name on the screen. The two best friends had gone an entire day without talking, which was highly unusual, but they would have to wait a little longer. Without a second thought, Holly ended the call, and looked apologetically at Maud.

'Sorry about that,' she said. 'It was my friend Jamie. She's the one whose hen do I was on when I met Evan, actually. She's getting married in under two weeks, and normally, she is the most chilled person you'd ever imagine. We thought she'd be the same with the wedding, but recently, she's started getting stressed. I think it's the fact that a lot of Fin's family are flying over from America, and trying to sort out that side of things would be stressful for everyone.'

'Two of you with American fellas. Are they a popular choice at the moment?'

'Actually, Fin introduced us,' Holly said.

'So they're friends? That was why he was on the do? Did you say it was his villa?'

'I know, it's crazy—' Holly stopped herself, remembering that she hadn't wanted to spend the entire evening talking about herself. 'Sorry, before Jamie rang, you were going to tell me about you. Why are you back here? What have you been up to?'

Maud nodded, once again, preparing to speak, when Holly's phone buzzed for a second time. Yet again, it was Jamie.

Jamie was smart enough to know that if Holly put a call through to voicemail, it was because she wasn't able to talk. The fact that she would ring again almost immediately afterwards meant there was something she needed to talk about.

'I'm really sorry, Maud,' Holly said apologetically. 'She obviously needs to speak to me. Do you mind? I'll just go outside. I'm sure it will be quick.'

Maud shook her head. 'No, don't be silly. Of course I don't mind. You go. I'm fine with the little one here.'

Holly glanced down at Hope in the highchair. A waitress had already brought her some breadsticks, which she was chewing away on happily. Hopefully, the call with Jamie would be brief, and she'd be back before Hope missed her.

Outside and standing on the quiet back street of Bourton, Holly felt like she'd barely pressed dial on the number when her friend picked up.

'Hey, is everything okay?' she asked.

A short, sharp breath travelled down the line, quickly followed by Jamie's voice.

'No. No, it's not okay,' she said. 'The wedding is off. It's all off.'

27

Holly couldn't stop apologising. She felt terrible. She had asked Maud to dinner, then turned up late and now was rushing out on her before she'd even had a drink. She was grateful they'd met at Maud's hotel. At least she hadn't had to travel.

'I don't know what's happened,' Holly said, as she bundled Hope back into the baby carrier, with the breadstick still in her hand. 'All she said was that the wedding was cancelled. I can come back afterwards?' she suggested, trying to salvage some of the night. 'Then again, I don't know how long this will take to sort out. You could come with us? Maybe you can help with whatever has happened.'

Maud shook her head. 'Don't be silly, dear. Your friend needs you. Go help her. I'm not going anywhere for a couple of days. Maybe I could catch you tomorrow evening. If it's not a rush?'

Holly nodded. 'Yes. Why don't you get the bar to ring me at the sweet shop tomorrow morning? If you're not planning on walking down? Or I can come up here?'

'We will work it out, love. It's not a problem. Now go help your friend.'

Holly wished she could drive. She wished she could put her foot flat on the accelerator and speed down to Jamie's house. But she couldn't. All she could do was walk as fast as the baby carrier would let her.

With every step, Holly's mind raced. Had Fin had done something? That was why most people called off weddings, wasn't it? When they found out something unscrupulous about their partner. But Fin? He adored Jamie, didn't he?

Holly tried to play devil's advocate. After all, she hadn't been a great fan of Fin when she first met him. She hadn't liked the way he swept into Jamie's life, and they'd become so serious so quickly. Of course, with her and Evan now in the same position, she didn't have a leg to stand on. Besides, all that had changed. Now, she thought the world of Fin. He couldn't have been more wonderful with her and Hope and their initial living situation, when Holly had spent the first few months of her child's life still living with them. Could she really have misread him that much?

When she reached her old house, Holly hammered on the front door. Immediately, Fin opened it.

Seeing Fin standing there all forlorn knocked the idea on the head of Jamie calling off the wedding because of cheating. After all, Jamie would hardly keep a guy around in the house after that. No, she would've kicked him to the curb.

'She's in the kitchen. With wine. I've had a glass too,' Fin said.

Holly did a double take. Fin having wine shocked her even more than the wedding being called off. He was a man who lived on kale smoothies, quinoa, and other concoctions that she couldn't name.

'What happened?' Holly took Hope out of the baby carrier and handed her straight to Fin, who was waiting with his arms out. Fin was undoubtedly Hope's favourite uncle and there were almost as many toys in this house as in Holly's.

'It's the venue. They called this morning—' he started as Holly marched through to the kitchen where Jamie was indeed tucking into a large glass of red wine.

'They double booked the place,' Jamie finished for him.

'Double booked?' Holly replied. 'What does that mean?'

'It means they've booked the same date for two couples...' Fin began.

'No, I know what double-booked means, but how could they have done this? You booked it months ago. You paid a deposit, didn't you?'

'That's exactly what we said to them. And they said they'll refund our money.' Bitterness filled Jamie's voice.

Just like Evan, Fin wasn't short of a few quid. Having the money refunded was nothing compared to not having their wedding day.

'I wouldn't mind normally,' Jamie continued. 'But all of Fin's family are coming over. They've paid for the flights. And they're not refundable. And so many people were staying at the venue for two of the nights. Where are we going to find rooms in peak summer season? We're not. It's a disaster.'

Holly knew that when a friend said something like that, you were required to offer solutions. To provide the level head that was needed during such an emotional time and show them that the situation perhaps wasn't as bad as they first thought. But Holly had nothing.

'What about other venues?' she said. 'Have you tried? Perhaps someone's called their wedding off last minute. Maybe you can get a space like that?'

'As much as taking someone's spot because they've cancelled feels like bad karma, we've tried,' Jamie responded. 'I've called over thirty venues since we found out this afternoon. None of them have a single date free on the days when both his aunts, uncles, cousins, parents, and grandparents are in the country.' Jamie let out a sigh.

'We chose that venue because they'd make it all easy. They'd do the food, photography, the cake. The whole lot.'

'And now, in one fell swoop, we've ended up with none of it,' Fin said, and took another long sip from his wine. He winced, like he really didn't like the taste at all, and was merely drinking it because it felt like the right thing to do.

'Okay...' Holly began to verbalise her thoughts as they came, hoping she might find a solution. 'If you can't get married there, what about mixing it up a bit? See if you can find a place to do a reception, people to do food, but then get married with registrar at a town hall somewhere else first. It doesn't have to be all at one venue?'

The two exchanged a look, indicating that they'd already spoken about this.

'That would be an option, yes – if there were any registrars free. But all the ones local to us are fully booked up. It's the summer. It's their busiest time. Unless they get a cancellation on the day, there's no way they'll be free. And we could look further away, but then everybody's got to travel more; not that we've even found anywhere for them to stay yet.'

Holly could see her friend was at her limit, but as painful as that was to watch, it was equally nice to see the way Fin responded. He was now up out of his chair, holding Hope in one arm while massaging Jamie's shoulder gently as he spoke.

'Something is going to come up,' he said, looking at them both as he spoke. 'I know it doesn't feel like it at the minute, but it will. Something will come up and this will all be fine. We just have to think outside the box, that's all.'

28

For the next hour, Jamie, Holly and Fin worked together to brainstorm ideas, while passing Hope between them so that she didn't get impatient.

Half an hour in, Holly knocked at next door and asked Ben to join them, too. However fearful she was that Georgia was going to open up the door, dressed in exquisite lingerie, she forced the thought down. From his days working in the bank, Ben knew more local businesses than anyone, and at that moment it was a case of 'more brains, the better'. Thankfully for Holly, he was on his own, and Hope was more than happy to have her daddy there to give her even more attention, meaning that Holly could continue talking to Jamie.

'Surely there are some people you've done work for...' Holly suggested. 'Renovations, that kind of thing, that have nice barns or gardens that you could ask?'

'I could, but I'd rather not,' Jamie replied. 'I don't want to become known as that kind of person.'

'You wouldn't. People know you well enough around here. They know you'd never ask for something unless you really needed it.'

'I don't think it's that simple,' Ben joined in. 'You need to have licenses to hold weddings in the UK. Venues have to apply for them and I don't think it's something that's that straightforward.'

'Well, what about the place you had your engagement party?' Holly asked, determined not to be beaten. 'That was amazing. I'm sure they must have a license for weddings.'

'They were the first place we rang,' Fin replied. 'But they've been booked out for the last two years. I know it's the Cotswolds, and it's beautiful here, but it's insane how quickly these places fill up. It was a miracle we got a booking in the first place.'

'Well, that's the whole point, isn't it?' Jamie said with a resigned sigh. 'We didn't get the place.'

Silence filled the group, and Holly wondered if she was the only one with a question in her head, or whether Ben was thinking it, too. But given how damp the mood already was, she decided she might as well ask.

'How did it happen?' Holly said. 'How did they make the mistake?'

At this, Fin and Jamie exchanged a look, both of them rolling their eyes.

'Would you believe it? Fin has the same initials and surname as the groom they've booked for the day. Freddie Micklethwaite, apparently. I mean, what are the chances? It's not even a million to one, is it? It has to be bigger than that.' Jamie fought back the bitter laugh with a gulp of her wine.

'So they thought they were dealing with the same people?' Ben asked.

'Exactly. The woman who spoke to us said she just assumed there was a work email and a home email. After all, they were both F. Micklethwaite.'

It was, like Jamie said, a million to one chance.

Down on the carpet, Hope let out a long yawn.

'Do you want to put her down at mine?' Ben said. 'You can stay here for a bit, have another glass of wine, then pick her up and I'll drop you back later.'

'Thank you,' Holly said. 'But don't worry, I'll walk back with the baby carrier. It's not far, and she always goes to sleep much easier after it.'

'Only if you're sure?'

She was about to reply that she was, when her phone rang. Her mother's name flashed up on the screen.

'Oh, crap.' She stood up. 'Sorry guys, I need to take this.'

'Is everything okay?' Jamie said, her own concern momentarily forgotten as she looked at Holly.

Holly glanced at her phone.

'It's fine,' she said, afraid they would think it was something serious if she didn't explain. 'Only I need to get a plumber.'

'Why? What happened?'

She hesitated. Then again, if ever people had needed to hear about someone else's disaster, it was today.

'Hope blocked the toilet.' Holly grimaced. 'She flushed two of Evan's bunnies down it.'

This time, Jamie's laugh was genuine.

29

Holly picked up the phone to her mother.

'Mum? Where are you?'

Her mother's face grinned back on the other side of the screen, with her father's face tucked in beside her. 'We're in France, love! We are just out of the tunnel. And look, the video call works. I told you it would.'

It was heart-warming to see her mother getting such joy from the simple act of a telephone call working from another country. A smile was plastered on to her face so high that her cheeks glowed, and they hadn't even got off the train yet. Still, there was a reason she'd called, and Holly wanted to get to the point as quickly as possible.

'Mum, did you hear from the plumber? Is he coming? Can he come tonight?'

'I spoke to the landlord, and he rang the plumber. He's got a little job to do first, but he said he'll be there about nine o'clock.'

With a slight sense of relief, Holly glanced down at her phone. It was already eight thirty, and she knew enough about tradesmen to know that 'around nine o'clock' could mean any time from now until gone ten.

'Thanks, Mum. Message me when you get to the hotel, okay?'

'Okay, darling. Give big kisses to Hope?'

'Will do.'

When Holly hung up the phone, she turned back to Ben.

'Change of plans. Any chance I can get that lift back?'

It took only a few minutes to gather their things, and a couple more to get Hope into the car seat. Some days, Hope would slip in and let herself be buckled up as though the car was her favourite place in the world to be; other times, it would be like wrestling a badger. That evening, it was closer to the latter, but with Ben on hand, it didn't take long and till they were all buckled in and headed home.

'Is that a Vespa?' Ben said, as he drove up Holly's driveway. The vehicle was exactly where Holly left it, still bright and shining. With all the commotion of the cancelled wedding, Holly had almost forgotten about it.

'It is,' Holly said, thinking that perhaps she ought to get one of the cover sheet things she saw people put over fancy cars and bikes. After all, the last thing she wanted was for it to get scratched up just sitting there.

'Whose is it?' Ben said.

'Sorry?'

'The Vespa? Who does it belong to? It's parked right in front of your house. You need to ask them to move it.'

'Oh, right?' Holly hesitated, wondering what to say next. It wasn't that she was worried Ben would judge her, but more, she supposed, that he'd judge Evan for buying her such an extravagant gift. But then, her only other option was to lie, and that was worse. Honesty was still the best route with her and Ben. That was their fundamental rule of co-parenting.

Still, there was a slight tingle of butterflies in her stomach as she told him. 'It's mine. It was a gift from Evan.'

Ben raised his eyebrows.

'That's a nice gift,' he said, then offered Holly a smile before opening the car door and slipping out. Holly waited a moment to see what else he would say, only he seemed to be done.

'Is that it?' she said, hurriedly unclipping herself and following.

'What do you mean?' Ben already had the back door open and was unstrapping Hope from her seat.

'It's a nice gift? That's all you have to say?' Holly wasn't sure why his answer left her feeling so enraged. Perhaps because it wasn't an answer at all.

He had already unbuckled Hope and was taking her out of the seat, but Holly blocked the way, offering him no room to get into the cottage.

'Do you think I'm being ridiculous?' she said. 'Do you think things are moving way too fast?'

'No,' he said, but his eyes went down to his feet. It was all the signal she needed. Her heart dropped.

'You do, don't you? You think it's moving too fast. You think I'm being ridiculous? I know it. I know it. I've fallen in headfirst. I don't know what's wrong with me.'

'You really do like to overreact in situations, don't you?' Ben said, handing her Hope so he could lean in and get her bag.

'So you weren't going to say you think it's going way too fast and I've lost my mind?'

Ben attempted to suppress a smirk and failed.

'What I was actually going to say to you was that Evan and I spoke quite a bit at your dad's party yesterday.'

A heavy weight of dread filled Holly's belly. 'When? I didn't see you two talking.'

'Well, it was when you were dealing with Aunt May. And Lenny and June had muddled up the vegetarian sausages with the meat ones.'

'Of course.' Holly remembered. She hadn't even had a chance to think about Evan during that chaos.

'Well, what did he say? What did you two talk about?' she said, focusing back on the moment.

'Well, *you* mostly. We spoke about you.'

That didn't make Holly feel any better.

Slipping past her, Ben walked over to the house, waiting for Holly to follow so that she could unlock the door.

'Think of it this way,' he said, as he put the bag down and turned to Holly. 'You and I didn't rush things at all. You and I were obscenely slow. From the first dates to the first kiss. I mean, we were painstakingly slow in getting our acts together even though we liked each other.'

'And you're telling me this, why?'

'Because at the end of the day, it didn't matter. We did things properly, ish. We knew each other well. We thought we knew exactly what we were getting into when we started our relationship, but it still didn't matter, because you and I weren't meant to be.'

Holly didn't know why Ben was saying all this, but if it was to make her feel better, then it wasn't working. What was he trying to tell her? That even when she thought she had a relationship figured out, she was wrong, so she should probably give up trying?

'So, you think Evan and I...'

'I think he's all in, Holly. He knows you. He gets you. He might not have spent that much time with you yet, comparatively, but he sees you. He gets what you're like. And he was really open about the whole situation with Hope. He wanted me to know that our relationship matters, too.'

'Yours and his?' Holly was even more confused by this statement.

'No, you idiot. Yours and mine. He was just saying how he wanted what was best for you and best for Hope, because he wasn't always going to get things right, but hopefully I'd be there to kick him in the right direction.'

'He really said that to you?'

'He really did.'

Holly's heart swelled. She hadn't even texted Evan that evening. Not since the incident with the bunny. But she would ring him later that night. She wouldn't mention this conversation, but just remind him again how lucky she felt to have him in her life.

She went in to hug Ben, only to notice the work van pulling onto the drive. A logo with a large water drop and a wrench was on the side.

'Looks like this is me,' she said, with a nod to the van. 'Let's hope this doesn't take all night.'

'Do you want me to stay? I can stay if you need?'

'No, I'm fine. I'm an independent woman, you know.'

'An independent woman with a stuffed rabbit down her toilet?'

30

'Explain to me again what happened, love.'

Holly and the plumber stood together in the bathroom, staring at the still-full toilet bowl. Hope had pulled herself up onto the side of her cot and was looking in from the bedroom, although Holly thought she should probably be in there with them; after all, it was all her fault there were there.

'My daughter flushed her bunnies down the toilet,' she said, grimacing as she spoke.

'Bunnies? As in rabbits?'

'Not real bunnies,' Holly clarified as the plumber paled. 'My daughter's cuddly bunnies. I think there are two of them. I wasn't watching, and she flushed them down the toilet.'

Relief washed visibly over the plumber's face as he nodded and leaned in closer to look at the bowl.

'And have you used it since?'

'The toilet? No. I assumed it would flood.'

'You're right. It doesn't stop some people, though. Well, it should be a fairly clean job then. If you don't mind?' He waved his hand a little, gesturing for Holly to leave. And although the motion of being shooed out of the bathroom in her own house annoyed her, she realised he needed the space to work.

'You're not gonna make too much damage to fix it, are you?' she said, walking back into the bathroom, only moments after stepping out of it. 'My landlord recently redid it all for me when I moved in. And he did everything I asked for, so I'd really like to not cause loads of hassle by chipping tiles, and that kind of thing?'

'Your landlord's a good man, don't worry. I'll do a good job.'

Holly nodded, leaving the room, realising she hadn't been given any assurances as to what a 'good job' meant at all. Given how small the upstairs of the cottage was, Holly knew any banging or hammering was bound to stop Hope from sleeping. Even white noise, which was her go-to during nap time, wasn't likely to cancel out this level of sound, so after a brief consideration, she decided it wasn't worth trying to get Hope to sleep when she didn't know how long the banging might go on for.

Gone were the days when Hope would lie on her back for hours at a time, flicking at the toys and smiling with delight. Now, she seemed to get pleasure only in crawling around chaotically. But it was a sign of how exhausted Hope was that she curled up on Holly's chest, without even a wriggle to get down.

'I haven't been very good about your bedtime these last few days, have I?' Holly said, as if Hope was going to respond like an adult, or a far older child. 'We'll get back into a routine tomorrow. Okay? But it's not all bad with Mummy, is it? We have a lot of fun. I thought tomorrow, we could go to the bird park. What do you think?'

Hope may not have understood everything, but she knew the meaning of the words 'bird park.' Her eyes lit up.

'Yes, we'll go to the bird park. And we'll see the penguins. Does that sound fun?' Hope went to smile, only for her mouth to open wider into a yawn. Her eyes scrunched shut as she dropped her head back down onto Holly's chest.

A deep ache spread through Holly. Her life was so busy that she rarely got time to do this. Time simply to sit with her child and appreciate what a little miracle she was. Even if she was about to cost her a hefty plumber's bill.

Hope's eyes had been closed for several minutes when Holly realised she hadn't heard the banging upstairs for a while. Did that mean it was all a lost cause, and the plumber had given up entirely, or, as she hoped, it meant he was done? She wasn't back in the shop tomorrow, given that she had Hope, but when you have a ten-month-old, not working doesn't equate to a lie-in. No, Hope would be up at the crack of dawn, regardless of whether or not it was a work day. And they would need a working toilet.

Now that the banging had ended, Holly headed upstairs and laid Hope down in her cot, before heading into the bathroom and finding the plumber brushing down his clothes.

'So this is what you're after, is it?' He handed her two sopping wet bunnies. The pink and the blue. Holly chuckled. Hope really wasn't into gender stereotypes at all.

'Thank you,' Holly said, intending to put them straight in the washing machine when she got downstairs. However, before that, there was a question she knew she had to ask. One that caused a knot to tighten in her stomach.

'So, how much do I owe you?'

The plumber crinkled his nose. 'Nothing. I was just told to put this on the account.'

'The account?'

He shrugged. 'Your landlord's, I guess. What do you usually do for things like this?'

There hadn't been a situation like this before, so Holly didn't know how to reply. The plumber took her silence as an answer.

'Look,' he said. 'I'm pretty certain I'm not meant to take any money from you now. If I find out I've done something wrong, I'll ring your landlord and he can sort it out with you. Does that sound okay?'

Holly went to nod, only to change her mind.

'Yes, yes, it would. The thing is... I've had a problem with my phone recently. Would I be able to grab my landlord's number from you?'

The plumber frowned. 'Did you not ring him to tell him about this issue?'

Holly realised how nonsensical she must sound. 'It's complicated to explain. But I don't have his number any more, so is there any chance I can grab it from you?'

'Yeah, don't see why not.' He pulled his phone out of his pocket and scrolled downwards until he found the contact. Then held it out for Holly. 'Do you wanna take it? Put it into your phone?'

The plumber looked at her expectantly as he waited for a reply. Only Holly couldn't speak. Even when he repeated himself, she stayed exactly where she was, only with the slightest tremble to her hand. All she could do was see that name on the phone. The name of the landlord, who Holly's mother had refused to let her contact. The one who had come to her rescue just when she needed a place of her own to stay, and allowed her to change the house however she wanted, including putting this brand-new bathroom suite in without having to pay a penny. And the name of that landlord caused her head to race.

Giles Caverty.

31

A lump filled Holly's throat, rising from her heart, stopping her from being able to breathe properly.

'You alright, love? Do you want me to write that number down for you or something?' the plumber said, his voice bringing Holly back to the moment.

Swallowing back the lump, she shook her head, hoping that the movement might cause her to see things a little clearer. It didn't.

She glanced back at the phone again, thinking that perhaps it was just a trick of the light that had made her see things wrong. But no, Giles's name and number were still there on that man's phone.

'Love? You wanna write it down?' the plumber repeated.

This time, Holly replied. 'No, no, do you know what? I have got it, actually. Yes. I do have his number. Sorry about that. Thank you.'

Before the plumber could respond, she turned and walked out of the bathroom. Her entire body was on autopilot as she headed downstairs, opened the washing machine door and threw the bunnies inside. A couple of minutes later, the plumber followed.

'Well, I'm all done, love. I'll just head off.'

Holly nodded. 'Thank you.'

Giles Caverty was her landlord. It didn't make sense. Or at least, she didn't want it to make sense. But actually, it made everything a whole lot clearer. This was why her mum had been so desperate not to pass on the number. Why she'd dealt with every little thing that came up. Because she and Giles had been in cahoots the whole time. June and Lenny had no idea what was going on, which is why they'd looked at Holly like she was mad when she'd tried to thank them for their help in finding the place.

When the initial shock faded, a new stream of questions raced through Holly's mind. Where did this leave her? And what did it mean when it came to her and Giles's relationship? The last time she'd seen him was less than a month ago, when he'd declared his love for her – again – and she'd chosen someone else over him – again. What did that mean? Was he really going to let her stay in a house, his house, knowing that there was no chance of them being together? What if he decided that if Holly didn't want him, then she would need to find somewhere else to live? Would he do that?

The spate of dizziness ended, fading almost immediately.

Old Giles probably would've done. The Giles that tried to sabotage her business. But then, that old Giles would never have bought a house and done such a good deed and stayed quiet about it. Old Giles didn't know the meaning of the word altruistic. He'd have wanted to tell the world and get all the accolades possible.

The knowledge that Giles was unlikely to kick her out offered Holly the slightest quiver of relief. She might not be homeless immediately, but she didn't know what she should do.

What she did know was that there was only one person she wanted to talk to about it.

They picked up on the second ring.

'Hey, you, I was about to call. Is everything okay? Have you taken your Vespa out again yet?'

Just seeing Evan's face on the screen was enough to cause a wash of calm to flood over her.

'Giles is my landlord,' she said.

She probably should have answered one of his questions before she delved into the depth of her despair. She should have maybe mentioned Jamie's cancelled wedding too, given how Evan was Fin's best friend. But right now, she needed him.

'Giles is my mystery landlord,' she repeated, just in case he hadn't heard her the first time.

'You mean Giles, the Giles who is not actually your ex, the one who confessed his love and dove into the water from his giant yacht with me to try to supposedly save you?' Evan's description was hardly succinct, but at least he confirmed he knew who Holly was talking about.

'Yes, that Giles. He's my landlord.'

'And you didn't know?'

'Does it sound like I knew?' Holly shook her head. 'I'm sorry. This is just freaking me out. My mum knew. My mum is the one that arranged the whole thing. The viewing, the keys. Dealt with him for the bathroom renovation. The landlord. That's all she's ever referred to him as. It was Giles all along. Why would she do that? Why wouldn't she tell me?'

A slight pause followed her question before Evan spoke.

'Well, the fact that he didn't tell you leads me to believe that he didn't want you to know. And your mum obviously thought that was a good idea.'

'But why not? Why wouldn't he tell me?'

Even on a pixelated screen, the frown line that appeared between Evan's brows was clearly visible. 'Is this one of those rhetorical situations where you're asking me a question but you don't really want to know the answer, you just want to rant and me to listen? In which case, I'm totally okay with that. Or is this one of those situations where you actually want real-life solutions? Even though you probably already know the answer.'

Holly paused. Did she really give rhetorical questions that she just didn't want answers to? Quite possibly. And did she already know the answer to this situation? Again, probably. But she needed to hear someone else say it, too.

'Why wouldn't he tell me?' she asked quietly.

Evan let out a short breath before he began. 'Well, would you have moved into the house if you had known?'

It didn't take Holly long to consider the answer.

'Like, I... Probably not. No. I wouldn't.'

'And did you need a place to live?'

Again, the question didn't take long to reply to. 'Maybe. I mean, Fin and Jamie are lovely, but they needed me out of their hair.'

'Then you have your answer. He did it because he knew you needed it. But he didn't want to tell you, because he knew you'd probably freak out like this, reject the help you needed, and then basically self-sabotage your and Hope's best chance of being happy.'

When Evan finished speaking, Holly groaned internally. Perhaps it was best to ask rhetorical questions after all.

'Okay, so I can get why he did that. It makes sense he didn't want me to know because he thought I'd overreact. But I do know now, so what do I do? I haven't messaged him since France. Do I message him and pretend that I don't know just like it's a casual "how are you doing, we said we were gonna meet up. By the way, I've got this really mysterious situation with my landlord that I don't know who he is?" Then I make out that I don't know who he is when Giles and I meet up, or is that too obvious?'

'Wow, this is serious babbling territory we're going into now.'

She shot Evan a glare through the phone screen. 'This is serious. I don't know what I'm meant to do.'

Another pause lingered, and though the frown line was gone, Evan continued to look at her with unwavering intensity.

'Do you want my truthful answer as to what I think you should do right now?' he said.

'Yes, yes, I do.'

Evan nodded. 'Alright, then. In my opinion, you should do nothing. It doesn't matter right now. One day, two days, or three weeks isn't gonna make any difference. You've been living in that house for what, six months? A couple more days or a week, it's not gonna make any difference. But if you rush into things, if you get cross with him or your mum, you'll regret it.' He looked at her so intently down the phone, it was almost as if Holly could hear the cogs turning in his mind. 'Just think things through carefully, okay? Although, in terms of grand gestures, my Vespa seems pretty tame now, right? I knew I should have gone with a cottage.'

'That isn't funny,' Holly said, fighting the urge to smile.

'It's a little bit funny.'

Holly shook her head again, though this time it was in laughter, as opposed to disbelief.

'I wish you were sharing my bed again tonight,' she said after a pause. 'It feels really empty in here without you.'

'Well, it's only two weeks to the wedding, and I'll see you then.'

The terror Holly was feeling about Giles and the landlord suddenly felt rather insignificant as she remembered the rest of the previous evening.

'Yes, well, about the wedding...'

32

Holly awoke to the sound of Hope babbling in her cot. It was, without doubt, Holly's favourite sound to wake to. A cross between singing, gurgling and talking. The nonsensical noises were more tuneful to Holly than any dawn chorus or personalised alarm clock could ever be.

She'd not had a great night's sleep. After telling Evan about the mess Jamie and Fin were in with the wedding, and with the whole Giles situation still weighing heavily on her mind, she had found it difficult to switch off. Even now, it was hard to believe she had slept at all, considering how exhausted she felt.

There was a time, when Hope was smaller, that Holly could have simply scooped her out of her cot, carried her back into bed with her, and got an extra hour's rest that way. But those days were gone. Besides, the last thing Holly wanted to do was waste a beautiful sunny day with her daughter.

As much as Holly loved working in the shop, some days there was nothing better than a full twenty-four hours with Hope, knowing that Ben or her mother weren't going to pick her up, or want her at a certain place at a certain time, so the two of them could spend the day exactly as Holly chose. That didn't mean the days were always easy, but not having Hope with her all the time made her more grateful than ever for days like this.

As was almost always the case on a Hope and Holly day, Holly started the morning with one of her most favourite activities. Baking.

'You want to sift the flour, Hope?' Holly said as she tipped flour over a bowl and shook the fine metal sieve beneath. 'If you don't, you're going to get lumps in your breakfast muffins. And we don't want that, do we?'

Hope wasn't paying as much attention as Holly would have liked to this cookery lesson. Instead, she was chewing on bits of banana in between sticking her fingers in the mixing bowl. Still, Holly hoped that by cooking regularly in front of Hope, she might gain a passion for the hobby, just like Holly had done. Childhood memories of her mother and her baking together, decorating cakes and biscuits for school bake sales floated into Holly's mind, but she quickly pushed them aside. She didn't want to think about her mum right now. She was still too angry at her.

Unfortunately, the fates had other ideas, and as Holly cracked the first egg into the mixture, her phone rang.

Holly took several deep breaths in while staring at her mother's name on the screen. Holly had known from the moment she had woken up that she wasn't ready to talk to her yet. But this was the first time her parents had been abroad since Holly could remember and they were bound to be nervous. It was only fair that she checked in on how they were doing.

'Holly! Look, look at the Atomium!' It was her dad holding the phone – at least, that's what Holly assumed, given it was his voice shouting at her energetically – although the camera was pointing directly at a silver globe in the sky. 'Isn't it magnificent? We got the Metro service here this morning. Can you believe that? Your mother and I, getting an early morning Metro in a foreign country? And we got coffee too. In takeaway cups. Very nice it was too, although your mother said hers was a bit strong.'

The anger Holly was feeling at the sight of the phone call ebbed away. Even she had to smile at her father's enthusiasm.

'So how's it all going?' she asked, relieved that she felt the response was going to be a positive one.

'Oh, it's wonderful, Holly. Marvellous. We are going around here this morning, and then this afternoon, we're going back to the city centre and doing a tour of some of the chocolate places. Then we've booked in on a chocolate-making course.'

'A chocolate-making course?'

'Yes, it sounded like fun. And your mother said she's always wanted to try it.'

'Well, that sounds great. I'm glad you're having a good time.'

'Oh, we are love. You never know, maybe I'll be able to bring a couple of skills back to the shop. I'm sure the customers would appreciate some handmade delicacies.'

Holly was tempted to remind her father that they had a full range of handmade chocolates from both Belgium and the UK available already, but she didn't want to dampen his enthusiasm. Besides, the longer he was on the phone, the more likely it was that Wendy would come and start talking to her.

'I better get going, Dad. I've just left Hope with the banana muffin mixture.'

'Don't you want to talk to your mother?'

'I'd better go. Love you both,' Holly said, then hung up before he could ask another question.

Placing the phone back on the table, she closed her eyes and let out a long sigh, trying to ignore the niggling ache in her chest. It had been a long time since she'd deliberately hung up the phone without speaking to her mother, but she was determined not to feel bad about how she felt. After all, it wasn't her fault. Her mother had brought this upon herself.

'Come on, Hopey,' she said, forcing some joviality into her voice. 'We need to get these muffins finished and in the oven. Because you know where we're going today, don't you?'

33

There were plenty of attractions in Bourton that had stood the test of time. There was the Motor Museum, nestled just next to one of the bridges; a perfect location, with the river running right beside it. Then there was the model village, with its miniature versions of all the old houses in Bourton. The sweet shop proudly sat in the centre of the High Street, and there was even a model village within the model village itself. But since Hope had come along, Holly's most frequently visited attraction had become the bird park.

Rather than using the baby carrier, Holly had taken Hope in her pushchair, the bottom of which she'd loaded with snacks, including the still-warm breakfast muffins, two of which Hope had eaten on the way. Holly had already received two morning messages from Evan, one telling her he missed her and would ring her as soon as he could, and a second saying that his day was now scarily busy, so would ring her in the evening when he was back at his flat.

As much as Holly would have liked to have spoken to him, she was more than happy to wait until the evening to talk. The last thing she wanted was to become one of those women who couldn't survive without hearing from her boyfriend every twenty minutes.

As she approached the counter to pay for their tickets to the bird park, a woman Holly knew named Kathy stepped out from behind the till and leaned down in front of the pushchair.

'Good morning, Hope,' she said, before tugging gently on the baby's hair. 'Look at you with all those gorgeous curls. You are lucky. Where did you get them from?'

Holly smiled politely. The close-knit community was what Holly loved about living in Bourton, but sometimes it could get a little claustrophobic.

'Just the two of you today?' Kathy said, straightening up to look at Holly, although straightening up was using the term loosely. Holly didn't know how old Kathy was, but she had been a constant feature at the bird park when Holly was a child. Now, with her white hair and worsening hunch, she was as stalwart a figure in Bourton as the bird park itself.

'Just the two of us,' Holly confirmed. Kathy's eyes twinkled.

'You know, my grandson is coming down next week. He's an architect. I think you and him would get on brilliantly. You should bring Hope down on your day off then. He'd love to meet you.'

Holly pressed her lips into the tightest smile she could form, given how badly she wanted to grimace. Another thing with living in a village like Bourton – gossip spread like wildfire. Everyone had known when she and Ben had got together, just like they'd known when they'd broken up, and the fact that they weren't staying together, even though they were having a baby. Holly had even heard her name whispered in conjunctions with Giles's once or twice in the pubs, but she'd ignored that.

That was another thing she loved about her relationship with Evan. It was entirely separate from the village. He knew no one and no one knew him. As far as the other shopkeepers and local gossips were aware, Holly was entirely single. And she was happy to keep it that way, even if it meant having to politely turn down a few unsolicited requests for blind dates.

'I'm sure he's lovely, but you know I've actually got a full week in the shop next week,' Holly said, keeping her lies to a minimum.

'You know, a lovely girl like you really shouldn't be on her own,' Kathy said, refusing to drop the point.

'Then it's a good job I'm not, isn't it?' Holly said, bending down and kissing Hope on the cheek and receiving the most wonderful smile in the world. Smiles and giggles. Some days, it felt like those were all she needed to live on.

'Oh well, you know I'm not going to give up,' Kathy said, reinforcing her point. 'But I'll let you go. Just one adult ticket, is it?'

'Yes, please,' Holly said with a grin. 'It's a proper mummy-daughter day.'

'Well, that sounds perfect to me. Here you go, have a bag of bird feed on me.'

'Thank you, that's very kind,' Holly said, before she trundled Hope into the park.

During each visit, Hope would find a new favourite animal to stare at for an unfeasible length of time. Sometimes, it was the red parrot stood by the entrance, chattering away. Those days irritated Holly slightly, considering she'd paid the full entrance fee, only for them to stand six feet from the gate the entire time. But other days, Hope wanted to go in further and spend her time looking at other animals.

That day, Hope was struggling to find anything to hold her interest. They went straight to the penguins, only for Hope to grumble and point to the flamingos. They managed a couple of minutes there before the grizzling started again. In fact, the only time she wasn't griping was when Holly was pushing the pushchair. Realising there was no point stopping and trying to make her daughter look at things, Holly opted to go away from the main part of the park and weave her way through the outer pathways. Thick foliage made a home for large dinosaur models, though when they reached the very outskirts of the park, the scenery changed.

Part of the hedgerows had been cut all the way back. Probably to make room for a new enclosure, although, for the moment, the lack of bushes and trees offered a view right out over open fields. The undulating land rose and fell, and there in the distance, surrounded by green, stood a large, Cotswolds stone building.

At a rough guess, it was at least three floors, and probably large enough for ten bedrooms, though, given how Holly hadn't seen it before, it was unlikely to be a hotel or pub. Which meant that it would have to be a private home instead. Would they have the license to hold weddings? she wondered. If they did, they were probably fully booked for wedding season. Nevertheless, on her way back out of the park – after Hope had spent a solid fifteen minutes staring at a flock of pigeons – the image of the house refused to shift from her mind.

'See you again soon?' Kathy said, as Holly walked back through the main gate. Hope was nodding off to sleep in the pushchair, and Holly had decided to head back to the cottage. With a little bit of luck, Hope would stay asleep long enough in the house to put a load of washing on.

'Of course you will.' Holly smiled in response to Kathy's question, before she moved to go, only to hesitate. 'Kathy, there's a house just across the fields. A big one. I don't suppose you know who owns it.'

'Do you mean the Manor House?'

'Do I?' Holly said, a little unsure. 'Possibly.'

Kathy nodded emphatically, implying that was definitely the building Holly meant. The old woman's face crinkled further as she chewed down on her bottom lip.

'Now, I do know. Give me a sec. My memory's not what it used to be. Some lord... Lord Canbury, I think.'

A lump formed in the pit of Holly's stomach.

'Any chance it's Lord Caverty?' she asked, a note of trepidation in her voice. Holly had known from their first meeting that Giles was from a wealthy background and if she remembered correctly, his uncle was the richest of them all. But she would have known if Giles was related to a lord, wouldn't she? Then again, she hadn't known he was her landlord until less than twelve hours ago.

'That's it! Lord Caverty,' Kathy said excitedly. 'He's got a nephew who comes into the village now and then if I'm not mistaken. God, I'd love to own a place like that, wouldn't you?' Kathy said dreamily. 'Imagine, all that space.'

'Imagine,' Holly said.

34

The bird park and baking were only half of the day's adventures Holly had planned for her and Hope. Back at the cottage, they enjoyed a picnic lunch out in the back garden, before a session of finger painting. Afterwards, while a small part of Holly would have loved to sit on the sofa, Hope was still full of beans. As such, they left the house again, this time to feed the ducks with a bag of oats.

'I thought you weren't coming in today?' Drey said, as Holly poked her head through the door.

'I was just passing,' Holly replied.

'And so you thought you'd come and check we hadn't run the place to the ground?' Caroline smirked.

It wasn't that Holly didn't trust Drey and Caroline to manage the shop. She did. Completely. But it was a force of habit to check in whenever she passed.

'Sorry.'

'No need to apologise,' Drey said, immediately moving away from the counter. 'You can just let me have some cuddles with this one, and all will be forgiven.'

For over thirty minutes, Drey cuddled and cooed over Hope.

Lifting her into the air and causing her to giggle with delight, while Holly and Caroline dealt with a deluge of customers. Secretly, Holly had been hoping she might have time to talk to Caroline about Giles and the wedding, but instead, there was barely a second to breathe as they criss-crossed one another on the shop floor hurrying to weigh out sweets and put them through the till.

So far, this summer had been even better than last year. If it carried on the same way, she would look at adding some extra shelving units, or at least updating the ones she had. Only when Hope started grizzling, from a mixture of tiredness and hunger, did Holly decide it was time to head back home.

That evening, the night-time routine consisted of four readings of *We're Going on a Bear Hunt,* followed by a quick read through of *That's Not My Fairy,* both of which Holly had read so many times, she could recite them word for word. Still, Hope loved those books. A soft, sleepy smile curled on her lips as Holly gave Hope her final kiss of the day, and lay her down in her cot, only for Holly's phone to ring downstairs.

As had become normal, Holly texted Evan a couple of times during the day just to check on him, but her messages had gone unread. She couldn't blame him; when she was at work, she would leave her phone upstairs, often not seeing his messages until hours later. They were like ships passing in the night, and they needed to set more anchors to ensure they could spend time together.

She raced downstairs to answer.

'How has it only been a day since I saw you? It makes no sense,' Holly said with a sigh. 'It feels like weeks.'

'I know. But hopefully, I'll get back soon. How are you doing?'

'Honestly...' Holly didn't want to unburden herself to Evan. Not when they hadn't spoken all day. But there were thoughts she just couldn't shift. 'I'm still mad. Really mad. The thing is, it's just so... so

Giles. Over-the-top gestures. The sweeping in when he thinks I need help.'

'But from what you've said, you did kind of need a place of your own to live?'

'That's not the point.' She huffed. Not for the first time, Holly wasn't interested in any rational arguments or logical explanations. She just wanted to vent. 'But I think it's Mum I'm most mad at. Surely, her loyalty lies with me. Surely, I am the one she should be keeping secrets for, not from. I mean, I told her about seeing Giles in France. I told her about spending the night on his boat.'

'Where nothing happened,' Evan interjected.

'Yes, I know. Nothing happened. But that's not the point. What I'm saying is I told her all these things, about how we had seen each other, about how I said I didn't want a relationship with him, and she didn't think to tell me about the house. Surely there was a point when she thought, "Oh, maybe I should tell Holly about the fact that her mystery landlord isn't really a mystery at all." She could have done that, right?'

'She could have, but maybe she wanted to talk to Giles about it first.'

Holly ponded the point a moment longer before letting out another long sigh.

'Maybe, but that doesn't change the fact that she shouldn't have lied to me. Honestly, I'm so mad at her. And I know that she and Dad are going to call soon and tell me all the wonderful things they've done, and I'm going to have to sound smiley and happy and like I don't know that she's been lying to me. And I hate it.'

'Then just tell her.'

Of all the ridiculous things Evan had said, that had to be the most ludicrous. There was no way Holly could do that. 'You think I should ruin her holiday by telling her now? I can't do that.'

'You don't have to ruin her holiday,' Evan replied. 'Just be straightforward about it. "Hi Mum, I spoke to the plumber about the landlord and discovered it was Giles. Thank you for trying to protect me, but honestly, Giles and I are fine now. You didn't need to do that."'

Evan finished his brief speech, and Holly had to admit it was good – straight to the point, no fuss. Yet she doubted she could deliver it in the same manner.

'That's not how Mum and I work. We talk things through face to face. I can't do this over the phone. I'll wait until she's back and then we'll go for cake or something. Or wine. Wine might be better.'

'It's up to you. I just don't want you fretting about it, that's all.'

Holly took a deep breath in and sipped her drink. 'No, I'm not stressing about it. Let's talk about something else.'

'Jamie and Fin's wedding? Any luck finding a location?'

Holly's mind immediately went to the large house she'd seen behind the bird park. Her jaw locked in response. How was Giles and his current stunt so impossible to get out of her head? Even when she really didn't want them there.

'Not a great topic of conversation, either. Any others you've got for me?'

'Well, how about Maud then? Did you catch up with her again?'

'Crap,' Holly said. This conversation was just getting worse and worse.

35

Holly's frustration and annoyance at her mother were replaced with anger at herself. Not to mention guilt. She felt terrible. Having told Maud to ring the sweet shop, and arrange a time and place to catch up, she'd entirely forgotten that she wouldn't be in the sweet shop that day at all. Given how busy and sunny it would've been, the likelihood of someone picking up the phone and taking a message was slim.

'Caroline.' Holly called her friend the second she got off the phone with Evan. 'Did Maud call while you were at the shop today?'

'Maud? As in the old sweet shop owner, Maud?'

'Yes, yes, that's the one.'

'No, not that I heard. Listen, Holly, Jamie rang me last night and told me what happened about the wedding. It's terrible, isn't it? I sent Michael to see if there are any council buildings that might be free. They sometimes have space for things like this.'

Holly's guilt deepened further. She hadn't even text Jamie that day to see how the hunt was going. She was failing on all levels of friendship at the moment.

'That would be fabulous if he could find somewhere,' Holly replied, though she didn't hold out much hope. Summer was the busiest time of the year for everybody. If the council could use those buildings to make some money, chances were that they, like everybody else, were already fully booked.

'Have you had a good day off?' Caroline asked, when there was nothing more to add about Jamie's situation.

'Yes, mixed. It was lovely to spend some time with Hope, as always.'

'And Evan? When is he coming back?'

'Soon, I think. I hope,' she added, aware of the desperation that echoed in her voice. 'Hopefully before the wedding.'

She still didn't know how it was possible to miss someone so much when they had barely spent any time together, but maybe that was why this relationship was different.

'I hear he bought you a Vespa,' Caroline said, interrupting Holly's thoughts.

'How do you know that? I didn't tell anyone.'

'Yes, you did. You told Ben and then Ben told Jamie and Jamie told me. So, when are you going to take us out for a ride?'

By the sound of it, Caroline was deadly serious, yet Holly couldn't help but laugh.

'I'm not exactly an experienced driver,' she said, 'and to be honest, I don't know when I'm going to next take myself out for a ride. But don't worry, I'll take you out with me as soon as I can.'

'That's a deal, and I'm holding you to it.'

The pair chuckled.

'Okay, well, I'd better go. I need to see if I can track Maud down. I don't know how long she's back in town for, and the last thing I want to do is miss her.'

'No worries. Ben's got Hope tomorrow, right? So, I'll see you at the shop. Did you want me to open up?'

Holly was about to say no, that it was fine, and she could do it, but early in the morning seemed like a great time to catch Maud if she was having breakfast at the hotel. It might be better than ringing so late at night, too. Knowing Maud, she was probably out, catching up with people. Yes, breakfast sounded a much better option.

'If you could do that, it would be great.'

'No worries, see you tomorrow. Love you.'

'You too.'

* * *

Holly arranged with Ben that she would drop Hope off at his house. It wasn't the normal way they did things, but she was planning on driving to see Maud, and it seemed silly not to drop Hope off at the same time.

'Any exciting plans this morning?' Holly asked Ben as she handed Hope over to him.

'Oh, you know us,' he replied nonchalantly. The fact was, she did know him. And she knew that their day would be full of planned activities, from water play in the garden, a visit to the soft play centre if the weather was bad, or a trip out on the back of his bicycle around the Slaughters if he felt like traveling a bit further. Ben was one of those parents who made Holly feel like she was never doing enough, though on the positive side, they were parenting the same child, which meant Holly didn't feel that guilty about lazy days with Hope either.

'Everything okay?' Ben said. 'Caroline said she's opening up for you this morning.'

'Since when did you and Caroline speak to each other constantly?' Holly asked with a genuine curiosity. First Jamie's situation and now this. It wasn't that the pair hadn't been friends, but she'd never realised they were the type of friends that rang each other. At least they weren't when she and Ben had been together.

'Since she and Michael have been trying to get a new mortgage,' he replied. 'She rings me nearly every evening. I've even got a special ringtone for her now, so I'm warned that it's her before I see it.'

Holly laughed. 'I'm going to tell her that this afternoon.'

'You wouldn't?' Ben's face quickly paled.

'Depends on how good a mood I'm in.' She winked.

36

As Holly parked up outside the Little Lodge, she couldn't help but feel another flicker of guilt. After all, having absconded Maud, and not been there in anticipation of her call at the shop, Holly was now invading her privacy at the hotel. She could only hope her friend understood that life had been a little more hectic this week than expected.

Holly pushed open the door to the restaurant, the bell jingling above her.

'You right there, love?' The man behind the bar smiled. 'Can I help you?'

Holly scanned the space. 'Yes, I'm looking for my friend. She was staying here last night. Actually, she's been staying here for a few nights, I think. I was just hoping I could come and see her. Have breakfast with her, you know.'

He frowned.

'Breakfast is for residents only.'

'Yes, yes, I know that.' Holly worked quickly to reword herself. 'I didn't mean that I was going to eat breakfast with her. I meant that maybe I could sit with her while she was eating her breakfast. I just want to catch up. She's only visiting for a few days, you see.'

The man's frowned deepened, as if Holly was secretly trying to do him out of a dozen miniature jars of Tiptree jam. Finally, he nodded over to the dining area.

'Suppose you can. Staying by herself, is she?'

Holly nodded.

'Then she's not come down yet. Only people down this time are families. You want me to ring the room?'

Holly went to reply, only to change her mind. The last thing she wanted was for Maud to rush. She had already inconvenienced her enough.

'No, it's fine. I'll just wait.'

The man offered her yet another gruff response, and Holly smiled as sweetly as she could. How was it when she was in the sweet shop, she spent all her time smiling at every single customer, then you would go into other places, and the people serving would do nothing but scowl? It was a miracle they got any service at all.

A few minutes later, Holly was sitting in the dining area, checking through the delivery schedules and orders for the shop on her phone. It really was a wonder of modern technology that she could work like this wherever she was. Still, when fifteen minutes became thirty, Holly considered asking the man if he could ring Maud's room, only to change her mind, and ring the shop instead, to tell Caroline she was going to be longer than expected. She had just hung up when she spotted Maud hobbling down the staircase, holding on to the banister gingerly.

Holly rushed across to help her and took her arm at the bottom of the stairs.

'Holly? What are you doing here? We didn't arrange to meet this morning, did we?'

'No, no, we didn't.' Holly shook her head as she led Maud over to the table. 'But I felt so bad about rushing out the other day, and then I completely forgot I wasn't at the shop yesterday for you to phone. And I was worried you might be leaving soon.'

A look of gratitude washed over the old woman's face.

'Thank... Thank you, Holly, love. That means a lot.'

Holly smiled in response, and Maud tried to reciprocate the gesture, but it seemed an effort to even raise her lips.

When Holly had met Maud the other night, her hair had been done, while blush had added a bit of colour to her cheeks. She'd even had a slight slick of lipstick. But there was none of that now. Maud's face was drawn and tired. Her skin was translucent, with a web of blue-green veins crisscrossing beneath.

When they reached the dining area, Holly pulled out a chair for her to sit down on.

'Let me fetch you a cup of tea,' she said.

Maud nodded, not even managing a word of thanks.

Even after all these years, Holly recalled how Maud had liked her tea: White, but with no sugar, 'because she was sweet enough'. At least, that was what Agnes used to say.

Checking that the grumpy waiter's back was turned, and she wouldn't be chastised for stealing, Holly grabbed another cup for herself and filled it with coffee from the percolator. Deciding that Maud also looked like she could do with feeding up a bit too, Holly grab a croissant and a pain au chocolat before heading back to the table and placing them down in front of her friend.

Given how chatty Maud had been at the shop the other day, and while meeting Hope, Holly expected her to start asking her questions about her life, or perhaps tell her about her trips abroad. Instead, she remained completely still, staring into the teacup. More people were coming and going into the dining room now. Plates were clattering, and children chattering, yet all Holly could do was look at Maud.

Finally, she found her voice, along with a deep sinking feeling which filled her stomach.

'Maud?' There was a tremble in Holly's voice. She didn't want to hear the answer to the question she was about to ask, but she knew she had to ask it. 'Maud, are you okay?'

The old woman lifted her head. Her eyes met Holly's and for a single second, Holly felt as though her heart was about to stop beating, when a small smile rose at the corner of Maud's lips. The first smile Holly had seen since she arrived.

'Actually, Holly dear, I hope you don't mind, but while I was here, I was hoping I could ask you for a favour.'

Holly didn't need to ask what the favour was. The answer was immediate, regardless.

'Of course you can. Anything. What do you need?'

The twinkle that had been missing from Maud's eyes all morning returned with a sparkle.

'It's more of a want than a need,' she said.

37

The last time Holly had seen Maud working in the shop, the old woman had been frail and defeated, no longer able to bear the weight of Agnes's memory, which the building held so keenly. She had let the shop fall into disrepair. Neglecting orders and bills left, right and centre. But the woman who donned the blue and white striped apron that morning made the old, frail woman from the past appear a figment of Holly's imagination. And it made her heart fit to burst.

This was the Maud Holly remembered from the old days, full of vitality, chatting away with the customers. She knew instinctively where all the various jars should be on the shelves and didn't think twice about chastising Holly for having moved something around.

'You can't just have a quarter of acid drops,' she said to one of the old regulars. 'You need to get at least a half. And don't forget the cough candy. You always used to love the cough candy.'

Holly had expected Maud to recognise the local customers, but she hadn't expected her to remember all their orders so accurately, or for it to have such an impact on their profits – Maud had persuaded them all to up their bag weight, or the number of purchases.

One by one, the customers gave in to Maud's masterful sales tactics, and Holly watched the sweets fly off the shelves.

'She's incredible,' Caroline whispered, as another customer left with three times what they had come in for.

'She is,' Holly replied. 'They both were.'

Holly looked at her old friend, working away. Her hands, which that very morning had struggled to hold a teacup steady with the weight of it, were carrying around the large jars and slipping open the paper bags for the sweets without the slightest bit of effort. Was it simply muscle memory, Holly wondered, or was it more than that? Something in built into her heart?

As energetic and enthusiastic as Maud started the day, it didn't take long before she began to tire. Holly could see it in her stance, which began to slouch, before her hands started to tremble by just a fraction.

'I think I'd better take her back to the hotel,' she said to Caroline. 'Will you be okay here for a bit?'

Caroline nodded. 'Of course, take as long as you need. I'll be fine.'

A moment later, Holly was standing beside the till with Maud next to her.

'Why don't you have a rest?' she said, as tactfully as she could. 'You can go upstairs. Or I can drive you back to the Little Lodge. I can always pick you up again and bring you back down this afternoon if that's what you'd like,' she added.

Maud smiled faintly. 'You know, I think I've had the perfect fill for me,' she said. 'Perfect. But yes, if you could take me back, that would be good. Thank you, love.'

After saying goodbye to Caroline, Holly drove Maud back to the lodge, having to help her both in and out of the car. The old, tired woman that had evaporated inside the sweetshop had returned and, as Holly guided her back towards the building, Maud leaned heavily against her arm. The old lady's footsteps were half the speed as when she had been moving from the scales to the till and calling out all the customers' orders. It didn't make sense that her strength could come and go again so quickly.

'When are you off?' Holly asked as they reached the door. 'Would you like to come down to the shop again? It would be great to have an extra pair of hands behind the till. Especially with Dad away.'

Maud smiled softly, her hand still resting on Holly's arms. 'I'm not sure I was that much use, really.'

'Are you kidding me? I've never seen Mr Bourn buy so much.'

That same twinkle from early in the day appeared once again in Maud's eyes, although a slight sheen glistened over it.

'Do you have to hurry off, love?' she said. 'Perhaps I could buy you a cup of tea. Or something stronger, if you'd like. It is nearly lunchtime, after all.'

Holly's automatic response was to say that she should get back to the shop. After all, there was always something to do, whether it was stock taking, or re-ordering, or just dusting the shelves and giving the place a proper sweep through. Yet as Maud looked up at her, her eyes still bright behind the tapestry of wrinkles, Holly couldn't help but think of Agnes, and what she would have given for another chance to sit down and talk to her. To hear about her adventures and escapades and life before the sweet shop. Holly wouldn't get that chance to sit down with Agnes ever again, and nor would she miss the opportunity with Maud.

'Of course. Of course.'

The early lunch crowd was already filling the tables outside, yet inside, they had their choice of seats. Holly headed to one in the corner, where the window was open, letting the breeze in.

'Why don't we get a menu, too?' she said. 'You didn't eat very much for breakfast. And I'll get these.'

Maud took a long breath in. Holly was certain she was about to insist on buying lunch, but instead, she smiled.

'That sounds nice. Perhaps we could share a plate of chips?'

'Perfect.'

While Maud took a seat, Holly disappeared to the bar to order the chips and two glasses of lemonade, one of which she placed in front of Maud before taking a long sip of her own.

'It was lovely, being at the shop today,' Maud said. 'Like it used to be. You know, for a second there, I almost forgot. It was like she was there still. Upstairs, squirrelling away.'

Maud's gaze drifted out the window. It was the same far-off look that she had worn at breakfast. But rather than speaking again, Holly just let the old women sit there until she was ready to talk. It would be impossible to imagine all the memories that had hit Maud that morning, back in the shop, and no doubt she needed time to process it all. For Holly, processing meant talking. And often baking too, but she knew that wasn't what all people were like. If all Maud wanted to do was sit and eat her chips in silence, then that was fine with her. Though it was only a moment later that Maud turned back to her, and Holly noticed the sheen that now covered her eyes.

'Maud?' A sickening dread crept up Holly's throat. There was something about Maud's look that told Holly that this was more than grief for Agnes. 'What is it? What's happened?'

Holly waited, willing Maud to remain silent. To keep that wistful look and not say anything and yet the old woman took a deep breath in, then let the air out with a sigh.

'I'm sick, my love,' Maud said. 'I'm very sick.'

38

Holly felt as if a knife had been thrust straight between her ribs. Maud, with all the dignity and grace she possessed, wiped her cheeks with the back of her hand, sighed gently, and then picked up her lemonade for a short sip.

'Now, don't look at me like that,' she said. 'I don't need you to look at me like that.'

Holly wasn't exactly sure how she was looking at Maud, but if she had to guess, she would assume it was with an expression of complete devastation. She couldn't bear it. It didn't make sense.

'What is it?' Holly asked, before quickly shaking her head. 'I didn't mean like that. You don't have to tell me anything you don't want to.'

Maud smiled gently. 'Oh, there's some long, complicated name that the doctors have given it, but it doesn't really matter, does it? It's gonna get me. That's what really counts.'

It was like someone had taken that blade and twisted it further still. Holly's eyes filled with tears, but she didn't want to let them show. If Maud wasn't crying, and she was the one that was sick, then the least Holly could do was have the dignity not to do the same. But it was hard. Harder than she'd ever known.

'You know, doctors have to give you the worst news,' Holly said, trying to sound as upbeat as possible. 'It's a thing, you know. They don't want to get your hopes up. That's all it is. I'm sure the odds are much better than they've told you.'

Once again, Maud smiled, a soft smile of gratitude, followed by another sip of her drink.

'Oh, I think it is as bad as they tell me. I can feel it, you know. Everywhere in me now. But it's okay. I'm okay with that.'

As Holly struggled to speak, Maud stretched her hands across the table. She felt so cold, Holly thought as she looked down at Maud's frail fingers, where her knucklebones protruded outwards, unnaturally harsh and angular.

'So, this is the reason you came back to Bourton?' she asked, trying to keep her voice steady as she spoke.

'I've got some things to sort out,' Maud replied. 'People I need to say goodbye to. People I need to give the middle finger to, too. It's fabulous what you find the courage to do when there are no repercussions.'

At this, Holly laughed. She couldn't imagine anything ever preventing Maud from sticking her middle finger up at someone if she wanted to, but it was good to see she still hadn't lost her sense of humour.

'I'm so sorry, Maud. I should've been more there for you. I wasn't there with Agnes, and now—'

'No, no, don't you go doing that.' Maud's expression changed to a firm pout. 'Don't you go blaming yourself for things you can't change. You were out there living your life. And I wouldn't have it any other way. And neither would Agnes. You know, those years back there with you in the shop, they were some of the happiest we had.'

Holly could feel her eyes welling with tears again. This time, though, she didn't try to stifle them.

'Me too,' she said.

'And maybe it was wrong of us. After all, you had your own family, bless them, but we used to think of you like a daughter. You know that. We couldn't have one ourselves. Fate wasn't on our side there, but we had you, and for a long while, it was all we could have hoped for. And I know Agnes isn't here to say it, so I'll have to do it myself, but we are ever so proud of how you've turned out, Holly. Ever so proud.'

It was more than Holly could take. Tears tumbled down her cheeks.

'Maud, please, you don't need to give up yet. You know they're always coming up with new drug trials, new medicines. Maybe we can explore that option? Maybe we can see if you qualify for a drug trial?'

At this, Maud let out a hearty chuckle. 'Oh, my love, they're not gonna put an old woman like me through something like that. It's just another shot in the dark. I've had a good life, a great life. Besides, I've missed Agnes, you know. It's been a long while and I'm tired of missing her. And maybe this way, just maybe, we'll get to be together again.'

For a while, they sat there, holding on to each other. At one point, the waiter came in and caught Holly's eye. For a moment, she thought he was about to say something, something gruff, like someone else needed the table and it was time for them to leave. Instead, he glanced between the two of them and silently exited the room.

'So, what now?' Holly asked, when she had finally wiped away all her tears. 'What are your plans? Are you coming back to Bourton permanently?'

Maud sniffed and straightened her posture a little.

'Well, the plan is to head back up to Scotland. I know Agnes's family would like to have me there. And I'd like to be with them too. But the thing is, Holly, like I said, we thought of you as a daughter. And I want to do right by you. And you know I got quite a lot of money from selling the cottage.'

Holly's chest tightened.

'Maud, I don't want to talk about this. I don't. Please, it doesn't feel right.'

'Well, I'm older than you, and I do want to talk about it, so you don't have a choice. Now listen, I don't have millions—'

'Maud, please, I don't need your money, if that's what you're going to say. You have given me so much in life.'

'Well, I don't have millions. Not even close. And there's all Agnes's nieces and nephews, too. But the sweet shop, they didn't get it the way you did. No one did.'

Holly continued to sob, tears streaming down her face.

'What can I do to help you now?' she asked, pushing Maud's comments away. She didn't care about money. She cared about her friends. 'I don't have to go into the shop again today; Caroline will be perfectly fine. Is there anyone you want to see? Anywhere you'd like to go? Stow? Moreton? I'll take you there. I can drive you.'

Maud smiled sadly.

'I'm just going to rest a little,' she said. 'Just for a little while.'

39

When she reached her car, Holly sat with both hands on the steering wheel and cried. These weren't the controlled tears that tumbled down her cheeks when she was talking to Maud; these were full-on, cascading sobs that she had no way of controlling. Ones that caused her nose to run and her throat to scratch. Ones that stung her eyes and made it impossible for her to see. Given that she was parked up on the road, where dozens of tourists were strolling by, she was sure some of them must have seen her in her broken-down state, but she didn't care. By the time she'd stemmed the flow of tears enough to catch her breath, she sent Caroline a message, confirming that she was going to take the rest of the afternoon off.

Holly could barely recall the drive back from the hotel to the cottage. It wasn't a long drive, by any means, but she did the entire journey on auto pilot, barely aware of anything around her. She desperately wanted to ring Evan. She wanted to sob down the phone to him and pour her heart out. But she'd spent the last two days whinging to him about Giles and her mother, and that wasn't the type of girlfriend she wanted to be. Especially not so early in the relationship. And so she headed back home, unsure of what she was going to do next. As it happened, she found the answer, standing there in front of her driveway.

She was going to go for a ride.

* * *

This wasn't the first time Holly had driven the Vespa on her own. In France, she'd got all the way from Evan's villa to the marina to see Giles on his yacht without anyone to help her. And she planned on driving exactly the same way as she'd done then. Very, very slowly. She had nothing to prove and no one to watch her. Still, her nerves were high as she fixed her helmet and climbed on top of the vehicle. The most difficult part, she recalled from her drive, only a couple of days before, was going to be getting out of her driveway. After a moment's deliberation, she dismounted and pushed the bike down towards the road, before climbing back onto the seat and switching on the engine.

Holly had intended to ride slowly, and that was how she started. She headed out of the village at an exceptionally tentative pace, before crossing over the Fosseway and taking the hill up towards Naunton. But as she twisted and turned through the country lanes, underneath the dappled patterns of light which fell through the broken gaps in the leaves, the idea of a steady sleep slipped from her mind. Somehow, being on the vehicle like this, so close to nature, was all it took to wash away her worries from the last few days. Giles being her landlord: the weight of it whipped from her as she took one corner. It was as if the air was sweeping away that worry like dust that clung to her clothes. With the next corner, which she took just a little bit faster, she let the fears of Jamie and Fin's wedding fly from her mind. They would sort it out like they sorted everything out. They would be fine.

With the next bend, she thought about her mother.

Wendy had lied to her. The thought caused a knot in Holly's chest, but she refused to let it settle. She and Wendy would be fine in the long run. Holly would need to own up to knowing and Wendy would need to apologise. It wasn't a conversation she wanted to have, but she would, and they would be okay, because that's who they were. She would forgive her mother. After all, she had only done what she thought was best.

With the next bend, Holly's thought shifted again as she twisted the throttle a fraction more. And this time, she thought about Maud. Or more precisely, she thought about losing Maud. Immediately, the tears welled in her eyes. With her helmet on, there was no way Holly could wipe them away, and she knew that if she wasn't careful, they'd start blurring her sight and making it impossible for her to see. But she wasn't going to let herself get to that state.

'You're fine, you're fine,' Holly was saying to herself as she rode, but the more she spoke, the shallower her breath became, and the faster the tears fell. She was less than a mile from Naunton. She had driven and walked these roads so many times, she probably knew them with her eyes closed. But they were narrow, lined with trees and full of thick foliage. Even one of the rare passing spaces didn't really offer a place for her to stop and regather herself. What Holly needed to do was get to the village. There would be space there, with its quaint church and wide verges. She just had to reach Naunton, then she could sit down and sort herself out. A few hundred metres, she told herself. That was all she needed, and she would be fine.

She would be fine. But Maud wouldn't. That was the thought that filled her head and refused to shift. It was still there, running through Holly's head as she turned the next corner. Maud would never be okay.

If Holly had been travelling slower, maybe it would've made a difference. If she'd been able to hear better, without her sobs wheezing in her ears, or could see through the blur of her tears, maybe she would've avoided it. But it was too late.

The instant she turned the corner, the car came into view. Holly yanked on the handlebars, twisting them as far as they could go, while twisting the brake and willing herself out of the car's path. Only there was nowhere to go. Not on a country lane this narrow. Even through the blur of tears and the panic of adrenaline, she saw the tree trunk, only a couple of metres in front of her, before her front tire collided with it. A shock wave ran through her body and in a second that lasted a lifetime, she was thrown from the bike.

40

Holly had never been in a proper car crash – or Vespa crash – before. In fact, the closest she'd got was a couple of years ago when her mother swerved to avoid a pheasant in the road and they ended up in a ditch. But both humans, the car and the pheasant, had been fine. Holly knew without a doubt that this wasn't anything like that.

Her head throbbed, and ears rang as it took her a moment to piece together what had happened. With a gasping breath, she realised that her chin was wet and instantly assumed the culprit to be blood, only to recall that she had been crying profusely before the crash happened. Those tears had stopped, but that appeared to be one of the few pieces of good news.

Another piece of good news was that Holly herself had not hit the tree trunk. The angle at which the Vespa had struck the tree meant she had been thrown into a leafy hedgerow, as opposed to another, more immobile object. Still, she could feel the stings where the thorns and branches had broken the skin and the way her head was throbbing implied there probably was a cut there after all. Wanting to assess how bad the damage was, she placed a hand down on the ground and tried to push herself up to standing, only to yell out in pain.

'Jeez!' More thorns and twigs dug into her palm, but that wasn't the issue. The issue was with her arm.

Rolling herself onto her knees, she tried again to lift herself up, only for a sharp pain to shoot down to her elbow.

'Stay where you are. Stay where you are,' someone said. 'You shouldn't move. Should I call an ambulance?'

'An ambulance?' Holly said.

With a concerted effort, and avoiding placing any weight on her arm, she tipped herself onto her knees and pushed herself up to a standing position. Her legs were trembling, and she felt distinctly less than stable, but all the same, she glanced down at the bike. An ache rippled through her chest. The beautiful paintwork of her Vespa was no more. Instead, there were dents, scrapes, and paint chipped off in various places. The front wheel was twisted at completely the wrong angle. Another sob struck Holly, adding to the guilt and embarrassment she already felt.

'I didn't see you coming.' This time, Holly paid more attention to the woman who was talking to her. She was young – around the same age as her – and at that moment, so pale, she was almost translucent. 'I'm really sorry. These roads are so narrow, with so many trees. You can't see around the corners at all. I'm so sorry.'

'This wasn't just your fault,' Holly replied. She could barely remember the moment before the crash, and she was pretty sure that had a lot more to do with her not paying attention than any form of concussion. 'I should've looked where I was going more.' Another thought struck her. Suddenly aware that she had been entirely absorbed in her own injuries and worries, she looked the woman up and down. 'Are you okay? Is your car okay?'

The woman nodded rapidly. 'I'm fine. I just caught my wing mirror. My car is fine. Don't worry about it.'

'So, what do we do now?' Holly said.

The pair stood in silence for a second before the woman spoke again.

'I really think you should call an ambulance,' she said.

Holly was about to refuse, only then she realised just how much her arm was throbbing, although the pain seemed to come in waves, along with the dizziness that accompanied it. Unfortunately, the colour of her hands confirmed it was definitely blood now, trickling down from her forehead, but her left arm was in the worst state. The top layer of skin had been scraped off from her elbow to her wrist, and there was something not quite right about how it looked. Adding to the fact she couldn't put any weight on it at all, the obvious assumption was a broken bone. If this had happened to any of her friends, she would have sent them straight to the hospital too...

Holly pointed to her front pocket and spoke to the woman. 'Can you grab my phone for me? I'll ring my friend. She'll know what to do.'

'Are you sure you don't want me to ring an ambulance first?'

'It's fine. I'll ring one in a minute, but she lives close. She'll get here faster.'

The woman fumbled through Holly's pocket and grabbed her phone, after which she typed in the code Holly told her, then went straight to the contacts.

'Who is it you want me to call?' she asked.

Holly took the phone from her and scrolled down herself, using just one hand. There was only one person she could ring at a time like this.

41

'What happened?' Jamie asked. She had gone straight there, although it was a miracle she found them, given how Holly had started sobbing the moment she answered the phone. Somehow, she had now stopped, though it was probably more to do with a lack of tears than anything else.

'I just needed to go out for a drive. That poor woman.' Holly glanced over at the driver of the car, who was still standing on, waiting to see if she could be of help. 'She keeps apologising, and it wasn't her at all. If it was anyone's fault, it was mine. I can barely remember what happened. I was just thinking about Maud.'

'The sweet shop lady?'

'She's dying,' Holly said. 'Pretty soon, by the sound of it.'

'Oh, Holly, I'm sorry. I know how much she means to you.' Instinctively, Jamie went in for a hug, only for Holly to gasp as a bolt of pain shot up her arm towards her spine.

The waves of throbbing had become constant, and ever growing. And as much as she hated to admit it, Holly knew the woman was right. She needed to get to the hospital.

'Evan is going to kill me,' she said, as Jamie single-handedly pulled the Vespa out of the undergrowth and rolled it towards the back of her van. The beautiful paintwork was now chipped, the handlebars bent at a funny angle. None of it was sparkling any more.

'Too right, Evan is gonna kill you,' Jamie said. 'But not because his Vespa is a write-off. In fact, I'm going to kill him for getting you a Vespa in the first place. He's going to kill you for hurting yourself and ending up in a hedge.'

Holly could feel the tears welling in her eyes, and Jamie saw it too.

'It's fine. Come on, let's get you to the hospital. And take that poor woman's number, too. You can send her a box of chocolates or something. I think she needs them.'

* * *

Holly had heard about the current waiting times in A&E on the news, and expected to be sat around waiting for quite some time, but it was a testament to the place, or to her injury, that she was ushered straight through for an X-ray.

'You don't need to wait for me,' she said to Jamie, as she followed the nurse. 'And can you message Ben? He's got Hope tonight, so he doesn't need to know any of this.'

'So you want me to message Ben, to not tell him about this?' Jamie tried to clarify.

Holly found herself unable to answer.

'What I mean is—'

'Go and get your damn X-ray, will you?'

Unsurprisingly, the results of the X-ray showed that Holly's left arm was broken in two places.

'It could've been a lot worse,' the doctor said, as he pointed to the lines on the scan. 'There is no dislocation or movement in the bone, so it won't need pinning. Which, if you ask me, is a miracle. But it's good for you – no need for a nasty operation, and the recovery time should be quicker, too.'

At least that was something to be grateful for.

'So how long will it be?' Holly asked. 'I run my own business, and I've got a daughter on my own. I'm a single mum, sort of.'

'Well, I hope your business doesn't involve carrying heavy things. And as for your daughter, same there. You're going to be in a cast for six to eight weeks, and after that, we'll have a look at it.'

Six to eight weeks. Holly's jaw dropped, and another batch of tears filled her throat. Six to eight weeks meant she'd be in a cast for Jamie's wedding, if it was still going ahead, but really, that was the least of her worries. They were smack bang in the middle of the busiest summer in years at the shop, and while her job didn't involve heavy machinery, the large bags of sweets that she got from the suppliers weren't light, and she often found herself lugging ten kilos up the stairs in one go. Then there was Hope to think of. It was difficult enough handling her as it was. Getting her in and out of the car seat, not to mention the pushchair, the baths. How was she going to manage any of that with only one hand?

'And that cut on your head looks like it needs a few stitches too,' the doctor added.

While the X-ray didn't take long to happen, Holly had several hours waiting around for someone to stitch her up and fit the cast. By the time her arm was fixed up and seven stitches had secured the cut on her head, early evening was on its way.

Holly limped through the hospital, not because of the bruises on her leg, but because of the ones to her ego. She hadn't even thought about how she was getting home. The bus was the most viable option, but given how shattered she was, she thought she might just swallow the cost and grab a taxi instead. As it happened, she needed to do neither. There, still sitting in the waiting room, was Jamie.

'I told you you didn't have to hang around,' she said, feeling the tears she had only just stemmed swelling up once again.

'Don't worry, I've been using the time productively,' Jamie said. 'I've been looking up wedding venues that might have cancellations in Oxford or Somerset or even Warwickshire.'

'Any luck?'

Jamie shook her head. 'I've looked at Gretna Green too, but there's nothing at all. But we don't need to worry about that now. Let's get you home.'

42

Jamie offered to come into the cottage with Holly, to make a cup of tea or prepare a meal, given that Holly hadn't eaten all day other than a single bar of chocolate from the hospital vending machine. But despite her state, Holly shook her head.

'Don't worry, you've already helped me enough,' she said, as she clumped out of the car. 'Thank you for today.'

'Are you sure? I don't mind kipping on the sofa either, if you want someone to stay with you.'

Again, Holly shook her head. She was going to have this cast on for nearly two months; she knew she would have to learn to be independent sooner or later. Besides, she needed to ring people. She needed to ring Ben, to work out how they were going to handle things now. She needed to ring Caroline and Drey to see if they could cover a couple of extra shifts at the shop. And she needed to ring Evan, to tell him what she had done to the Vespa.

'I'll call you tomorrow, okay?' she said.

'Okay. Take care, alright?'

Jamie drove away with the Vespa in the back of the van. She had already mentioned on the way back that she had some mates who could probably repair it. Holly had nodded gratefully.

Yet she still felt numb. The painkillers the doctor had given her were strong enough to knock her out and if she took another one, she'd probably fall asleep where she stood. But she had things to do.

Holly rang Caroline and Drey first, both of whom offered to come around immediately and help. Holly told them the same line, that she was grateful for the offer, but she was just going to get some rest. And it was true. That was the plan at least, only she had a couple more people to speak to first, delaying the act of telling Evan just a little bit longer.

'Thank God it was only a broken arm,' Ben said. 'Do you realise you could have been seriously hurt?'

'Yes, thank you, Ben.' She tried not to sound annoyed with him. Of course she knew how close she had come to something far more serious. And the thought shook her to the core.

'Well, you're okay, that's what matters. What about the other people who were involved? Was the woman okay?' It didn't surprise Holly that this was the next question out of Ben's mouth. After all, he was always looking at the bigger picture.

'She's okay, shaken up,' Holly told him. 'I've got her number now, so I'll text her. At least it's my left arm so I can still write and use my phone.'

'Well, don't worry about logistics. We'll work out the days, but for the nights, Hope can stay with me for as long as you need.'

This brought tears to Holly's eyes. Sad tears. It wasn't that she wasn't grateful for everything Ben did, but the last thing she wanted was for Hope to spend extra nights with Ben. She found it tough enough when Hope was away as it was. She was only now beginning to not jolt awake in the middle of the night, panicking that her daughter wasn't with her. The thought of not being able to put her to bed in the evening, or hear her babbling in the morning, was enough to start the tears streaming again.

'Don't worry about this, Holly,' Ben reassured her, having clearly worked out what had caused the long pause on Holly's end of the line. 'If it helps, I'll come round to you at bath time and put her to bed at yours instead. And then I can come round early in the morning, if you need help getting her up for breakfast. Unless you want to move in to mine for a bit, or longer – I'm guessing it might be a while. I'm sure Georgia would understand, though.'

Holly managed to smile through the tears. She wasn't entirely sure how she'd feel if Evan wanted an ex to move in with him for two months, even if they were hurt, but the fact that Ben made the offer was enough to make her heart swell. It was a mystery how her life had turned around. All those years she'd spent with Dan not appreciating her, never wanting to do anything for her, and now she had all these men trying to help. And they weren't even together.

'Have you told Evan yet?' Ben asked.

Holly shook her head, only to remember they were on a voice call. There was no way she could cope with a blurry-eyed face call after the day she'd had. Even to her closest friends.

'No, he's my next call. I've had a couple of missed calls from Mum and Dad too when I was in hospital, but I've just sent them a message saying I was busy. If they see the state I'm in, they'll probably want to come home. And they've only got a day left of their holiday.'

'Well, I'm here for anything you need.'

'Thank you, Ben.' Holly paused, ready to hang up, when she found herself wanting to say more. 'Ben, this is probably the painkillers talking, but you know I love you, don't you? In a completely platonic way. Like absolutely not romantic at all, in the slightest. No way. But I love you. You know that, right?'

'I love you too, in exactly the same way, Holly. I'll speak to you in the morning. Sleep tight.'

43

When the conversation with Ben ended, Holly couldn't avoid the inevitable any longer. She moved over to the cupboard to fetch herself a glass of wine to help with the nerves, only to remember what the doctor had said about drinking on painkillers. After putting the wine glass away, she poured herself a glass of orange juice instead, before sitting back down, picking up her phone and hitting the video call button.

Evan answered immediately.

'Hey, I was just about to—' His jaw dropped. 'Holly, what happened?'

'I had a bit of an accident.'

Evan's face, which was already white with shock, paled further still. 'Please don't tell me this was on the Vespa. Please don't tell me you hurt yourself on the Vespa. I would never forgive myself. I shouldn't have bought it for you. It was a ridiculous idea. Stupid.'

Holly was desperate to hold back the truth. To say that she fell down the stairs at work. Or tripped over one of Hope's toys. But there was no way she could lie to him. Not about something this big.

'It wasn't stupid. You did the most beautiful thing in the world. And I loved the Vespa. I loved it so much, and now... And now...' Her voice trailed off as tears remerged. 'I'm so sorry, Evan. I'll find a way to repay you. I promise.'

'Repay me? Are you joking?' He was shaking his head as he stared at her. 'I don't care about a Vespa. I care about you. Are you okay? How bad is it?'

Holly twisted around the phone and lifted her arm to show him the cast.

'I was lucky. It doesn't need to be pinned. But I don't know how I'm going to do anything. I don't know how I'm going to work, and I don't know how I'm going to pick up Hope and cuddle her.'

The thought of Hope set her off crying again. The type of tears she had never shown in front of Evan before. Ugly with staggered breaths, that involved an embarrassing amount of snorting and gulping too.

'And it's Maud,' she said, trying to stifle the sobs. 'I wasn't thinking properly because of Maud. She's dying.'

'Maud is dying?'

'And she wants to leave me some money, but I don't want that. I just want her to be okay and I want to be able to hold Hope and I don't want the beautiful Vespa to be broken. I want to cuddle you, too. I really need a cuddle,' she added.

Evan's eyes gazed at her through the phone screen, the saddest expression gracing his face.

'When are you going to America again?' Holly asked, knowing she sounded more like a child complaining about her parents going away for work than a girlfriend who was going to miss her boyfriend.

'I was just packing my suitcase now.'

Holly nodded. Even in her painkiller-addled state, she knew she didn't want to be clingy. She wanted to come across as strong and independent.

She drew a deep breath into her nose.

'I should let you get to it, then. I'm going to try to run a bath, have a sleep.'

'Are you sure? I can chat a bit longer.'

She shook her head. 'It's probably best if I get to bed soon. I'm not sure how well I'm going to sleep.'

'Okay. I love you.'

'I love you too.'

'And ring me if you need anything.'

'I will.'

Once she had hung up, she downed the rest of the orange juice in one, before she went over to the cake tin. She might not be able to drink wine, but nothing was going to stop her from eating every one of the breakfast muffins she had made the day before with Hope.

Later that evening, Holly knew she was going to fall asleep on the sofa. Several times, while her eyes sagged, she considered moving upstairs and climbing into her bed, but she didn't have the energy. The sofa was perfectly comfortable. She'd found it odd when she'd first moved in that the landlord would provide such an expensive sofa when he was renting the place out to a woman he knew had a baby. But now it made sense. Of course Giles would want Holly to have a comfy sofa. Though at least now she felt less guilty about the stains Hope had made on it.

Her thoughts were twisting and turning as she finally drifted off. And any fears she'd had that she wouldn't be able to sleep were quickly alleviated, as the painkillers did their job.

The sleep was dreamless, and she could probably have stayed in her dormant state for several hours more, had she not been jolted awake by a loud bang.

Having fallen asleep where she was, Holly hadn't even drawn the curtains, but outside was pitch black. Her first thought was of the time; during the summer months, it didn't get dark until after ten, which meant it had to be after midnight. She looked down at her phone and saw that it was 1:30 a.m., but what was more surprising than the time was the fact that Evan was calling her.

Confused, she picked up her phone. 'Evan?'

'I'm sorry. I've woken you up, haven't I? I was knocking and you didn't answer.'

Holly frowned. 'Knocking?'

'Yes, and it's still quite cold out here. So do you fancy letting me in?'

Holly moved to push herself up, only to remember the pain in her arm. The painkillers had obviously worn off by now.

'Are you okay?' Evan's voice echoed from outside. 'Can you open the door? I really wasn't joking about the cold.'

Realising that this wasn't some bizarre type of prank, Holly dashed to open the door. There, outside, shivering and beautiful, was Evan.

'What are you doing here?' She tried to hug him, only to find herself one arm short. 'I thought you were meant to be on a plane to America tomorrow?'

'I was, but then I thought, how can I possibly get on a plane when I'll spend my entire time worrying about you? So, I decided to bring my suitcase here instead.'

As he spoke, he wheeled his suitcase inside. It was substantially larger than the one he had brought when he came to stay before.

'I thought maybe I could give you a hand with Hope. It would give me a chance to get to know her a bit better and spend some time with you, too. Although I'll be honest, from what I've seen so far, I'm pretty sure you're a horrendous patient.'

Once again, Holly's eyes welled up with tears, although, for the first time all day, it wasn't out of sadness, but out of gratitude.

'Have I told you I love you recently?'

'I'm fairly sure you told me the last time we spoke on the phone. But I don't get tired of hearing it, so you can say it again.'

'I love you.'

'I love you too.'

44

As much as Holly wanted to stay up and chat with Evan all night, she knew she needed more sleep. Whilst sleeping on the sofa had been one thing, sleeping in the bed with her broken arm was agony. Perhaps it would have been easier if she'd had the entire bed to herself, but she doubted it. It was simply impossible to find a comfortable position. Until that day, she never realised how much she moved her arms in her sleep, how much weight she put on her hand, or how much she desperately wanted to scratch the skin on her forearm, although that could have just been because of the cast.

When Holly woke up for a second time, she somehow felt even less rested than when she had gone to sleep. She rolled over, finding the other side of the bed empty, and Evan's suitcase open wide at the foot of the bed. The enticing aroma of bacon wafted up from downstairs.

Grabbing her dressing gown, Holly headed down to find the source.

'Ben rang,' Evan said, as she appeared in the kitchen. 'He's changed his morning appointments so he doesn't have to go in until eleven thirty, so he'll drop Hope off here at eleven.'

Holly opened her mouth, confused by the drowsiness of sleep and the facts that were bombarding her so soon. And Evan wasn't done yet.

'We also knew that you'd probably kick up a fuss, so Ben and I made a collective decision together that you don't have a choice in the matter. He's coming at eleven and no sooner. You can't drive over there to get Hope, and I'm not going to either. Which means we've got the morning to try to sort things out, find some space in your closets and drawers for all my stuff, and get ready for Hope this afternoon.'

There was too much information to take in in one go. Rubbing her eyes, Holly tried to backtrack on what she just heard.

'Sorry, did you say space in my closet? How long are you planning on staying for?'

'I don't know right now. I've got my laptop, so I'm going to have to set up some kind of working area in your dining room, if that's okay? There's room at the minute, but I didn't want to my put stuff out there yet. Not without asking. I figured you might have you own way of setting things up. Besides, if it's a huge problem, Ben has said I can use the office in his house during the day while he's at work.'

This was all too much. She stepped towards Evan, lifting her hands in the air as she spoke.

'I'm sorry, you're going to use the father of my child's house to work in?'

'Only if you don't want me to work here, although Ben and I both agreed that it's probably best if I stay here in the cottage, until you get used to looking after Hope one-armed.'

Holly shook her head. She wasn't surprised at Ben trying to take control of the situation. That was what he did. It was one of the reasons that had them destined to fail in a long-term romantic relationship together. But she hadn't expected Evan to follow suit.

With a deep breath, she stepped forward and placed her hands on his chest.

'Look, I appreciate you wanting to help. But this is too much. You and Ben taking control—'

'No, that's not what I'm trying to do,' Evan cut across her before she could finish. 'I promise you. And if you say you don't want me to be here and assure me you can handle Hope and the shop the same way as normal, even with a broken arm, then that's fine. I'll go. I can be on the next flight to the States if you think you're okay. But people trying to help you is not the same as taking control. That's all I'm trying to do. Because that's what you do when you love people. You help them.'

There was a way he spoke that had an abnormally calming effect on Holly. Like she could tell he wasn't just saying the things to appease her, but because he really meant them.

'You have to admit, you and Ben talking to each other about this stuff is weird,' she said, still not willing to let the matter go entirely.

'I don't think so. I think it's merely two grown-ups working together to make the best of a crappy situation. Better than us yelling at each other. Now, how crispy do you like your bacon?'

Being waited upon was a luxury Holly had not experienced before, and she wasn't sure she liked it. To start with, she couldn't remember ever feeling so completely useless. Wanting to prove she was capable of something, she stretched up to the cupboard to grab some plates for the food, only to yelp in pain.

'Will you please go and sit down?' Evan insisted, pressing his hands on her shoulders and turning her back toward the living room. 'Or better still, go find the drugs the doc gave you. They told you to take them for a reason, you know.'

As much as Holly wanted to object, she knew he was right. Painkillers first. After that, she could keep a better eye on what Evan was doing in her kitchen.

Sharing a kitchen wasn't something Holly was great at doing, and when Fin had moved in with Jamie, she'd been more than a little peeved to find him shifting around her pots and pans. Yet, on first inspection, Evan seemed to be keeping the area pretty tidy. Not to mention he was doing an incredible job of frying the bacon to the point of perfect crispiness.

When he turned around, she saw the bowl in his hand.

'What are you doing? I thought we were having bacon sandwiches.'

'What? No way. It's bacon and pancakes all the way here. Though I think I might have done a bit much; I'm always starving after a morning run.'

Holly shook her head, not sure that she had heard him correctly.

'You went for a morning run? When?'

'About half five, I think. I bet there are some amazing routes around here. I didn't do anything too exciting though, just a couple of laps around the village to hit a 10K.'

Holly wasn't sure if she was impressed or horrified by this knowledge. Of course, she knew he was keen on exercise; the water skiing in France had shown her that. Even so, getting up at five thirty rather than lying in felt like insanity to her. She just hoped that wouldn't be his plan every day. Especially not on days when they would get to lie-in together.

'Go, sit down, have a drink,' he said. 'The food is nearly ready.'

45

After finishing the food, Holly wanted to be helpful and at least wash up, but it wasn't as easy as she'd hoped. With her left hand in a cast, she had to use her right to wrestle with the dishcloth and the crockery simultaneously. More than once, she nearly smashed a glass, but Evan, to give him his due, only asked once if she wanted him to take over. After her response, he didn't ask a second time.

'I'm going to get you a bigger frying pan,' he said, as he patiently waited to dry each item one by one and put them away. 'You could only do a couple of pancakes at a time in that one.'

'There's nothing wrong with my one. I like it. It's small. Like the cottage.'

'Which is cute, but honestly, a big frying pan would be far more efficient.'

'How about we see how we cope with your clothes in my wardrobe before you start messing with my kitchen, too? Trust me, that's the quickest way to end this relationship,' she laughed.

'In that case, the small frying pan stays,' Evan said, as he bent down and kissed her gently.

Everything took longer with her arm in a cast. Washing up took forever, as did a shower, and finding something to wear proved a near impossibility. Thankfully, after a few minutes searching, she found a sleeveless blouse she could fit her cast through.

Holly was still upstairs, having just dressed herself, with Evan's aid, when there was a knock on the door.

'I'll go get it,' Evan said.

'Really, I'm fine,' Holly said, jumping into action only for a pain to shoot through her side. Tears pricked her eyes as she dropped onto the bed and massaged her thigh. She might not have broken her leg, but the bruises were something else. She'd thought they were large when she got home, but they had only spread further, and her leg was unusually swollen. On one hand, she was grateful it was summer, and she didn't have to try to squeeze herself into jeans, but on the negative side, she suspected she'd get more than one question if she wore shorts in the shop.

'I'll get the door. You follow behind at your own pace,' Evan said, kissing her lightly on the lips before he bounded down the stairs.

The door clicked open.

'Ben, buddy. Good to see you. Thanks for doing this.'

'No problem at all. How is she?' Ben's voice floated up to meet her.

'Pretty banged up.'

'But her hearing is fine,' Holly interjected, having reached the halfway point of the stairs. 'So she doesn't need you to talk about her.'

Ben looked up, and his jaw dropped. 'Jeez, Holly. Should you be up and about? That cut on your head looks pretty bad.'

'Good luck getting her to stay in bed,' Evan said, before turning and looking at Hope. 'Okay, little one, it's time for you and me to get acquainted. Now, why don't you come and show me how those bunnies fit down the toilet again?'

'That is not funny,' Holly said, to which Evan responded with a grin so cheeky, she wasn't sure if she wanted to kiss him or hit him.

'I need to get off. I've got a meeting to get to,' Ben said, stepping back out of the cottage. 'But if you need me to have Hope this evening, I can. Georgia's coming over. We were going to go out to Cheltenham and watch something at the cinema, but really, her taste in films isn't that great, so I'm fine to have Hope.'

'Thanks, buddy,' Evan said, holding Hope on one side of his hip, while extending his other hand to shake Ben's. 'I appreciate it.'

When Evan closed the door and returned inside the cottage, Hope was still in his arms, looking quite bemused by this person she barely recalled. Not as bemused, however, as Holly herself.

'Buddy? Really?' she questioned. 'You and Ben are *buddies* now?'

'Like I said. Just two mature adults, making a situation work,' Evan replied. 'Now, how do I mix up this formula stuff?'

There was no way Holly could describe the rest of the day as easy. Hope was used to her mum's undivided attention when they were in the cottage and was more than a little perplexed that she didn't get picked up every time she demanded it. She was, however, seemingly aware of the object around Holly's arm. She prodded it several times and was perfectly happy when Holly allowed her to pick up one of her colouring crayons and scribble on the cast.

To give Evan his due, it didn't take long until he got the hang of things. He was baffled that Holly didn't own a thermometer to check the temperature of Hope's formula, especially when it specified the required temperature of water to make it. Feeding Hope solids wasn't any better, as there was no rhyme or reason to which bits of avocado she would put in her mouth and which she would throw onto the floor. He was, however, far more talented at finger painting animals than Holly would have expected, although after his fifth painted caterpillar, Hope had lost interest.

'Look, I think she's getting stir crazy,' Evan said. It had reached five o'clock and Hope had refused to be picked up for the last thirty minutes. They had tried water play outside. They tried Evan building towers for her to knock down. But she simply wasn't interested. Instead, she had crawled constantly, either to the door, where she banged repeatedly on the glass or to get Holly's shoes, which she carried over to her mum. 'Why don't I take Hope outside for a bit? She and I can go for a walk by the river?'

'I don't think that's a good idea,' Holly responded.

'Why not? I don't have to go far. And I can keep her in the pushchair. I don't think she wants to do any more finger painting. Or tower building. I think she wants to get out of here.'

Holly considered the idea. Her head was pounding, probably from the stitches, but there hadn't been a minute of quiet in the house since Hope had got home. Half an hour of quiet was probably just what she needed.

'Okay, but don't go far.'

'Deal.'

'Just don't let her out of her chair, even if you're by the river and feeding the ducks,' she said, as Evan and Hope headed out. 'She's impossible to get back in.'

'Don't worry, she will not be coming out of the pushchair.'

'Because if you do, you will have to carry her and push the pushchair all the way back home. And that's not easy to do. Believe me.'

'I heard you, Holly. She will not be coming out of the pushchair.'

'Okay, thank you. And I love you.'

'Love you too.'

The sense of quiet that filled the cottage when they left felt almost as eerie as the noise that had filled it beforehand. With a deep breath, Holly sat down on the sofa, exhausted. She wasn't expecting them to be gone for long. Maybe half an hour at most. But she figured she could use that time to get an early nap in. That was what she thought until her phone rang and her mum's name flashed up on the screen.

46

Holly stared at the name on her phone. The relaxed calm she had been feeling only moments ago had already drained from her body. She knew her mother hadn't heard about the accident. There was no way Jamie or Ben would have told her. And she had no intention of accepting a video call. But that didn't ease the twinge of dread she felt. Her parents only had one night left in Brussels before they were coming back to the Cotswolds, at which point, Holly knew she had to confront her mother about Giles. Either that, or let it fester. And that was without dealing with her parents' reaction to the crash. Maybe she would see if they wanted to extend the holiday a little longer.

Holding her breath, she stared at the name for a second longer before cancelling the video call request and redialling as a regular phone call.

Her mother answered immediately.

'Holly, dear? Is everything alright? We can't see you.'

'Sorry Mum, yes. I'm just out on a walk with Hope. Towards Rissington. You know what the reception is like here. How is Brussels? How was the chocolate-making workshop? Are you ready to come back?'

Holly hoped the influx of questions would deter her parents from asking too many of their own. The tactic worked, as her father chimed in.

'We went to the model village, Holly. But it's not like the one in Bourton. Oh no, much better than that. It's got miniature places from all around the world. A miniature Eiffel Tower, a miniature White House, and guess what? A miniature Arlington Row!'

'Arlington Row?' Holly replied, admittedly a bit surprised. Arlington Row was a tiny row of houses in the Cotswold village of Bibury, only a short drive from Bourton-on-the-Water. It was certainly picturesque and featured on dozens of postcards of the area, but she couldn't imagine it was famous enough to appear in a model village in another country. Apparently it was.

'We're having a wonderful time, love. I wish we could stay for longer. We're even thinking next time we might go to Bruges instead. I spoke to your mother about extending the trip, actually. I told her you wouldn't mind if we did an extra couple of days. Get the train up there, then come back later in the week. But she didn't want to leave you in the lurch any longer than we planned. But it wouldn't be a problem, would it, love?'

Holly's heart soared with the idea, only for it to drop again. While having her parents stay away longer would be a great way to avoid the inevitably awkward conversations she had to have, it would be a logistical nightmare. Ben had likely shifted his meetings to later in the week because he'd assumed her mother would be back to look after Hope. And there was only so long that Drey and Caroline could hold down the fort while she was out of action without needing a day off. But this was the first time her parents had been abroad, and after everything they'd done for her over the last ten months, she owed them this.

'I'd manage. If that's what you want to do,' she reassured them.

'Don't be silly, love,' her mother said. 'Your father is being ridiculous. We've paid for the tickets and we'll just wait for another cheap deal to come up. Besides, it will be something else to look forward to. Now, how are you? And how was Maud? Did you meet up with her? Was she... okay?'

There was a slight pause in the question, and it reminded Holly of how surprised her mother had been to hear that Maud was back in the village. Suddenly, it struck. Her mother had known something was wrong with Maud and hadn't said anything. That was why she had acted so strangely when Holly mentioned her before. The lies on her mother's tally chart were stacking up, and it was all Holly could to not to call her out then and there.

Instead, she moved the phone away from her mouth. 'Sorry, Mum, what was that? I think I'm losing you. Look, I'll ring you in the morning, okay? Love you. Love you lots.'

She hung up the phone and swallowed back a wave of anger.

After the phone call, Holly wanted nothing more than a glass of wine, or at least a nap to wash away the feelings of guilt and distrust. Once again, knowing that a cup of tea and the last breakfast muffin were her only options, she had just put the water in the mug when her telephone rang again. This time, she opened it up on to the video call.

'Hey, you.' Holly's face flicked into an automatic smile as she saw Evan on the screen, though it didn't stay that way for long. For someone who was the epitome of calm, there were more creases on his face than the day he'd been trying to hide the Vespa gift from her.

'Hey, babe. Is there any chance you could come down to the village for me? We're just on the green, opposite the shop,' he said, his voice quivering slightly.

Holly's stomach performed a multitude of somersaults.

'You let her out of her pushchair, didn't you? I told you, she's a nightmare to get back in.'

Holly was looking around on the floor, searching for her shoes, although the only pair she could see were trainers with the laces undone, and she wasn't sure it was even possible to do up shoelaces with just one hand.

'Actually, it's not that,' Evan said, his voice bringing Holly's attention back to her phone. 'Hope's still in the pushchair. And she's fine. Absolutely fine.'

'She is? Then what's wrong?'

Rather than responding, Evan panned the screen around. There, still sitting in her chair next to him, was Hope, with a big smile on her face as the river flowed lazily behind her. But Evan didn't stop panning around. As the image continued, Holly saw Kathy, the woman from the bird park next to him, and then there, beside her, a very stern, very tired-looking police officer.

47

Holly didn't bother doing her laces up before racing down into the village, in something between a fast walk and a jog. She wasn't a runner at the best of times, but the cast, combined with the loose trainers and numerous bruises, meant even she knew it was a disaster waiting to happen. Still, at the fastest pace she could manage, she couldn't remember the walk into the village ever taking as long as it did then. Every step she took seemed to be blocked by one person or another, either walking their dog, cycling, or merely stopping in the most awkward place possible to get a photo.

By the time Holly reached the green, she was dripping with sweat that was only partially to do with her sprint down there.

Just as he'd said, Evan was standing opposite the shop, next to Hope, who was sitting in the pushchair, while an unusually stern-looking Kathy and the police officer Holly had seen on the phone stood by. But they were no longer the only people there. A small crowd had gathered on the pavement and the nearby bridge, peering over one another, trying to get a glimpse of the action.

'Hey, babe, sorry about this,' Evan said, but Holly didn't have a chance to reply.

As soon as Hope saw Holly, she stretched out her arms and cried. Without even thinking about her arm, or the fact she wouldn't be able to get her back into the pushchair, she reached down and unclipped her, fighting down the pain as she hoisted her onto her hip.

'Hey, what's all this fuss for, baby girl? Don't be so silly.'

'See, I told you. That's the mother,' Kathy said, bringing Holly back to the moment.

'Yes, I'm her mother.' Holly turned and looked at the old woman, only for Kathy's eyes to widen in surprise. It was only then that Holly realised how much of a state she must look. It wasn't just the cuts and bruises. She hadn't even bothered to brush her hair when she left the house. Not to mention she was dressed in her comfy joggers, which, in winter especially, she used as full-on pyjamas. Then there was also the cast on her arm and the stitches in her forehead.

'Good lord, woman, what happened to you?'

Holly shook her head, dismissing Kathy's question. The last thing she wanted was the entire village knowing what she had done, though knowing Bourton, half of them already did. She turned to Evan.

'What happened?' she asked. 'Was it Hope?'

'Hope's fine, babe. Don't worry, everything's fine. A misunderstanding, that's all.'

Beside them, the police officer cleared his throat. Realising that if the police were at a situation, she probably should have spoken to them first, Holly turned around.

'What happened, officer? Is everything alright?'

The policeman's eyes lingered on the cut on Holly's forehead before he cleared his throat for a second time. 'Madam, is this your child?'

Hope was currently snuggled up on Holly's shoulder, the brief crying spell from only moments ago abated by a hug from her mum.

'Yes, she's my daughter.'

'And do you know this man she was with?'

Holly looked at Evan, whose eyebrows were raised, and she couldn't decide if he was finding the situation amusing or something else altogether. She was about to say that yes, she knew him, he was her boyfriend, but before she could get a word in, Kathy was speaking again.

'I've never seen him in my life, and I can tell you that much. I've lived in this village for over sixty years. And the baby. She didn't want to be near him. Poor thing. She was trying to get out of her pushchair and would have made a run for it, if she could have walked, that is. Terrifying. Absolutely terrifying.'

'She was trying to get out of the pushchair to see the ducks,' Evan said firmly. 'Holly, will you tell this very helpful, and well-meaning lady, that you told me not to let her out of the chair?'

'So you know this gentleman, ma'am,' the police officer said.

'I told you I've never seen him before in my life,' Kathy replied.

The policeman inhaled slowly as he forced a smile. 'Madam, I was talking to the mother.' He looked at Holly. 'You know this gentleman?'

Holly nodded rapidly. 'Yes, yes, absolutely.'

'And you were aware your child was with him?'

'Yes, he took Hope out of the house so I could get a bit of rest. It's been a stressful couple of days.' She lifted her arm to reinforce the point.

'Your house?' Kathy said indignantly.

Ignoring the old woman and looking at the exhausted police officer, Holly smiled apologetically.

'I'm really sorry. This is obviously just a big misunderstanding. Evan is my boyfriend.'

'Boyfriend!' This was more than Kathy could take. 'She's never said anything about having a boyfriend to me.'

Holly turned and looked at the old woman, not sure whether she should feel guilty or annoyed at the comment.

'Well, he is.'

Kathy still wasn't having any of it. Her head shook, lips pursed together in a pout.

'Well, I've not seen him around.'

'I'm not what you'd call local,' Evan said, offering his deepest American drawl. This wasn't the first time Holly had heard him turn on his accent just to make a point, but she couldn't help but smile.

'Is that everything, officer?' Holly said. 'Because if it's okay with you, I'd really like to get my daughter home. It's bath and bedtime now.'

As if understanding what was required of her, Hope scrunched up her nose and opened her mouth, giving the widest yawn possible.

Looking almost as tired, the officer let out a sigh.

'Yes, of course. It's fine. You get going.'

48

Evan had tied Holly's shoelaces for her, so she had one less thing to worry about as she carried Hope back to the cottage.

'So I'm guessing that's enough to put you off moving here?' she asked, as she paused outside the front door to get her keys out. Thankfully, they had seen the funny side of the situation – unlike Kathy, who had huffed off. Holly suspected it was more out of embarrassment than actual anger, but either way, she was going to give the bird park a wide berth for a while.

'You think one overly curious, nosy old woman would be enough to scare me off?' Evan laughed. 'Believe me, we get those where I'm from too. I think you get them everywhere. Besides, you know Kathy will love me soon enough. Everyone loves me when they get to know me.'

'Is that right?' Holly stepped forward, and Evan wrapped his arms around her waist.

'It is, though it happens there's only one person in this village whose opinion I actually care about.'

He shifted closer, but Holly crinkled her nose. 'You know that's not actually true. I mean, there's Fin and Jamie, not to mention Hope.'

'Stop trying to ruin the moment, will you?' he said, as a smile twisted on his mouth. Happy to oblige, Holly closed her eyes and leaned forward.

They fell into a kiss. Sleepy, and full of weariness, but utterly perfect. Or at least it would have been, had Hope not started crying the moment their lips touched.

'Hold that thought,' Holly said.

When they got inside the cottage, she disappeared upstairs to put Hope to bed. Given how sleepy Hope now was – and how much Holly didn't want to ask Evan for help so quickly again – she decided they were going to miss bath night. A wash with a flannel around all the important places more than sufficed, and was quickly followed by a book, though Hope barely made it through the first repeat of *Bear Hunt*.

When Holly came back downstairs, half an hour later, Evan was working away on his laptop on the dining room table. She stood beside him and draped her right arm around his shoulder, before kissing him lightly on the ear.

'She asleep?'

'For now.'

Breaking away, Holly pulled out one of the dining chairs and sat down next to him. Despite having slept in later than she'd done for years, she was exhausted. As much as she and Evan had laughed at Kathy's busybody-ness, it meant that now she was going to have to deal with the village gossip about her new boyfriend, along with everything else. And the fact that her parents were arriving home tomorrow meant she wouldn't be able to delay the inevitable that much longer.

'Do you want to watch a movie?' Evan said, breaking her thoughts.

'A film?'

'Yes. Do you want to watch one? I have about half an hour's work to do if that's okay? We can put the movie on after that.'

'You need to do work now? This evening? Sorry, yes, of course you do. Ignore me. My mind is all over the place.'

Although coming to Bourton and waiting on her hand and foot clearly meant that Evan had neglected his business for the day, he pushed his laptop lid halfway down and turned on his seat so that he was facing Holly. Pressing his lips together, he placed a hand on her knee.

'Holly, can I say something? Something about your mum and the cottage... because it's clearly eating you up.'

Holly took a deep inhale, which she let out with a sigh. There was no point in her saying she was fine with it all. Evan knew that wasn't the case. And frankly, anyone's opinion on how to deal with the matter had to be better than the thoughts going through her head. Which, at that moment, consisted of burying her head in the sand and ignoring it altogether.

'Go for it,' she said.

'Well, do you really need to mention this at all? So what, Giles is your landlord and your mother was keeping it from you? They were obviously only doing it because they thought that was best. Why don't you just stay quiet and pretend you never found out? No harm's been done.'

So, it turned out Evan was having exactly the same thoughts as her. But rather than Holly feeling relieved or it reinforcing that it was the right thing to do, a familiar knot formed in her chest.

'I know. And on the one side, you're right. It's what I keep thinking. But I can't let it go. I can't. I'll just end up resenting my mum for keeping all the secrets. To be honest, there's a lot I'm feeling she's keeping from me at the moment, and it's not good.'

Evan nodded, but he didn't pry into what those other things

could be. And Holly was grateful. She couldn't bear to think about Maud right now, too.

'In that case,' Evan said, 'why don't you ask Giles about it first? Maybe talking to him will be enough, and you won't feel the need to discuss it with your mum. Or maybe you'll find she didn't even want to keep this from you at all.'

'So you're pushing me to see Giles again?' Holly winked, yet Evan simply rolled his eyes.

'I think it's pretty safe. I mean, I did nearly get arrested for you today.'

'I don't think I'd go that far.'

'Oh, I definitely would.' He smirked. 'This is a story I'm going to tell our grandchildren.'

'Is that right?'

'Yes, absolutely.'

They leaned in and kissed. It was the type of kiss that meant you forgot about the sofa and the film you were going to watch. Or even the work that was waiting on Evan's laptop after he'd spent all day with her. At least, that's the type of kiss Holly suspected it would've been, had her phone not started ringing. Her instinct was to ignore it, but her eyes pinged open reflexively, and there, on the table, she saw Jamie's name flashing away.

'I should get this,' she said.

49

'How's the patient?'

Despite all the chaos going on in her own life, Jamie's first question was checking on Holly. Of course it was. That was the type of friend she was.

Holly answered truthfully. 'Okay actually, but I'm only on day one and it already itches. I'm dreading to think how much my arm is going to stink when I finally get this thing off.'

'Not to mention tan lines. I mean, summer really is a bad time to do that.'

'Thank you.'

'And you know you're likely to lose a lot of muscle strength, too? It's crap, but it's just an effect of not using the muscle at all.'

Holly wasn't overly grateful for Jamie's input on the situation at that moment, though it wasn't like she was a weightlifter or anything. She was sure she would be fine.

'What about you? Hopefully, you're ringing with some news? Any luck with the wedding?'

'Yes, and no.' Jamie let out a sigh, implying it wasn't all as sorted as Holly hoped it would be. 'We've found somewhere for the family to stay, on the days when they were meant to be at the wedding venue.'

'That's good, isn't it?'

'Yes, sort of. It's a new glamping place that's set up by Naunton. They weren't meant to be opening till the week after, as they've had some delays with furniture and things, but I've told them as long as there's a bed in each tent then we're happy.'

'That's good, and what about weddings? Can you get married there?'

There was a slight pause, in which Holly assumed Jamie was shaking her head.

'No, they're not registered for that yet. And even if they were, we still haven't got anyone that can do the wedding. No registrars are available. At least not one that we have a contact for.'

'So, do you have a plan?'

There was another brief pause, although this time, Jamie's sigh rolled through the phone.

'Really, we're thinking it's just going to be a big party. Like a second engagement party, but this time with everyone. We've spoken about it, and we can't ask everybody to fly back here, so I think we might just fly out to the States for a wedding. Taking my mum and dad with us. It's not ideal. I want you guys there, too. But I know I can't ask you to fly all that way. Especially not with Hope.'

Holly's stomach was heavy with disappointment. She'd been with Fin and Jamie since the beginning of their relationship. There were family. And as guilty as she felt, she couldn't help but be a little upset if she wasn't involved in the actual big day.

A thought flashed in her mind: Evan had more than enough money to fly them all out there.

As fast as the thought arose, she quashed it again. That was exactly the type of relationship she didn't want, using him for things she couldn't afford. The fact the thought had even crossed her mind made her stomach churn with guilt.

'There's still over a week to go,' she said, forcing her focus back on Jamie and Jamie alone. 'A lot can happen in a week. Lots of these places must have last-minute cancellations. You know, the day before type thing. The type you see on soap operas.'

'I know, but it feels really mean, waiting for something like that to happen.'

'I guess.'

Silence threatened to fall, but before Holly could speak, Jamie was asking her questions again.

'So Evan is living with you? How's that going?'

Holly looked across to the dining room table, where Evan, once again, had his laptop out and was typing away. As luck would have it, at the exact moment she looked at him, he glanced upwards and caught her eye. A knowing smile flickered on his lips.

'Are you talking about me?'

'Maybe?' Holly said, before focusing back on the conversation. 'It's only been a day, but he seems to be settled in very well. He is currently doing some work. And I had to give up some of my wardrobe space for him.'

'I'm not even sure you had much wardrobe space in that cottage. That really must be love.'

'Yes, I guess it is.'

Jamie chuckled. 'And your mum and dad are getting back tomorrow? That must be a relief.'

Holly paused. A relief? Is that what it was? It didn't feel like that. It felt like a load of stress she didn't want to think about.

'What time are they getting in?' Jamie continued.

Holly let out a sigh. 'Early afternoon. I was going to pick them up from the station, but I guess I can't do that now. Not if I can't drive.'

'I can drive you,' Evan said, once again poking up from behind his laptop. 'It's time I got to know my way around these damn lanes.'

'I guess that's what we're doing then,' Holly said, before speaking back to Jamie. 'Apparently, Evan is driving me there. Anyway, hun, I better get going. I need to go check on Hope. But keep me up to date on the wedding situation, won't you? Let me know if anything crops up.'

'Of course I will. Love you.'

'Love you too.'

As she put down the phone, she turned to Evan.

'You really don't have to pick Mum and Dad up tomorrow,' she said. 'They actually like using the bus to get around.'

'It's fine. Like I said, I need to learn my way around here. And it might help soften the blow of them seeing you with your arm in that thing.'

Holly dreaded to think how her mother would respond to seeing her in a cast. She'd got through her entire childhood without a single broken bone, and now there she was, two fractures in one place, after what was definitely a reckless drive. Still, part of her wished her mum would just get the bus. That way, she could delay seeing her a bit longer.

Obviously, Evan knew what she was thinking.

'Look, why don't we pick them up, then when we get to your parents' place, you and your mum can go for a coffee, and talk it over. I'll chat to your dad about the holiday. Male bonding time, that kind of thing. You know, the sooner you face her, the better. Unless you're going to talk to Giles first?'

Holly dropped her head onto her chest as she let out a groan.

'Can I let you know tomorrow? I don't want to think about any of it tonight.'

A smile spread across Evan's face as he pushed his laptop lid back down for a second time. 'Is that right? Well, maybe I can think of some way to distract you.'

50

Holly woke with butterflies in her stomach. Not the excited ones, when it felt like something good was going to happen, but the tight, twisty ones. The ones that tightened into knots and made her feel a little nauseous. Immediately, her mind rattled through all the current stresses in her life, from Maud to Jamie's wedding and to the shop and her mother. Turning around in the bed, she jolted at the time on her phone. She and Evan had stayed awake until the early hours talking and kissing, and she'd known she was going to struggle to get up in the morning. Still, it was a surprise to see it was already gone nine. And while Holly could easily believe that she had slept in to such a time, she couldn't believe the same of her daughter.

With as much speed as she could manage, she raced downstairs, to find Hope already in her highchair, while Evan was standing over the hob.

'We wondered if you were going to join us,' he said, as he whipped up another batch of pancakes, this time with the addition of blueberries. 'Hope, you need to stay a morning person. We'll win your mum round, won't we? These are the best hours of the day.'

Hope babbled away as she took a piece of her chopped-up pancake from her tray table and stuffed it into her mouth.

Already salivating from the smell, Holly picked a freshly cooked and still-warm pancake from the plate next to Evan and took a bite.

'I was expecting Ben by now.' Evan said. 'He is having her today, right?'

Holly waited till she'd eaten and swallowed her mouthful before she spoke.

'I told him not to worry until later on. You don't mind, do you? It's just, he's had to rearrange his work quite a bit for me. And this way, I could give him a couple of hours extra to get jobs done.'

'Of course I don't mind. So, we've got a beautiful morning. What are we going to do?'

'Well, I can't ride a bike, but what about a walk? You said you wanted to learn the local areas? Let's head to Slaughter.'

Lower Slaughter was one of the little villages in easy walking distance of Bourton across the fields and was easily one of Holly's favourite places. Somehow, with all the memories that Bourton held for her, both good and bad, Slaughter held only good ones.

Her parents used to take her there frequently when she was a child. Sometimes, they had picnics or sat on the edge of the stream with a fishing net, trying to grab the little minnows that darted in the water. Other times, they wouldn't get as far as the village, but would just walk along the hedgerows, collecting ripe blackberries that she and her mother would later use to make crumbles together.

But her memories hadn't stopped with her parents. She and Ben had once gone on a cycle ride there, on one of the days when she wasn't sure if she even liked the man, let alone envisaged having a child with him. But even when they knew the relationship was fading, she'd found solace in the place. The wheel of the old mill had long since stopped turning, but they served some damn fine ice cream. And the shallow water was fine for Hope to sit on the edge of the river and watch as the ducks and swans paddled by.

Unfortunately, in order to walk there, Hope needed to get into her pushchair first, and it was something she had no intention of doing.

'You just need to hold her in there a little better,' Holly said, peering over Evan's shoulder as he struggled to work out where all the straps went. 'Hope, honey, please don't be silly. We're going to go to Slaughter. To see the ducks. You want to see the ducks, don't you?'

Even the magic word wouldn't stop Hope from squirming as she kicked out her legs and twisted around, making it impossible for Evan to do the belt up. Given how much she was kicking, Holly didn't think it was wise that she got in there and try to help.

'I don't understand how she's so strong,' Evan said, catching her under the arms as she attempted to dive out of the side of the chair. 'Have you looked at getting one-on-one training for her? Weightlifting, perhaps. I think she's a shoo-in for the Olympics.'

Holly would have laughed. After all, Evan was doing a good job of trying to manage the situation. Only Holly knew there was no managing it. When Hope was in one of these moods, all she wanted was to be carried. And that was fine, when Holly had both working arms. She would slip her in the baby carrier, do up the straps around the back, and be off, ready to walk as many miles as she needed. But she couldn't put the baby carrier on now. And she could hardly ask Evan to wear it. Could she?

'There must be some other solution,' Evan said, whipping Hope out of the pushchair and holding her against his chest. Immediately, she stopped her grizzling. 'I can carry her like this. This is fine.'

'You can't carry her like that,' Holly said. 'She feels light now, but in fifteen minutes, your arms are going to hurt.'

'So what other option is there?' he said.

Holly grimaced. 'Just so you know, you asked for this.'

51

The moment Hope saw the baby carrier, she was all smiles, although the giggles and laughter soon shifted to confusion as Holly and Evan worked together to increase the lengths of the straps to make it fit him. It took a couple of attempts. Apparently, Holly's explanations of how to fit it weren't the clearest and with only one hand, she wasn't much practical use either, but after ten minutes of trial and error, Hope was securely strapped to Evan's chest, and they were off, on their way for their first family walk.

'I think this is one of the best things about living in England,' Evan said, as they crossed the main road and immediately found themselves in the middle of an empty field with just a single path cutting through the middle. 'Going for walks.'

'You can go for walks in the States, surely?' Holly said. She always saw posts on social media of influencers in America hiking on amazing trails or standing with their arms stretched around ancient, gargantuan trees.

'Oh sure. I mean, some of the scenery is the best in the world. But it's so vast. So massive. I love that. I do. But I love the small scale of things here too. How life feels so much slower. Not to mention you have great pubs you can walk to.'

'We do have great pubs,' Holly said, thinking that perhaps a pub lunch would be in order after the walk.

With her right hand holding Evan's left, they continued their way down the path to where it reached a thicket of trees. Only a short walk later, they were in the village.

'There is no way this is real,' Evan said, as he slowly took in the scene. 'It looks like a film set.'

'Oh, it's definitely real. And there's a man who makes the most amazing homemade ice cream in one of those cottages there,' Holly said, pointing at the house Ben had taken her to over a year ago.

'Could you imagine waking up to this view every day?' Evan said, as he reached the river. 'I mean, it feels like you've stepped back in time, right? That you could be two hundred years in the past. It's insane.'

It was true, some of the houses in the village dated all the way back to the sixteenth century, the golden-yellow limestone still glinting after all those years.

'Look, there's one for sale there.' Evan pointed to a cottage a little way down the path where a large *For Sale* sign was fixed in the small garden outside. Without another word, Evan picked up his pace, marching him and Hope towards it. As fast as she could, Holly followed suit.

'This would be perfect for us,' Evan said, standing back and surveying the building. The traditional Cotswold stone home was three storeys high, with dormer windows on the roof and large bay windows on the ground floor. It was perfect, Holly wanted to say. But there was also a definite issue.

'I think something like that would be way out of my budget,' she responded. 'And that was if I actually had a budget. Which I don't.'

'I think we should book an appointment. Just to look around.

You never know, we might have completely different tastes in houses. And then how would we ever live together?'

'If it has a bath in it, I'm happy,' Holly said simply.

'In that case, I'm pretty sure it'll fit the bill. And if not, we could put one in it.'

For another half an hour, they walked around the village before heading to the Country Inn for the pub lunch Evan had been so desperate for. The large establishment had to have one of the best pub locations, right by the edge of the path, with the river running through the grounds and an expansive beer garden which Hope met with delight, crawling on the grass to her heart's content.

Thankfully, getting Hope out of the baby carrier was easier than putting her in it.

As they ate, Holly noticed the other families around them. Some children were eating meals with their parents, others were riding bicycles on the path beside the garden and one pair of siblings were in the water, with fishing nets in their hand, as they swept them back and forth, much the same way Holly had done when she was a child.

Is that what she and Evan looked like with Hope? she wondered. Just a normal family, enjoying a day out? And wasn't that what they were? Somehow, after so little time, that was what it felt like. They were a family.

Even with Ben, Holly couldn't remember feeling the sense of ease. The sense of 'this was how it should be'. This family. But she did now, as she realised what had been missing in all her other relationships. It wasn't about the attention, or the gestures; it was about that feeling of security. That feeling that even if you messed up and trashed the most beautiful gift anyone had ever given you, they would forgive you, because they knew you. Because you were a team. She and Evan were a team. Suddenly, Ben wanting to introduce Hope to Georgia also made sense. Of course, he wanted her to be part of Hope's life. He'd wanted them to be a family as soon as they could, just like she did with Evan.

'I know it's only been one day, but I like having you in the house,' Holly said, verbalising her thoughts. 'I think, even when my arm is healed, we need to do it more. We need to do this more often, the three of us.'

'Is that right? How often are you thinking?' he said, his glance momentarily shifting from where Hope was crawling on the grass to look at her.

'I don't know. But very often.'

She couldn't ask him to move in with her, could she? No, he lived in London. That was where his life was. Besides, it would be a ridiculous thing to suggest this early on. Yet she wanted to. Just like she wanted to ask whether his comment about looking around the house together was a joke, or if he was serious. Not that she had any idea how she could afford another mortgage on top of the shop's, but still she should probably know if she was going to have to start saving even harder soon.

Taking a deep breath in, she opened her mouth, hoping the right words might just spill from her lips, when she glanced at her watch. Somehow, the morning had raced away with her.

'Mum and Dad's train is going to get in soon. We should probably leave now, if we're going to pick them up,' Holly said.

The knots that had escaped her whilst they were walking returned with a sudden ferocity.

'Don't worry,' Evan said. 'Let's get Hope back to Ben's. You've got this.'

52

On the one hand, Holly couldn't believe how fast the morning had gone. The walk back had been slightly slower than the way there, although Hope had simply slept all the way on Evan's chest. After checking that Ben was going to be home, they detoured and dropped Hope at his en route.

With that done, she and Evan had just enough time for a cup of tea before they headed off to fetch her parents from the station.

'How are you feeling?' Evan asked, as he opened the passenger door for her.

'Terrified,' Holly answered truthfully.

'Well, that's ridiculous.'

'Believe me, it's not.' Holly raised her eyebrows, to which Evan only shrugged.

'This won't go anywhere near as bad as you think. In an hour's time, you'll probably be laughing about all this. And then you'll realise that being terrified was completely pointless. Come on, we should go, lest you want to leave your mum at the station for an hour. Just for payback.'

'It's tempting, but we should probably get going.'

Holly found it odd being a passenger in her own car, particularly with Evan driving. As judgemental as she was, she couldn't help but think of how he was used to driving on the other side of the road, both in France and America. She knew he lived in London now and had done for years, but he didn't own a car there, was happy to jump into black cabs for wherever he needed to go. Still, she'd made sure he'd got comprehensive insurance on her car, and, despite her reservations, he seemed to be a perfect driver. She just needed to work on her passenger skills. That was all. Especially as she was likely to be stuck in the situation for a while yet.

They took the Fosseway for almost the entire journey. The straight, Roman road passed around the outskirts of Bourton, then Stow-on-the-Wold, before it cut straight through the centre of Moreton-in-Marsh. Even with the busy road going through the middle of it, Holly had always considered Moreton one of the prettiest towns in the area, with its ivy-covered restaurants and large, Cotswold stone town hall that stood in the centre, dominating the view with its clock tower. It also had the advantage of having a train station, unlike many other small towns in the area.

As they headed over the final bridge, Holly's nerves took another upward turn, which surged further still as they parked up at the exact moment the train arrived.

We're back!

A message pinged up on Holly's screen only a moment later, and she placed her phone on the dashboard and took a deep breath in.

'Shall I come with you? I can help with their bags?' Evan asked. 'They might need a hand.'

'No, it's fine. I'll be fine. I should probably see them on my own first. You know, with all of this, and everything.' She gestured to the cut on her forehead.

Evan grimaced.

'They're going to kill me, aren't they?' he asked.

'No,' Holly replied, although she sounded far from convincing.

With another deep breath in, she kissed him on the lips before climbing out of the car and heading down to the platform.

The position of the car park allowed Holly to spot her parents before they saw her, giving her a chance to observe just how much good the break had done them. They were deep in conversation and their smiles were wide as they held hands. In fact, they were so absorbed with gazing at one another, they seemed oblivious to everything else in the world. Holly couldn't remember seeing her father so relaxed. Not since his heart attack, at least. It was as if those few days away had somehow wiped the wrinkles from his face. From both their faces. Although those wrinkles and worry lines reappeared the moment they looked up and saw Holly.

'Hey, how are you? How was the break?' Holly asked. She smiled widely, hoping that just like on the phone, a large smile and some questions might divert attention from the massive cast and stitches on her forehead.

'Oh, my goodness.' Her mother dropped her bag as she raced towards Holly. 'What happened?'

She fingered the stitches on Holly's forehead, causing Holly to wince in pain. Her mother's eyes welled with tears.

'Holly, why didn't you let us know? What happened to you?'

'It's fine, Mum. It's a broken arm and a few stitches, that's all.'

'But how? What on earth happened?'

'It was an accident.' Holly wondered momentarily if she could just keep things vague and get away with it that way.

'What do you mean? Do you mean a car accident? Is the car okay? Was Hope in it? Oh my goodness, where's Hope?' Her mother was in near hysterics now as she scanned around as if Hope might somehow appear on the platform.

Holly placed her hand on her mother's shoulder.

'It wasn't a car accident, Mum. I was on a Vespa.'

'A Vespa?' Her mother frowned, her hysterics replaced with confusion. 'What do you mean, a Vespa?'

'Evan bought me one, you know, as a present.'

Holly's father, who had remained entirely silent until that point, let out an almighty roar.

'Why the hell did he do that?'

Holly could feel a heat rising to her cheeks. She had hoped that she might manage to keep control of the situation and stop her parents from getting too upset or angry. So far, she hadn't managed either of those things.

'A Vespa?' Wendy interjected, before Holly had a chance to respond. 'You don't know how to drive one of those! What were you thinking?'

'It was a lovely gift, Mum. And I do know how to drive... Well, sort of. I've driven with Evan before in France. I just got a bit carried away, that's all. I had a bit of bad news. It's not Evan's fault for this.'

Apparently, her explanation did not have them convinced, and it was a sign of her mother's anger that she didn't even bother to ask what the bad news was.

'It's just irresponsible, Holly. What were you thinking? Getting on one of those things. You can't mess around like a child now. You're a parent.'

The guilt Holly had been feeling was replaced by a sudden spurt of anger.

'I know I'm a parent, thank you. Like I said, it wasn't a big accident. This is the exact reason I didn't tell you – because I knew you were going to react like this.'

Her mother opened her mouth, ready to protest, but Holly wasn't having any of it. She had already heard enough.

'Look, it's done now. And Evan is waiting in the car for us. So either you can stay here yelling at me, or we can drive you home and you can tell me about your holiday.'

She turned around, ready to move, only to find her parents' gaze locked on one another, their expressions still thunderous.

'Evan?' her mum said. 'Well, we're not getting in a car with *him*.'

53

Holly tilted her head, sure she couldn't have heard her mother correctly.

'You won't get into the car with him? That's ridiculous? He wasn't even driving the Vespa. He was in London when it happened.'

Her mother's face remained just as hard and fixed.

'He's obviously irresponsible. The fact he would think so little of your own life, when he apparently cares about you, makes me wonder how reckless he would be with us in his car.'

That was all Holly could take. She snapped.

'*Apparently cares about me?* Really? You know, he was meant to be in New York right now. He has meetings there for ten days and he cancelled them all on the spot, so that he could come to Bourton and help me with Hope.'

'Quite frankly, I think that's the least he could do, given how he's practically left you immobile.'

Holly gritted her teeth. She would not get into a fight with her mum here. She couldn't. She had already gone over the exact things she wanted to say, time and time again in her head, and if she mentioned Giles and Maud now, she would likely say something she regretted.

Taking a deep breath in, she looked her mother squarely in the face.

'I'm sure you're very tired from travelling, and from the exciting couple of days you've had. And I understand seeing me like this is probably quite a shock, but we – Evan and I – have taken time out of our day to come and pick you up, so we could see you. Now, get in the car.'

Holly couldn't remember a single time in her life when she had told her parents what to do – other than when her father had got lost in one of his long conversations with a customer in the sweet shop and was completely oblivious to the queue forming behind them. For a split second, Holly had no idea how they were going to react. For a second, silence filled the platform around them, before her mum turned to her dad and let out an audible sniff.

'Fine then,' she said, picking up her suitcase and rolling it towards the car park. 'But don't expect me to be happy about it.'

The journey back to Northleach felt impossibly slow. Holly remained in the front, still seething from the earlier conversation, and no matter how much Evan tried to make conversation with Wendy and Arthur, they only responded in grunts.

'Holly tells me you did a chocolate-making course?' he said, still trying to sound upbeat, despite all his questions about the travel and the hotel falling flat only minutes beforehand. 'Are we going to get to try some of those soon?'

'Doubt it.' Her father's response was as blunt as it was brutal and made Holly wince almost as much as someone touching her head.

Evan looked at her quizzically, his eyes asking the simple question of what he'd done wrong. After all, they'd been fine the last time they met.

'The Vespa,' Holly mouthed, only to grind her back teeth together in frustration. Of course, she'd known her parents would have a go at her for taking the Vespa out when she wasn't ready. But to have a go at Evan for it was ridiculous. He hadn't made her go out. And she could have just as easily crashed her car in the mood she'd been in after learning about Maud. It hardly seemed right to blame Evan. But she wouldn't have that conversation with them now. After all, she and her mother needed other words first.

Evan nodded understandingly, but when he opened his mouth to speak, Holly shook her head to stop him. The mood her parents were in, it would probably make things worse.

When they reached Northleach, Holly gave Evan the directions to her parents' house. Once there, he jumped out and opened her door, before going to Wendy's, only for her to snap the door open in front of him first. It was a wonder she didn't hit him with it. Or with her suitcase, which she swung out of the boot on her own after refusing his help.

'Thank you for the lift, but we were perfectly fine getting the bus,' she said, in what was the most awkward and false display of gratitude Holly had ever heard. Wendy turned and pulled the suitcase up the path to the front door. 'Holly, I will ring you later. I think we need a serious conversation.'

Holly's skull was throbbing from the way she had ground her back teeth together the entire journey back from the station. This unpleasant side of her mother was nothing like the Wendy she was used to. Of course, Holly understood exactly where the protectiveness came from, but that didn't excuse it. On the plus side, being mad at her mother was going to make having the conversation about the cottage a whole lot easier.

'Actually, Mum, I was hoping you and I could go for a drink. There's something I need to talk to you about.'

Her mother frowned. 'Now? I'm very tired, love. Your father and I have been travelling all day.'

'Now,' Holly said. 'This can't wait. Evan is fine to wait around with Dad, isn't that right?'

There Holly was, using that tone again. The tone implied she would not pander to them, and that even though she was their child, she wasn't taking no for an answer in this matter – though she did feel a slight flicker of guilt at inflicting her father on Evan, given the mood her dad was in. When Evan had mentioned some bonding time, Holly was sure he hadn't been imagining the evening would start like this.

Thankfully, her dad nodded his response.

'I don't know how long we're going to be, but make sure he gets a cup of tea, Dad, okay?' Holly added. 'Mum and I have some things we need to discuss.'

54

Holly didn't wait for her mother to reply. Instead, she turned on her heel and walked down the path and onto the pavement, heading towards the centre of the village. If she didn't follow, then they would have it out here, outside her own home. Possibly in her front garden. Holly was a few strides down the road when her mother called out to her.

'Can you at least slow down a bit?' she asked, before muttering just loud enough for Holly to hear. 'Honestly, I don't know what's got into you.'

It took all of Holly's restraint to bite down on her tongue and not say anything, although she slowed her pace enough for her mum to catch her up.

'Are you going to tell me what this is about?'

'Not yet. I need a drink first.'

They walked to the Wheatsheaf. The iconic pub in the centre of the village had been there long before Wendy and Arthur moved from Bourton. Holly knew it was frequented by the locals, but she herself had never been.

'Why don't you get a seat, Mum? I'll go get the drinks,' Holly said. This time, her mother nodded and did what Holly had asked without an argument.

At the bar, Holly ordered two glasses of wine, a large one for her mother to drink, and a smaller one for her to swirl around in the glass while inhaling the aroma. It wasn't the first time she had ordered wine in a pub and not drunk it. When she had been pregnant with Hope, Ben had banned alcohol in the house, not even allowing a single morsel to pass Holly's lips. So instead, she would often use her time with Giles to sneak out to a pub somewhere outside Bourton, and simply sniff at a glass of red wine. That had been enough then, and hopefully it would be now, too.

She paid for the drinks, then sat down at the table, where her mother was sitting, her arms across her chest.

'If you want me to apologise, I'm not going to. It was a completely irresponsible gift for him to give you.'

Holly sucked a deep breath in.

'We're not discussing the accident,' Holly said. 'Blaming Evan is simply churlish. I'm the one who was irresponsible for riding it when I wasn't in a good place. But that's not what I'm here to talk about. There's something else you and I need to discuss.'

Holly paused, waiting to see her mother's reaction. To most people, nothing had changed. She looked as cross and steadfast as always. But Holly noticed the way her mother swallowed more than normal, and how her lips pursed ever so slightly. She was worried.

'Did you know that Maud was sick, Mum?'

Holly watched as a look of relief flashed across her mother's face, only to be replaced by a look of deep sympathy.

'Oh, Holly, darling, I'm so sorry.'

'I don't want your sympathy, Mum. I want to know if you knew.'

It was her mother's turn for a deep inhale. Pinching the stem of her wineglass, she lifted the drink slightly off the table, before putting it down again without taking a sip.

'I didn't know for certain,' she said quietly.

'But you knew? You'd heard, and yet chose not to tell me anything.'

Wendy unfolded her arms. For what felt like the first time since they had picked her up, she looked Holly in the eye, rather than at the cut on her forehead.

'It wasn't that simple, dear. I heard some village gossip. What was I meant to say? That a woman in the supermarket was telling a cashier that she heard the old woman from the sweet shop was sick? I didn't know if that was Maud. Besides, I knew if it was true, she'd tell you. Which I assumed she did. I'm sorry, love. How bad is it?'

'It's bad. She came to Bourton to say her goodbyes.'

'Oh, darling. I'm so sorry. If there's anything—'

Holly lifted her hand in the air, stopping her mother from carrying on. She shook her head. She didn't want to get into Maud. If she was thinking about Maud, she wouldn't be able to think rationally about the next part of the conversation. And this needed all the strength she had got.

She picked up her glass, moved to take a sip, then remembered she shouldn't be drinking and took a long breath of the aroma instead. That was going to have to do.

'That's not the only reason I wanted to talk to you,' Holly said, placing the glass back down on the table. 'I wanted to know when you were going to tell me that Giles Caverty is my landlord.'

55

Holly could feel her heart all the way up in her chest. She had thought over what Evan had said to her the night before, about confronting Giles before speaking to her mother. And while it made sense on one hand, who knew when she'd next be able to physically see Giles? Just like with her mother, it wasn't the type of conversation she wanted to have on the phone, but the way he flitted in and out of the country, she might well have to wait months before he was back in the Cotswolds and free to speak. And there was no way she could go that long without confronting her mother. So she had made the decision that it was the sooner, the better. However, as her mum sat there clutching the stem of her wineglass, Holly wondered if she'd made a mistake.

For a full minute, neither of them spoke. Wendy's eyes remained wide in disbelief as she stared at Holly, while Holly raised her eyebrows ever so slightly, showing she wouldn't say anything until her mother admitted the truth. Finally, her mother's throat crackled, emitting a strange sound somewhere between a gurgle and a gasp, before she finally said anything intelligible.

'Did he tell you? I didn't think he was going to tell you.'

Holly's back teeth clenched again. She took a deep inhale, followed by a long exhale, as she tried to breathe some of the tension away.

'I'm not talking about Giles right now, Mum. I will deal with him. I will get to him. What I want to know is about you. Why didn't you tell me?'

This time, her mother picked the wineglass up and lifted it all the way to her mouth. Never could Holly remember seeing her take such a large gulp before and for a second, she was worried she was going to polish off the entire drink. While her mother didn't down the entire thing, the glass was a good third emptier when she placed it back down on the table.

'Well?' Holly pressed. 'Why didn't you tell me?'

'What do you mean, *why didn't I tell you*?' Her tone was as exasperated as Holly's. 'How could I have told you?'

'How could you not?' Holly could hardly believe her mother was being this stubborn. And once again, her mother's arms were folded across her chest.

'Would you have rented the house had you known he was the landlord?'

'Probably not.'

'Exactly.' A look of satisfaction crossed her mother's face, but Holly wasn't having it.

'That's not an excuse, Mum. I had a right to know. Do you not understand how it makes me feel, knowing you kept this from me? Not to mention all those lies you made up about a friend of your neighbours.'

Wendy let out a short huff. 'What was I meant to say? That I bumped into him at Tesco when I was with Hope, and he asked how you were doing?'

The comment caught Holly by surprise, enough for her to catch her breath.

'You saw him when you were with her? With Hope?'

Her chest tightened, causing a lump to force its way up her throat. Holly wasn't sure why this piece of information upset her so much. After all, the last time she and Giles had spoken, he'd mentioned wanting to meet Hope. And she'd been happy for that. She wanted him to see Hope again, given that the only other time they'd met had been inside the hospital ward when she'd just given birth. But she'd wanted him to meet Hope on her terms. With her there. Not in a supermarket where he could plot with her mother.

'Holly, dear.' Her mother's voice softened for the first time since she'd picked her up from the station. Wendy reached out a hand to Holly, but Holly didn't take it. 'It was a coincidence, that's all, love. And Hope was fast asleep in her pushchair. I doubt he could even see more than her nose.'

Holly tried to envision the scene. In her mother's defence, Holly had bumped into Giles herself at the same supermarket. That was how the two of them had rekindled their friendship. Even so, she needed to know more.

'Tell me,' she said, punctuating her words clearly. 'Tell me exactly what happened. What he said. What you said. How I ended up with the cottage. I want to know it all.'

56

Holly's mother took a deep breath in as she reached for her wineglass, though this time she was far more measured with the sip she took. Still. A pause stretched between them. Holly had asked for it all. She wanted to know every part of how her mother and Giles bumping together in a random supermarket would end up with Holly renting a house that he owned.

It took her mother a moment or two longer to figure out where to begin.

'I was buying a chicken,' she started. 'Or it could have been a beef joint. No, it was a chicken, I think. For our Sunday roast. You know how we like our chickens for our Sunday roast?'

'I don't need to know about the contents of your shopping basket, Mum,' Holly said, a little sharper than she expected to. 'I just want to know about Giles. What did you and Giles talk about?'

Her mother nodded again.

'Well, he was the one who spotted me. He came up and said hello. Asked me If I remembered him, which I did of course, from when he helped us with the car.'

Holly nodded along as she pictured the scene in her mind. The way Giles would approach her mother, probably with his hand outstretched. All manners and charm. And she knew exactly what incident with the car Wendy was talking about. Giles had had to pull the pair of them out of a ditch just outside Northleach once, when a pheasant had startled them on the road.

'And then what?' Holly pressed.

'Well, then he asked after Arthur, how he was doing with his heart, and so I told him. And then he asked about you. About you and Hope.'

Holly's throat was tightening for reasons she couldn't explain. Perhaps it was all the memories with Giles. The way he had intertwined himself so deeply, not only with her life, but with her parents' too, since she moved back here. She'd never realised it before.

Her mother paused, staring at her glass, though she left it where it was.

Holly prompted her to carry on. 'What did you tell him about me?'

'Darling, you're saying it as if I did something unsavoury. But it wasn't like that. He asked me how you were doing and I said you were doing well. I said that you and Ben were doing a great job of parenting Hope, considering you weren't together any more.'

Holly bit down on her tongue. She wasn't sure why it mattered that Wendy had mentioned Ben and their situation, but it seemed yet another invasion of their privacy. But then they had obviously spoken about more than that, as Holly had ended up living in Giles's house.

'What then? What did you talk about after that?'

Her mother let out a long sigh, then continued. 'We probably talked about a few other things. I can't remember what exactly, but Giles asked about your living situation and if you were still with Jamie. And I said yes, it seemed to work okay. But I mentioned I was a bit worried about Jamie and Fin getting married. Then... then...' Her words stuttered and stumbled and Holly could tell this was where they got to the crux of the story. The part she had been waiting for her mother to tell her since they sat down.

'What did you say, Mum?'

With a deep breath in, Wendy visibly steeled herself before she spoke.

'I said that you were struggling, that a bit of room and privacy would be good for you and Hope. But I said that there wasn't much available to rent, at least not within your price range. That's all. It was true. I wasn't saying anything bad, Holly. I wasn't saying you needed him.'

'So what, then he just swept in and gave you the keys to the cottage?'

She bit down on her lip. 'Not exactly. He told me he might be able to help, and asked for my phone number, in case he heard of anything.'

Of course, Holly had known it hadn't been a single encounter at the supermarket that would have resulted in her having the cottage, but she didn't know if she wanted to find out just how far this web of lies went.

'So you spoke to him again?'

Wendy exhaled loudly, as if it was physically paining her to have to recount it all.

'We had conversations, just brief ones,' she continued. 'He rang me a week or so later. Said there was a property in the village that he was thinking of getting as a buy-to-let. He'd had his eye on it for months, he told me, but it was only a small place, and he wanted to know whether I thought it would work for you and Hope before he bought it.'

Holly only then realised how tightly clenched her muscles were. With deep breathing, she forced them to loosen.

'So you mean he bought me the cottage? He bought the cottage for me and Hope to live in?'

'I don't think it was like that, darling. I really think he wanted some property to invest in.'

It was a sign of her mother's naivety and lack of knowledge about Giles that made her think that. Deep down, Holly knew that was exactly what Giles had done. He had bought the house for her. Still, she drew in a lungful of air and forced herself to steady her thoughts. She hadn't come here to get mad at her mother. She'd come to make things clear, to put things right, so she didn't harbour this anger within her. But it wasn't all that easy.

'So, how often have you spoken to him? Do you still speak to him?'

'No, not really. Only when you need something. Like with the bathroom, you knew I was in contact with him then.'

'I knew you were in contact with the landlord,' Holly corrected her. 'You said he didn't like to speak to other people.'

'He made me promise, love.' She looked at Holly, her eyes pleading. 'He didn't want you to think he was doing this because, you know, because he wanted a relationship. He was worried that if you knew it was him, that's what you'd think and you'd end up not taking the house. I don't know, you're gonna hate me for saying this, but I think I made the right decision in not telling you.'

The she sat back, straightening her shoulders, at which point Holly matched her pose inch for inch, as if there was a mirror placed between the two of them.

'I do. I think it was the right choice,' her mother said, reinforcing her point, nodding as she spoke. 'You and Hope have been so much better off since you moved into that cottage. You and Ben have some space apart, Fin and Jamie have got some space. You're more independent, you're happier. I know you see it. Darling, tell me you won't stay mad at me about this. I don't want to fall out. I know I shouldn't have lied, but you're a mother now.'

It was a change from how her father had spoken the words 'you're a parent' only a while before at the station. Then it had been an accusation, a reason not to do something. Here, it was a defending reason.

Holly picked up her wine glass, swirled it around in her nose, and then lowered it back onto the table without taking a sip.

'I'm not going to stay mad at you for this, Mum. At least, I don't want to. I don't like what you did, but it ends now. All the secrecy and everything, it ends now. But I need you to know I'm still angry. And that's not going to fade straight away.'

'I understand love, I do.'

With her mother still waiting for her to say more, Holly plucked her phone from out of her bag and began to type a message on it.

'What are you doing?' her mother asked, the deep furrows of concern reappearing on her forehead.

'What do you think I'm doing?' Holly said. 'I'm messaging Giles. I've had this talk with you; now I need to have it with him.'

57

Now that Holly had decided to contact Giles, she didn't want to waste any more time. While her mother sipped nervously on her wine, Holly fired a message straight off.

When are you back in the UK? I'd like to meet for a drink.

She ummed and ahhed for a moment about whether she should place a kiss on the end and decided against it. Kissing Giles was something she had fastidiously avoided, even if it was just a letter in a text.

As she placed her phone back in her pocket, she looked back up to find her mother still staring at her, worry lines still on her face.

'Honestly, love, you know I wouldn't do anything I thought would hurt you, don't you?'

'Of course I know that, Mum.'

A wave of guilt rolled through Holly. Having cleared the air, she now felt bad for having laid it on so thickly. After all, her mother looked terrible, and all the relaxation of the holiday had seemingly ebbed away.

'If there's anything I can do...'

Holly didn't have to think for long for a reply. 'Actually, there is.'

'There is?' Her mother looked surprised by this comment.

'Yes. You and Dad can ease off Evan. The way you were in the car was, quite frankly, embarrassingly rude.'

Her mother's face hardened. 'Holly, you could've been seriously injured.'

'And if I had been, it would've been my fault. I was the one who went for a ride. Please, Mum, you can't sit there and in one breath ask me to forgive you for only doing what you thought was best for me and not accept that I'm a grown woman who can make their own mistakes. You made mistakes. So did I.'

Holly considered telling her mother the truth about the accident – that she had been so upset over finding out about Maud and Giles and how her own mother had been hiding all those things from her. Those were the real reason she crashed. But her mother was the closest to broken Holly had ever seen her, other than her dad's heart attack, that was. She didn't need Holly piling more things on top of her.

'Think of it this way,' Holly said. 'If you're not willing to be pleasant to Evan, then we've got a lot further to go to fix this relationship than I thought.'

Holly never imagined she'd use threats of this nature with her mother, but maybe it was time she put boundaries in place. She appreciated all the help she gave her with Hope and how her father helped at the shop. But her mother seemed to have forgotten that Holly wasn't a child any more. Holly was responsible for making her own decisions and if her mother wasn't willing to accept that, then perhaps there were other parts of their relationship that needed addressing.

Across the table, her mother continued to pout, and for a

second, Holly thought she was going to refuse, when she finally spoke.

'Fine, I'll talk to your dad. But it won't be easy to forget this.'

'Really, Mum?' She offered her a withering gaze, only for Wendy to shrink beneath it.

'Fine.'

'Great. Then can we get back, please? I think my boyfriend probably needs rescuing. I don't want to imagine how Dad's been treating him.'

* * *

As it happened, her father hadn't been giving Evan a hard time at all, or at least not verbally.

When the front door clicked open, Evan came rushing through from the living area into the hall.

'Are you okay?' he asked, looking from Holly to Wendy and back again.

'We're good,' Holly said, giving him a quick peck on the cheek. 'Mum, I think you have something to say to Evan, don't you?'

Holly watched as her mother pouted. It was hard not to laugh. She had never seen much of herself in her before, yet the way Wendy's bottom lip protruded was almost identical to how Hope sulked.

'Evan, I'm very sorry for giving you a hard time when you were so kind to come and pick us up from the station,' she said. 'I realise the Vespa, though sadly misguided, was a well-intentioned gift.'

'And...?' Holly pushed her. There was still more her mother needed to say.

'And no one is to blame for the accident other than Holly herself,' she said, with a sigh that sounded more like that of a petulant teenager than a grown woman.

'Thank you, Wendy. No hard feelings here,' Evan said, at which Wendy grunted.

'Well, I'm going to put the kettle on,' her mother said shortly afterwards, and squeezed past him into the kitchen.

'Sorry,' Holly said the second they were alone, dropping her head onto Evan's chest. It wasn't exactly the heartfelt apology she had been hoping for, but it was something. 'Where's Dad?' she said, when she lifted her head back up. 'Has he been awful?'

Evan shook his head. 'Not at all. I haven't seen him. He went out into the garden when we got in. Said he needed to water his plants. I offered him help, and he said he didn't need it.'

'Did he at least make you a drink first?' Holly asked, yet again embarrassed by her parents' rudeness.

'No, but he showed me where the kettle and the teabags were.'

Holly forced herself to take a deep breath in before turning and heading into the kitchen, only to find her mother standing just inside the doorway, clearly eavesdropping.

'Mother... Will you?'

'I'll talk to your father now,' she said, before hustling outside and disappearing into the garden, no doubt to fill Arthur in on both the contents of hers and Holly's conversation, along with his requirements to apologise and be nice to Evan.

Holly let out a deep sigh of relief. 'I'm so sorry. They're not normally like this.'

'Don't be silly. They're your parents. They're going to be protective of you. How did it go talking to your mum? Did you say everything you needed to?'

Holly shrugged. 'Pretty much. I mean, it's tough. On the one hand, I understand why she did it. But it's going to be difficult to forget. I think she thinks everything's going to go back to normal with us straight away, and I don't think that's going to be the case. Not for a while, at least.'

'Well, someday soon, when you and I get our own house, big enough for all of us, this is going to be a thing of the past.'

Holly leaned into him, allowing Evan's arms to wrap tightly around her. For a few minutes, they stayed there, completely at ease, and Holly found herself wishing all life could be as simple and perfect as that hug.

It was only when they were back in the car that Holly checked her phone and saw she had a message. The name was enough to make her stomach somersault. Giles. Giles had messaged her back already, although the sight of his name didn't affect her nearly as much as the contents of the text:

I came back last night. Fancy brunch tomorrow?

58

Deep down, Holly had assumed Giles wouldn't be able to meet up. After all, it was the summer, and therefore, fair to assume he would be out chartering his yachts to the wealthy holidaymakers in the south of France. If she was honest with herself, she'd expected nothing more than a quick apology reply, saying he'd try to catch up when he was next back. Or perhaps even no reply at all. She certainly hadn't expected this. Breakfast. Tomorrow.

'Delay him, if you're that worried about it,' Evan said, as they opened up the door to the cottage. It was Hope's night at Ben's again, and somehow having Evan there made it feel even stranger. Like the house wasn't completely quiet, but it didn't have Hope's laughter in it either.

'I can't delay him. I need to speak to him about this. The sooner I get it over with, the better. No, this is good. I told Mum I was going to speak to him. And that's what I'm going to do.'

'And what are you gonna say?'

Holly drew a deep breath in. This was different from talking to her mum. Giles had been the instigator, the one who swept in like a knight in shining armour. She needed to make him see she didn't need that, and even if she had, he couldn't be that for her. But she had to admit, her mother was right. Having a cottage to live in had made a massive difference in her life, and she wanted Giles to know that she was grateful. So somehow, she just had to find the right balance between gratitude and extreme annoyance. Easier said than done.

'I've no idea. But at least it'll be over and done with.'

That night, she struggled to sleep. She never realised how much she moved her arm before, or how much she liked to lie on it. And it didn't help that Evan was there, taking up an uncomfortably large portion of their bed. When she'd been single, having a standard double hadn't seemed small at all, but it was easy to see why people chose king and super king options, particularly when they had boyfriends. Around 3 a.m., she woke up and headed downstairs, where she flicked on the TV, and then finally drifted back to sleep around four-thirty, just in time for Evan to appear downstairs, ready for his morning run.

'I'm sorry,' he said, as his footsteps creaked on the staircase. 'I didn't mean to wake you up. I didn't hear you come down last night. Why don't you head back up to bed?'

Holly nodded groggily. Back to bed sounded good, and, in her daze, she dragged herself back upstairs.

It felt as if she had barely closed her eyes when Evan was waking her up again, but this time with a cup of tea in his hand.

'What time is it?' she asked.

'Eight thirty.'

She bolted upright.

'Eight thirty? Are you sure?'

Evan made a false pretence of glancing at his watch.

'Yes, definitely eight thirty. What's the problem? I thought your dad was opening up today?'

'He was, but I forgot to check with him. Besides, I want to see

Hope before Mum picks her up from Ben's. Just give her a quick cuddle. I do that sometimes.'

'No worries. Just grab a quick shower. Or bung some clothes on and have a shower when you get back. That way, we can be out of here in ten, can't we?'

It was amazing to be with a man who didn't sweat the small stuff. If you were running late, you just ran a bit faster; if you were feeling tired, you just took a nap. Evan's approach to life was as refreshing as it was enviable. And considering how badly this week could've gone, Holly was amazed at how easily it went. Still, she wanted to go straight from seeing Hope to the shop and then to Giles, which meant she needed to look good.

'I'm pretty sure you don't make this much effort when you're deciding what clothes to wear for me,' Evan said, as Holly rummaged through her wardrobe.

'That's because since you've been here, I've mainly been wearing my pyjamas,' Holly replied. 'And anyway, it's different with Giles. I need to look professional. I need him to listen to me. If I dress too fancy, he'll make a joke of that; if I dress too slobby, he'll make a joke about that too. I need to find a happy medium.'

In the end, she settled on a summery dress, with deep pockets, that had the added advantage of being able to fit her cast through the armhole.

Her first stop was Ben's to give Hope a big morning cuddle.

'How are your mum and dad? Did they have fun on the trip?' Ben asked, as he packed a day bag for Wendy to take with her.

'Oh, absolutely. Loved it.' Holly decided not to mention everything that had gone down between her and her parents the night before. As much as she didn't like keeping secrets from Ben, she suspected his reaction to Giles owning the cottage would be even more vehement than her own.

'Well, your mother will be here any second. I'm sure she'll tell us all about it.'

Holly's stomach tightened. She wasn't quite ready to talk to her mother again just yet. And certainly not with other people there. As such, she made her excuses.

'I should get going now, actually,' she said. 'Evan's gone ahead to the bakery, and I said I'd meet him there before I go to the shop.' She kissed Hope again on the forehead, then the cheeks and then the belly, which resulted in a loud giggle. 'And I'll see you this afternoon, gorgeous.'

Just as she'd told Ben, Evan was at the bakery, but had already reached the front of the queue and had ordered half a dozen pastries.

'How are you feeling about today?' he said, handing her a pain aux raisins. 'About brunch.'

Holly considered the question. 'Less terrified than yesterday.'

'Well, that's something.'

It was a relief to discover her father was already opening up the shop, straightening the jars of sweets and setting up the bags and scales ready for the first customers.

When he saw Evan, his face flushed with embarrassment.

'Evan, I've been told I owe you a proper apology. And Holly is probably right. We did get a bit heated yesterday.'

Holly was grateful her dad hadn't tried to avoid the situation.

'It's fine,' Evan assured him, shaking his hand. 'You're right to be protective. She's a wonderful woman. And I promise I will postpone the parachute jump I had planned until next year.'

Arthur's eyes bulged in shock.

'He's joking, Dad, he's joking.'

'Oh, right,' he said, letting out a strained chuckle. 'Of course it's a joke.'

Holly took a deep breath in. Later today, she must remind Evan that not everyone shared the same sense of humour as he did.

'Dad, I'm going to do some accounts work upstairs for a bit, but I'm going to need to head out in an hour. You'll be okay here, right? Just for a couple of hours. Evan is going to be at the cottage working if you need him.'

'Is that right?' Her father was eyeing Evan with suspicion yet again, possibly still from the parachute jump comment. 'So you can do that, can you? Work wherever you want? Must be nice.'

'Yes, it's not bad,' Evan said. 'I mean, I have to go into the office sometimes. Either the London one or the New York one. But most of the time, I can set up wherever I fancy.'

'Looks like you're fixing yourself here a fair bit,' her dad added, with a quick quirk of the eyebrow.

'Well, I think that might be the plan,' Evan replied, glancing at Holly, only to add hurriedly, 'Not that I want to rush anything, of course. We have to take our time.'

Holly felt a prickle of disappointment at the statement, along with a pang of relief. She was grateful she hadn't mentioned moving in together yesterday at Slaughter when Evan clearly still had doubts about it.

Besides, she already had enough on her plate right now.

59

Holly felt a little guilty for choosing somewhere smack bang in the middle of Bourton to meet Giles.

Since the incident early in their relationship, where he had tried to sabotage her business by planting a dead mouse among the chocolate hedgehogs, people in the village had viewed him with scepticism. Rumours had travelled fast and, as such, he had made a concerted effort to avoid the village. Yet Giles was not one to let the opinions of others get to him, and when Holly walked into the Riverside Café, he was sitting there at a table in the far corner with a grin on his face. A grin that dropped the moment he saw her.

It was clearly something she was going to have to get used to while her arm was in a sling and the bruises were still prominent, but thankfully, the stitches were doing their job and her face looked a little better.

'What did you do?' The first words out of his mouth were almost an exact copy of what her parents had said to her the night before. 'Oh my God, that looks serious.'

'A Vespa accident,' she said.

Unlike her parents, this response caused a smirk to flicker on his face. 'The new man bought you a Vespa?'

'I didn't say that.' Holly was mildly affronted by this comment, however truthful it was.

'You didn't need to say it. You told me about the Vespa in France, remember? You loved it and he's got money. If I'd been him, it's what I'd do. The perfect present. So, how many times had you been out on it when you crashed?'

His smirk was so irritating. That know-it-all-ness of it drove her mad, but at the same time made her want to wrap her arms around him and squeeze as tightly as she could. If nothing else, Giles always made her smile.

'If you must know, it was my first trip out. Or at least, first trip on my own.'

'God, he must feel like crap.'

'Yes, you could say that. He's moved into the cottage with me to help, given that I can't do much.' She lifted her cast-laden arm to show what she meant. 'My mum and dad are absolutely furious with him, obviously. Not a great impression to make right at the beginning of a relationship.'

'Oh, I'm sure they'll soften. He seems like a good guy. How are things at the cottage? Can't imagine there's much room for you both there. It's pretty small.' He sounded so casual, Holly wouldn't have even noticed the slight inflection in his voice, had she not known what it meant. But he had brought it up now, so it seemed an appropriate time to confess.

'I know.'

Her short sentence lingered in the air between them as she waited for a reply. Giles's face crinkled in confusion.

'What do you mean?'

'You know what I mean. I know. And there's no point denying it. I confronted Mum yesterday. And she cracked immediately.'

His gaze went down to the table as he chewed on the bottom of his lip. When he looked up again, a wide grin was plastered on his face.

'Well, I'll be honest with you – I thought Wendy would crack way before now. You're not mad, are you? I didn't know what else I could do.'

Unlike her mother, there were no deep, heart-felt apologies here. But then again, it wasn't like he really had much to apologise for. Other than keeping things a secret.

'I was mad. I was furious,' Holly replied.

Giles feigned a wounded expression. 'How can you say that? I am the most perfect landlord in all existence. I let you refit the bathroom, and I paid for it all.'

'Yes, but not because you're the perfect landlord. It was because you're you, Giles. And I hate myself for not seeing it.'

'Oh, don't be so hard on yourself. I take it this means you're not gonna pack up and leave me without a tenant?'

'Well, I don't have anywhere to go.'

'If that's the case, I could probably get at least 50 per cent more rent than I'm charging you. You know that, right?'

If Holly hadn't known it would hurt, she probably would've thumped him, but instead she just grinned.

'Thank you. I mean it. I'm grateful.'

Giles's smirk finally dropped. 'You're welcome,' he said, his tone earnest. 'And it's yours as long as you want it. If you wanna pack up tomorrow and move in with this new fella, then I'd say you're insane, but fine. If you want to stay there till Hope's eighteen and off to university, that's fine too. I'm not gonna sell it, not as long as you want to be there.'

'Thank you.'

It felt like there should be more she could say to this, something else she could add. More than a simple 'thank you', and yet there wasn't. The pair of them fell into silence. Holly never used to mind being silent around Giles. It used to be calming, peaceful. And it still was in some ways. Yet today, she couldn't help but feel like she should be saying more.

'So, what have you been up to? Lots of yacht trips?'

'Yes, it's been busy. But there's been some bad weather. It's put a bit of a spanner in the works this last couple of weeks.'

'Sorry,' Holly replied. She knew how much bad weather could affect business at the sweet shop; it was likely to be a thousand times worse with Giles and the boat.

'So, is that why you're back here?' she asked. 'Because the weather's too bad to work?'

'No. Would you believe it, Faye has got engaged?'

'Really?' Holly had a soft spot for Giles's sister, Faye, particularly after she'd been the midwife present at Hope's birth, and had let all Holly's friends stay in the room.

'Yes. To a man I've never met.' His face dropped into a scowl.

'Oh.' Holly let out a low noise. 'I guess you're not too happy about that.'

'No, of course I'm not. I need to thoroughly scare the man away and see what he does then. Test his mettle.'

'Is that right?'

'It is. And if he comes back, then we'll know he's worth it.'

'I'm sure Faye will thoroughly appreciate your intervention,' Holly joked. 'Well, sounds like it's time for chaotic wedding plans.'

'Jamie and her fella?' It wasn't surprising that Giles had immediately jumped to the right conclusion. After all, he had been there for part of the stag and hen do only a few weeks before and it wasn't like Holly had many friends who were getting married. 'What happened?'

Holly wasn't sure if she wanted to get into it or not. After all, it was Jamie's business, not hers, but she didn't see any harm in telling

Giles what had happened. She was pretty sure most people in Bourton knew anyway, as they had asked everyone and anyone if they knew of any solutions.

'The hotel double booked the wedding.'

'What? Can they do that?' Giles looked genuinely shocked by this news.

'Apparently, the man had the same surname and initials as Fin. What are the chances? Anyway, these other people were booked in first, so Fin and Jamie are out of a place to get married. It's a right mess. They've got all the family coming over from the States and they've searched everywhere, but it seems like everything is fully booked and there are no registrars available to do the service. Basically, the entire thing's a complete mess.'

Holly expected this news to elicit more of a response or perhaps sympathy for her friend's situation, but Giles was staring at her fixedly. Unblinking.

'What? What is it?' she asked. 'Is there something on my face? Other than the stitches?'

The silence expanded. Holly found herself on tenterhooks, waiting.

'Giles?'

Finally, he took a deep breath in.

'My mother is a registrar,' he said. 'I think she could do it. I think she could marry Jamie and Fin.'

60

Holly shook her head, not convinced she had heard Giles correctly.

'Your mother is a registrar?'

'She used to be, full time. She doesn't do it so much any more, now that she's older. Tends to just do odd ceremonies around the busy season, but she's still licensed to do it. We were talking about her doing Faye's wedding, actually. Assuming I approve of this guy.'

Holly shook her head. That didn't make sense. A registrar was, well, a normal job, and Giles wasn't normal. He was wealthy. Borderline aristocracy. She remembered what Kathy had said about the Manor House on the edge of the village belonging to Lord Caverty. Had she been wrong to assume that was a relation?

'I don't get it. I thought all your family were... your family are...' She struggled to find the words to explain what she meant without coming across as rude. Fortunately, Giles had no such qualms.

'You thought all my family were landed gentry?'

'Pretty much,' Holly admitted.

Giles laughed.

'On my dad's side, yes. On my mum's, no. Her brother is an electrician, unlike my uncle on my father's side, who pretty much has people to switch on lights for him.'

'Why did I not know this?' Holly asked, still confused. Then again, she didn't know why she should. The only member of his family she had met was Faye.

'I guess you didn't take as much interest in my life as I took in yours,' Giles replied with raised eyebrows.

Holly didn't care how much it hurt her arm. She reached across and thumped him on the shoulder anyway.

Giles leaned back in his chair and let out a light chuckle that somehow turned into a sigh. 'I don't know. I guess that's not the part of the family I talk about. It doesn't help me with the line of jobs I do. When I'm talking to people, you know. Anyway, my dad died years ago, left his share of the estate to me. Faye is only my half-sister, different dads. She is very much more like Mum, hence the midwifery.'

Holly was struggling to take it in. How could there be so much she didn't know about Giles, given all the time they spent together? How could there be two such different sides to him?

'Mum and Dad got married really young, had me way before they should've. And then got divorced. I grew up a pretty angry kid. I was angry at my mum for not being happy with the life my dad could provide for her, and I was angry with my dad for not doing more to keep the family together. So I spent most of the time with my uncle. When Dad died, well, that was probably when I became the worst version of myself. Which carried on for several years, until I met this charming lady who ran a sweet shop, and I pushed my antics a bit too far. That, you could say, was my low point and the start of my reinvention.'

Holly sat back in the seat, aghast, as she struggled to take this all in. She really hadn't asked him anything about his life at all. How?

Still, she was only just considering this when the other thought re-entered her head.

'So, your mum, she's really a registrar? Do you think she could do it? Do you think she could do the wedding?'

'I don't know the ins and outs. I'd have to check with her. But assuming Jamie and Fin have got the right paperwork, I can't see why not.'

Holly's mind was whirring at a thousand miles an hour.

'But that still doesn't help the situation with the venue. They've found a place for their family to stay in, but they're not registered for weddings. Jamie already told me as much.'

Another smile formed on Giles's face. That sly, slanted smirk that always meant he had another trick up his sleeve. Often, Holly dreaded what it meant because he was bound to be up to no good. This time, however, she was desperate to hear what he had to say.

'Do you know what?' he said after an excruciating pause. 'I might be able to help with the wedding venue, too.'

61

Back at the shop, Holly couldn't sit still. Unfortunately though, with her arm in a cast, she wasn't much help when it came to weighing up sweets.

'Are you okay, love?' her father asked, coming over to help her out. 'Why don't you stay upstairs? I'm fine down here, and to be honest, you're not that much use.'

Holly shook her head. 'No, I'm waiting for a telephone call. And I need to stay distracted. I need jobs to do.'

'Well, to be honest, right now all you're doing is making more work for me,' he replied, straightening a jar she just moved.

Holly let out a deep groan, at which her dad stepped towards her and placed a hand on her shoulder.

'Holly, go upstairs. Please.'

Finally relenting, Holly headed up to the stock room where she sat down, opened up her phone, and looked at old photos of Hope, while wondering if she ought to dock her salary for the day.

At lunchtime, Arthur called up, saying he was going for a break, and she headed downstairs to the till. The summer rush meant it was busy, but even the slightest lull had her checking her phone.

Giles had told her he would ring her as soon as he knew whether his mother could do the ceremony, but he had given her no indication as to when that would be. Half an hour, an hour? That's what she thought at first, but when three hours had passed and she'd still heard nothing from him, her stomach was a mass of knots. More than once she thought about calling him, or at least sending a message, but she didn't want to nag. After all, she knew him well enough to be sure he was already doing everything he could. It wasn't like her pestering would speed anything up.

After her dad's lunch break, Holly took her own brief one, before heading back upstairs to continue her pacing until three fifteen, when her father called up for a second time that day.

'Holly, love, there's someone here to speak to you.'

Holly jumped up from her seat so fast she nearly banged her head on a shelf, but she didn't stop. Racing across the floor, she took the steps two at a time. What did it mean that he'd come to the shop? It meant that his mother couldn't do it, didn't it? It was always better to give bad news face to face. That was what she thought, at least, until she reached the shop floor.

A familiar face was standing in front of the till, but it wasn't Giles.

'Maud?'

Holly rushed over and wrapped her one working arm around her old friend, who, just like everybody else, focused solely on the cast and stitches.

'What happened?' Maud asked.

'Don't worry about that,' Holly assured her. 'How are you? I'm sorry I haven't seen you since the other night. I meant to ring the lodge, but as you can see, I got a bit distracted.'

Maud shook her head emphatically. 'Don't be silly. It's fine, not a problem at all. I was just coming to say that I'm off back to Scotland this afternoon. I've got a taxi picking me up in half an hour.

And I wanted to give you this.' She pulled an envelope out of her handbag and held it out to Holly.

'What's this?'

'Nothing, just a bit of what we talked about. Don't look at it now. Wait till I'm gone. Okay, you know what I've told you, but I don't want any tears, got it?'

The adrenaline Holly had felt only minutes before was suddenly replaced with something else. A heavy weight. An inevitable fate. This was the last time she was going to see Maud.

The thought choked in her throat. Holly could feel her eyes welling up, her breath shallowing in her lungs. How could this be the last time she would ever see her friend? It didn't make sense.

'Maud, I don't know how I can ever thank you for everything you've done for me,' she said, wiping the tears from her cheeks.

'Don't be silly, you just have a grand old life. Do you understand? And I want you to know that we are very, very proud of you.'

Holly didn't want her to leave. Knowing that when they said goodbye, it would be the last time she ever saw her was enough to make Holly's heart hurt. She went in to hug Maud again, trying to breathe in every fragment of her she could, when her phone started ringing in her pocket.

'I... I...' She reached down, only to hesitate. Even if it was Giles, he could wait for now. Everything could wait, except Maud.

'It's fine, love,' Maud said, as she gently wiped away her own tears. 'Look at me, breaking my own rule and turning into a blubbering mess on the shop floor. You go answer your call. And don't forget to put that somewhere safe.' She pointed to the envelope.

Holly nodded and kissed her friend once more. Then, without a word, Maud closed her eyes, breathing the smell of the sweets and chocolates. The moment could only have lasted a few seconds, yet Holly knew that it held a hundred thousand memories. No doubt some of the best, and some of the worst. An ache throbbed through

Holly's chest for all the moments she had shared with Agnes and Maud under this roof, and gratitude that she was given that chance. When she opened her eyes again, Maud offered Holly one last smile before she turned and walked out of Just One More, for what they both knew would be the last time.

62

Given how emotional Holly was, she had no intention of answering the call on the shop floor, although by the time Maud had gone, her phone had stopped ringing.

She reached the top of the stairs and folded the envelope from Maud, and slipped it into her pocket before taking out her phone. A single missed call from Giles glared on the screen with a bright-red notification.

Wasting no time, she took a deep breath and called him straight back.

'Giles?' She could barely hear herself speak, the way her heart was drumming in her chest. 'Have you spoken to her? What did she say?'

A pause followed her questions.

'You know, most people usually start a telephone call with some sort of pleasantry. Rather than lunging straight in.'

'Believe me, you don't want to try joking with me. Not after the day I've had.'

'Sorry. I apologise,' Giles said, sounding genuine, although an apology wasn't what she was after at that precise moment.

'Did you speak to your mum? What did she say?'

'She said, okay,' he responded.

Holly waited, certain that there had to be more to add. *Okay* couldn't be the full contents of anyone's conversation. Especially a conversation with Giles.

'Okay what? What does "okay" mean?' she asked, unable to hide her exasperation.

'Okay, means okay, it should work. She told me to pass on her number to you, so either you can message or Jamie can. Jamie, I suppose. Mum said they might need to check a couple of dates, like, if people are staying the whole week, the ceremony might have to take place on a weekday rather than a weekend, but yes. It should work. Mum can officiate the wedding.'

If Giles had been there in person, Holly would have squeezed him in the tightest hug she could manage with one arm. But as he wasn't, all she could do was grip on to her phone and stamp her feet on the ground, so much so that the wooden floorboards creaked beneath her. She stopped when she realised this, though she could do nothing to stem the tears that tumbled down her cheeks.

'So, I guess I should get off the line?' Giles said. 'I assume you want to tell Jamie as soon as possible?'

Holly stopped bouncing and perched on the edge of the table. Of course she wanted Jamie to know, and the sooner the better, but she couldn't ring her up. And this wasn't a case of not wanting to share the news down a phone line. It was more a case that she didn't think she should be the one to tell her at all.

'You need to do it,' she said, knowing as soon as she spoke that it was the right thing to do. 'You've got to be the one to tell them. You're the one who's fixed it all.'

'We hope,' he added. 'Like I said, she might have to change the day to earlier in the week.'

'Trust me, she's not going to care about that at all. So you'll do it? You'll come and speak to them?'

Even on the phone, she could hear the crack in Giles's throat.

'You want me to tell Jamie? Jamie hates me.'

'I'm not taking no for an answer. You have to tell her. This is because of you. Besides, maybe this could finally stop the silly feud between the pair of you and you could actually become friends.'

A slight hiss reverberated down the line. Maybe at another time, Holly would have thought she was pushing it too far, but not today. Today she could feel it in her bones. Even the broken one. This was fate's way of bringing all the people she loved finally together.

'You know she won't even let me into her house?' Giles said, still not convinced.

'Don't be ridiculous. Of course she will. Right, she's at work now, shall we say five thirty at hers? Obviously I'll message Fin too, to make sure he can be there. They both have to be there. Can you do that? Five thirty?'

'It doesn't sound like you're giving me much choice,' Giles grumbled.

'You're right, I'm not. I'll see you at five thirty at Jamie's. Do not be late.'

'Hold on,' he said, before she could hang up. 'There was that other thing you asked me about, too.'

63

Rounding up the troops wasn't just a case of Jamie and Fin. Obviously, Evan and Hope were going to be there too, and it didn't seem fair not to include Ben, given that he was next door. However, once she'd rung Ben to check that he could make it, she'd felt bad that Caroline wasn't included too, and so had rung her and extended the invite. With them all gathered in Jamie's kitchen, it made for one of the fullest houses Holly could remember in some time.

'Why won't you just tell me why you've turned up here?' Jamie said, looking decidedly frantic.

'Because it's not my place to tell you,' Holly said, unable to suppress her grin. 'But it's good news, I promise. And he'll be here any minute. He better be...'

'And who is it we're waiting for, exactly?' Fin asked, a question Caroline clearly seconded from the way she was nodding her head.

'The guest of honour.'

'This is ridiculous, Holly. Even for you.' Jamie scowled.

Holly hadn't even let Evan in on the secret. No, the first people to hear the news had to be Jamie and Fin, and they needed to hear it from Giles. But she was starting to think that he had chickened out. After all, it was already five thirty-five, and she'd been quite insistent that he needed to be prompt.

She picked up her phone, ready to call him and yell, when the doorbell buzzed.

'I'll get it!' she said, and raced to the front of the house, closing the door to the kitchen en route so that they couldn't see out into the hallway and spot Giles.

'You're late,' she said, as she let him in.

'And you clearly didn't trust that I'd turn up. Had you got all nervous and started babbling yet?'

She slapped him on the arm. 'Just hurry up. Everyone is waiting.'

'What do you mean, everybody? I thought you said it was only going to be Jamie and Fin.'

Holly decided not to say any more. Instead, she opened the door, and walked through into the kitchen.

All eyes stared straight at them.

'Is this some kind of joke?' Jamie said. 'What's he doing here?'

The comment was definitely loud enough for Giles to hear, but when Holly turned to look at him apologetically, he apparently hadn't heard. It looked as though he wasn't listening to anyone. Instead, he was staring at Ben, or more precisely, Hope in Ben's arms.

'Wow, she's gotten so big,' he said.

He took a step forward and stretched out his hand towards Hope, only for Holly to slap it away.

'You can give her all the cuddles you want in a minute. First, you need to tell them. Now.'

In all her years of knowing him, she couldn't remember seeing Giles this nervous before – except on the occasions he had professed his love for her. And it would've been amusing had it not been for the butterflies flitting around her stomach and the extreme confusion on everybody else's faces. If he didn't spit it out soon, she knew she was going to, but she gave him one more moment.

'Giles?' she said again.

He took a deep breath in.

'So, I don't know how much Holly has told you?' he started.

'Nothing,' Jamie said immediately. 'She's told us nothing at all. Honestly, we have no idea why you're here.'

'Well, my mum is a registrar.'

The confusion on everyone's faces turned into something far more pensive. Holly could feel the collective tension wrapping around them. Ben and Caroline were exchanging looks, whereas Fin and Jamie were holding one another's hands, while Evan's attention was solely on Holly.

'Go on…' Holly said.

Giles nodded, swallowing visibly. 'Well, she's been part-time now since she went into semi-retirement. But she can still do weddings, she's registered and as it happens she's got some free spaces late next week. Which means…'

Jamie was close to tears, her hand covering her mouth as she looked from Fin to Holly.

'Is this a joke?' she said.

'No,' Holly replied, feeling the tears well in her eyes.

'It's not a wind-up?'

'It's not a wind-up.'

64

Holly couldn't remember when, if ever, she'd seen Jamie mute, and yet there she was, stunned into silence, staring at Giles.

'She can marry us?' she managed.

'Assuming you've submitted all the correct information to the local registry office, then yes, she can.'

Jamie started blinking, unusually rapidly, and may have stayed that way for quite some while, had Fin not reached out and tapped her on the shoulder.

'That doesn't change the fact we don't have a venue, does it? You know, these rules in the UK are far more stressful than in the States. There you can just get married in your backyard.'

Jamie's face fell.

'He's right. We don't. It doesn't matter if we have a registrar or not, even the town halls are full at this point.'

'I know, he's right,' Holly said, 'but Giles has got a solution to that, too. Go on, tell them.'

She was bouncing with anticipation now. Hope, who so far had been sitting quietly on Ben's lap, began bobbing up and down too, mirroring Holly's excitement. Already fairly adept with the one-arm grip, Holly reached out and took Hope with her good arm, then continued bouncing around holding her as she waited for the others to hear what Giles had to say.

'My uncle has a place, an estate. You might have seen it. It's just outside the village, behind the bird park.'

'I've seen it!' Holly said, unable to keep her energy in check. 'Or at least, I think I have. They were cutting down some hedges one day when I took Hope for a walk there, around the back paths. It's massive.'

'Thank you for that insight.' Giles shot her a quick roll of his eyes. 'Anyway, he got a license for weddings a few years ago. He's only had two or three, I think. But he kept the license running, figured it could be a money-maker at some point if he ever needs it. As well as a place for his nieces and nephews to tie the knot, if we want to.'

'And we can use that?' Fin asked. 'He won't mind?'

'He's never there, but I know he won't mind. I've checked with him just in case.'

Jamie was once again frozen to the spot, though her eyes were locked on Giles, utterly unwavering in their gaze.

'This isn't some trick? You're not screwing with me?'

'I promise, I'm not. Here, take my phone. You can have a look at the messages on there from my mum. She messaged me to confirm it was all good to go ahead and wants me to pass on her number.'

He held his phone to Jamie, but she shook her head.

'Just promise me. Promise on Holly's life this isn't some sick game you're playing to totally mess with me?'

Holly wasn't entirely sure she liked Jamie's method of seeking assurance, particularly given that Evan was there with her, but it got her point through well and clear.

Giles took a step towards her.

'I swear on Holly and Faye's lives. And baby Hope's. This is not a trick. I'm not saying it'll be perfect, though. My uncle's place is dated, to put it nicely. Your best bet is probably using the garden and ignoring the house altogether. And you'll need to sort out the catering and that kind of thing.'

'We can do that.' Jamie was immediate with her response. 'We can get it all. We just need a venue and a person, and if we've got that... if we've got that...'

She couldn't finish her sentence. Holly could only imagine how she felt. Around the room, both Caroline and Ben had both remained silent, though tears glazed both their eyes. Finally, Fin reached out and took Jamie's hands, and it was like all the rest of them had just disappeared. Was that how Evan looked at her? Holly wondered briefly, only to know immediately what the answer was. He did. He looked at her like she was the only thing in the entire world that mattered.

'Looks like this is going ahead,' Fin said quietly. 'It's happening. The wedding is happening.'

The shriek that erupted around the kitchen was enough to make Hope jump in Holly's lap. But while Caroline and Holly danced on the spot, Fin remained where he was, squeezing Jamie so tightly it was as if he wanted her to crack her ribs. Then, without warning, he let go and turned around and stretched out his hand, straight towards Giles.

'We don't have words for this, dude. This is insane. Crazily insane.'

Giles nodded. 'I'll be honest, it's just nice to be seen as the good guy for once.'

Holly's heart was so full, she couldn't believe it hadn't burst yet. Still, the tears that had lodged in her throat were forcing their way up when Evan placed a hand on her waist.

'This looks like a perfect happy ending,' he whispered into her ear.

'It does, doesn't it?'

Then, as if the moment couldn't have got any better, Jamie turned around and wrapped her arms around Giles.

Holly's jaw dropped. As long as she had known Jamie, her friend couldn't stand to even be in the same room as the man, and yet there she was, hugging him. Of course, it was exceptional circumstances, and in no way did she expect it to become a regular feature of their relationship, but the fact it had happened at all was a near miracle.

When Jamie finally let go, she turned around and faced the rest of the room, her cheeks shining.

'Who's up for some champagne?'

65

Given all the painkillers she was on, Holly declined a glass of champagne. But it didn't matter in the slightest. She got all the joy and entertainment she could want watching her friends there together. In the midst of all the excitement, Caroline had rung Michael, who had brought the children round, but they weren't the only additions. As it was Holly's night with Hope, Georgia had turned up just after six, expecting Ben to be home alone as normal. When he hadn't been, she had rung his mobile.

'I'm so sorry. I'm just next door. I'll be there in one second!' He lifted his champagne glass to his lips as if he was hastily going to down it, but before he could take a sip, Holly accosted him.

'What are you doing? Invite her in.'

Ben's forehead crinkled with a frown. 'Are you sure?'

'Of course I'm sure. Jamie won't mind. And Georgia's going to come to the wedding, isn't she?'

Ben nodded, before leaning forwards and pecking her on the cheek.

'Thank you.'

Somehow, Georgia being there made the entire thing complete.

The way both Ben and Hope's face lit up when she came into the room was all the proof Holly needed that she was part of the group. Or would be with time.

The glasses clinked, while Jamie and Fin fielded one frantic call after another, and Holly watched on, her heart the fullest she could ever remember it being. These people were her chosen family, and she loved all of them with all her heart. Never once had she dreamed they would all be together like this. Happy. Ben and Evan. Jamie and Giles. There was nothing more that she could have wished for in the world.

And for Hope, despite all the excitement – and with the bonus of Caroline's children to fuss over her – it didn't take long before she started getting tired. Not wanting to disturb the festivities – but definitely not ready to head home either – Holly moved her into the living room, where she sat on the sofa. Immediately, Hope nestled into her shoulder. Hope cuddles really were the best cuddles in the world, even when Holly only had one functioning arm.

Sometimes, when Holly held her daughter, she found it impossible to believe where the time had gone. She was so big, and she wasn't going to stop growing. At some point, she would be too big to curl up on her chest, or worse still, might not even want to.

'We'll always cuddle, won't we, Hopey?' she asked, though she had only just finished speaking when the living room door creaked open.

'I'm not disturbing anything, am I?'

Giles stood in the doorway, holding a full glass of champagne.

'Of course not. Come in.'

She shifted in her seat so she was sitting more upright. When her eyes met Giles's, she couldn't help but smile.

'So, Giles Caverty, the hero of the story, again,' she said. 'You know this is almost becoming a theme.'

'I know, and it's such a shame. The villain always gets the better costume.'

Holly laughed out loud, but the sound was cut short when she noticed how intently Giles was staring at Hope. He had been there the first day she had born, ready to start a life with her. With both of them. And when she turned him down, on his boat in France, it hadn't just been the loss of Holly that had hurt him, but the loss of Hope too. The baby he had hoped to be some kind of father to. She never really realised that until that moment.

'Do you want to hold her?'

He opened his mouth, as if he was about to object, but instead he nodded ever so slightly.

'If you're sure she won't mind?'

'She won't mind. Come here, Hope.' Holly shuffled her daughter off her chest and onto her right arm, before she shifted around in the seat. 'I want you to meet your Uncle Giles.'

66

By the time they got home, Evan was drunk. It was, Holly realised, the first time she had seen him in such a state, though somehow it only made him more endearing. Unfortunately, it meant that she had had to push Hope back in the pushchair, single-handedly. Literally.

'You know I love you? I love everything about you.' His words slurred, and he swayed slightly while he walked.

'I know. You've told me quite a few times this evening,' Holly joked.

'But that's because I mean it!'

She had left Ben and Giles talking about the old times, when they had still been friends, and hopefully repairing one or two bridges.

'It's ridiculous, because I don't even know you that well. But I know that when I know you more, I'm just going to love you more.'

It was hard not to smile.

'You need an early night,' Holly said as she opened the door to the cottage. 'Somehow I don't think you'll be going for your 5 a.m. run tomorrow.'

'I will definitely be going for my run,' Evan insisted, as he knocked himself on the doorjamb not once, but twice. 'This is no good. We need a bigger house,' he moaned.

Holly laughed. 'I think doors are the same size in all houses.'

'No, that's not what I mean. I mean, you and me, we need a bigger house. What if we have more children? They can't all sleep in a room with Hope, can they?'

Holly's heart leapt, but she quashed the feeling almost as quickly as it had formed. Evan was drunk. People always said things they didn't mean when they were drunk. In the morning, most likely he'd have forgotten he'd even mentioned it.

'Right,' she said, when she reached the kitchen. 'I need something to eat. If I give you my phone, you can find the local Chinese takeaway. Order us a few dishes. I'll put Hope to bed.'

Holly opened the phone app and handed it to Evan. To her surprise, he began scrolling through the menu. Still, Holly seriously doubted he'd have ordered anything by the time she'd got Hope into bed.

Upstairs, she went to the bathroom and ran the bath, checking there were no cuddly bunnies on the floor as she placed Hope down beside her. After checking the temperature, and adding the baby-friendly bubble bath, she took her daughter into the bedroom and lay her down on the bed to undress her.

'Well, that was a lot of excitement today, wasn't it?' she said, unbuttoning the short-sleeved onesie. It was far harder to do with one arm out of action, but better that she tried on her own than have a drunken Evan helping her. 'Your Aunty Jamie and Uncle Fin are getting married, your daddy and Uncle Giles are friends again, and Mummy and Evan... Well... What do we think about Evan?'

Hope remained surprisingly still for Holly as she reached the last button, but rather than undoing it, Holly paused and looked her daughter in the eye.

'You do like him, don't you? He loves you. He really does, and he hasn't even spent that much time with you yet. But I think he's a good one, Hopey. I think we could have found ourselves a really good man here, who will take care of your mummy and make her happy. That'll be okay, won't it?' She paused. She may not have had anything to drink, but she was still feeling decidedly blurry-eyed and soppy. 'How do you think we ended up with so many good people in our lives, Hope? I know you don't know this yet, but you are such a lucky girl, because we are surrounded by love. We really are.'

As if responding, Hope reached up to her, and Holly, thinking her daughter was going to offer one of the strange opened-mouth kisses on the nose she had been giving recently, bent down.

Hope's moves were so swift, Holly barely saw it happen. One second Hope was looking at Holly, the next she had rolled over and grabbed a handful of paper from Holly's pocket.

'Hey, cheeky!' she said, scooping Hope up with one arm and laughing. 'Were you trying to pinch that? Well, you can't have it. That's important. That's for Mummy.'

As gently as she could, Holly prised the envelope out of Hope's hands. Her eyes lingered on her name. During all the excitement, she had forgotten that Maud had given her this. For a second, she contemplated opening it there and then, but she was in such a good mood, and her heart was the lightest she could remember in a long time. The last thing she wanted to do was to cast a shadow over that. Besides, whatever words Maud had written deserved her full attention, and there was no way she would get that until Hope was in bed. So, having taken the envelope, Holly placed it in the side drawer of her bed.

'Come on, bath time, you,' she said, picking up Hope and planting a large kiss on her belly.

* * *

When Hope was in bed, Holly headed downstairs to find Evan fast asleep on the sofa. His arm was slung over the side, his head tipped all the way back. She took the phone from him and placed it on the table before heading over to the kitchen. She only needed one hand to make scrambled eggs, after all, and there was no need to spend money on a takeaway when it was just her eating.

Aiming to stay quiet and not disturb him, she opened the lower cupboard where she kept her pans, only for everything to fall out with a clatter.

She jumped back in surprise.

'What! What happened?'

On the other side of the room, Evan was on his feet with a look of utter bemusement on his face, which quickly changed to fear.

'Holly? What happened? Are you okay?'

Holly shook her head, the shock of the sudden clattering replaced by confusion as she tried to understand why she now had dozens of kitchen utensils scattered around on the floor. Something didn't make sense. Everything fitted so neatly, normally. And there was always plenty of room. As she went to pick up the mess, her eyes fell on one particular item. Shiny, new looking, and very, very large. With her one hand on her hip, she turned around and faced Evan.

'Did you buy a new frying pan?'

As he looked at her, his bottom lip protruded ever so slightly, as if he was a sulky teenager.

'What can I say? I like my pancakes.'

Holly let out a sigh that turned involuntarily into a grin.

'Fine then. But as you're awake now, you're the one making the scrambled eggs.'

67

The week and a half before the wedding passed at an unprecedented pace, with everywhere Holly turned filled with a chaos of the best type. There were dress fittings, which for her included needing to find a way to fit her cast into her outfit, cake tastings, meetings with caterers – not to mention putting together the sweet platters which Jamie had asked Holly to do. Jamie, who hadn't thought she would be doing anything so last minute for the wedding, had several tiling and handyman jobs booked in that she didn't want to cancel and had sent various groups in her place. Caroline went with Fin to check out the caterers, while Holly accompanied the groom-to-be for a final check of the flowers, not to mention a supermarket run for all the champagne they were going to need for the day.

And most of the time, wherever Holly went, Evan was there too. Like an oversized, but very welcome, shadow. Holly had become accustomed to them spending their days together. Sometimes, she would come home from the shop and find him in the cottage, tapping away at his laptop or on a video call to an office on the other side of the world. But other times, he was playing with Hope.

Hope, it appeared, had taken to him even quicker than Holly, and while her parents had yet to forgive him entirely for the Vespa incident, progress had been made over a Sunday lunch when he brought a sweet potato dish he had made from scratch.

Their little family was as close to perfect as she could have hoped. There was just one issue: it couldn't last.

'I'm looking at my schedule for the next two months. I need to be in New York, then San Francisco, then I'm back in the UK for two weeks before I go to Dubai,' Evan said, looking at the calendar on his phone. 'Those are the ones I can't say no to.'

It was the evening before the wedding and, if they were sticking to the previous schedule Evan had given her, he was going to be leaving in forty-eight hours. Just the thought was enough to make Holly's heart ache.

'New York, San Francisco and...?'

Holly struggled to keep track of the places in her head. In the space of two months, Evan was going to visit more countries than she had done in her entire life.

'Dubai, but that's only for three nights. Nothing major.'

'Okay.'

She tried to sound casual, like nipping over to Dubai really was something casual, not the major event it would have been for her.

She wanted to see if Evan was going to say any more but he was back tapping away on his computer, every now and then stopping to swipe at his phone.

'I was thinking, when I get back, I can just come back here. There's no need for me to go to London other than for a couple of days. And I can get the train up easily enough.'

'Are you sure?' Holly said, trying to not sound too excited. It would make a huge difference to how much time they could spend together if he wasn't staying in London between travelling.

'Positive. Although maybe we could spend a couple of nights

there together? I'm sure Ben wouldn't mind. I've already said he and Georgia can use the apartment the next time they're planning a trip to the city.'

'You did?' Holly said.

Evan lifted his head from his computer, a look of concern on his face.

'Crap, I did it again, didn't I? Pushed myself into your life. You know, I'm sure he won't even ask about it. They never mentioned the double date again.'

'It's fine,' Holly said, standing up and planting a kiss on his lips. 'I like that you're friends with my friends.'

What she didn't like was the fact that a life with Evan meant not seeing him so much of the time, this lifestyle of grabbing a few days here and there, when they could. And it wasn't like the three of them could stay in the cottage long term. There was only just enough room for Evan and his giant suitcase. Holly could only imagine what it would be like if he wanted to move everything else in, too. Besides, she couldn't ask him to move in permanently, anyway. That would be ridiculous.

Since the time he had come back drunk, he hadn't mentioned anything more about their long-term future. Certainly not wanting extra children. And with the wedding and their imminent separation at the front of both their minds, it was hard to focus on anything else.

'Whilst we're discussing when I come back, Hols, there's something I want to talk to you about,' he said, only for Hope to let out a sudden squeal from her highchair. A second later, her plastic plate hit the ground, scattering the remains of her dinner on the floor.

'Okay, I'm coming, I'm coming.' Holly turned back to Evan and darted across to Hope, swallowing hard. Why did those words 'I want to talk,' fill her with so much dread? A thousand possibilities whirred through her head.

'Hey, you, what's going on?' Holly said, picking up the plate and the scraps of food. 'Are you ready for some fruit now?'

After tidying up the mess, she grabbed a banana from the fruit bowl and began to chop it up, keeping her back to Evan as she did so. Whatever serious conversation he wanted to have, she hoped she could delay it a little longer. After all, it wasn't like he'd bring up anything serious on Jamie's wedding day. Would he?

68

'Crap.' Evan spun around in the bedroom, knocking the lampshade that was hanging from the ceiling and sending the light fitting spinning for the second time in five minutes.

Holly had initially thought it would be easier to get ready at home, rather than at Jamie's. After all, Jamie already had a full house, as her mum was over, as well as Zahida and Naomi.

Besides, Holly needed to make sure Hope was suitably fed and ready with changes of clothes and snacks for the day. The real reason she had wanted to stay at the cottage, though, was to give her and Evan a little more time together before he left the following day. How someone could feel such a mixture of elation and sadness at the same time was a mystery to her. But that was the state she was in.

Unfortunately, the three of them trying to get ready in the same cramped space, with only one bathroom, was a disaster waiting to happen. Along with the light fitting taking a continual beating, Hope had immediately got lipstick on her first outfit, and while Holly was trying to find something else for her to wear, Evan was busy crawling on the floor.

'What are you doing?' she asked, trying to step over him.

'The button just popped off my cuff,' he said. 'Hold on, don't move. It's there.'

After reaching under the bed, he stood back up with the small, white button in his hand and frowned.

'I guess I have to sew it back on. Do you have a sewing kit?'

'It's fine,' Holly said, lifting Hope up with the one-handed manoeuvre she'd now mastered, and placing her on the bed. 'I've got a needle and thread here. I'll have it back on in a second. Give me the button and take your shirt off.'

Evan offered her a small smirk, only for Holly to raise her eyebrows in response. This wasn't the time.

As instructed, Evan stripped off his shirt and handed it to Holly, just in time to reach down and grab Hope before she tried to throw herself off the edge of the bed.

'Can you take her downstairs? I just need a bit of space to do this.'

With a wide grin, Evan looked at Hope.

'Come on, trouble. Let's give Mum a bit of space.'

When the room was empty, Holly took a moment and sat down on the edge of the bed. She wasn't going to let her sadness seep into Jamie's day. After all, it wasn't like it was permanent. Evan would be back in just over a fortnight, although he wouldn't be able to stay anywhere near as long this time. Hopefully, she could sort the shifts at the shop to make sure she had plenty of time with him. She could always get Drey back in, or hire another person for a couple of days, if that was what it took.

Pushing back the thoughts, she opened the drawer to the bedside table and shuffled a few items around in search of the small sewing kit she kept there.

It didn't take long to find, but the moment she moved to lift it up, a white envelope dropped from the edge of the drawer. Holly didn't move. Her hand remained poised to pick up the sewing kit, yet all she could look at was the envelope, now lying flat, with her name penned in beautiful, cursive writing staring up at her.

Somehow, she hadn't thought about the letter Maud had given her since she slipped it into the drawer over a week ago. But now that it was there in front of her, Holly wondered if that had been deliberate. Opening the envelope would mean admitting that Maud would soon be gone for good, and that was something that Holly didn't want to face. But then, Maud technically hadn't told her to wait till she had passed away to open the letter. Just until she wasn't in front of her. What if there was something Holly needed to read, to talk to Maud about before it was too late?

'Is everything okay?'

Holly turned around to find Evan looking at her from the doorway.

'Yes, yes.' She pushed the letter to the side and pulled the kit out instead. 'Here, let me get to that button of yours.'

'I just wanted to grab Hope's clothes. I figured I could get her dressed downstairs and give you a bit of space.'

'Thank you. Yes.' She handed him the dress while planting a long kiss on his lips.

'What was that for?' he asked, when they finally broke away.

'Just because.'

It took less than two minutes to sew the button back in place, and when Holly came back downstairs, Hope was dressed in her new, blue outfit, with the corresponding bunny in her hand.

'I packed the yellow one, too,' Evan said, with a nod to the nappy bag. 'Just in case she needs another outfit change.'

Holly nodded, but she didn't reply. Instead, she simply handed him his shirt.

'Hols.' Evan put Hope down on the floor beside him. 'I know

you've got a lot on your mind today, but there's something I really want to talk about before I go.'

A heat flooded through Holly's cheeks. It didn't matter how much she tried to push this conversation away, she knew she would have to face it eventually. She just wanted to put it off for as long as possible.

'Later. Can we talk later? I said to Jamie we'd be there at ten. It's already five to.'

Evan pressed his lips tightly together. Whatever he wanted to discuss, it was obviously more serious than Holly wanted to deal with, if he was refusing to let it go like this. Finally, he offered a small nod.

'Okay, we'll talk later. Let's get you in the car.' He lifted up Hope and carried her towards the door. 'You got everything?'

Holly was about to reply that yes, she had everything she needed, but she hesitated.

'Actually, can you just hang on for one second? There's something I need to do.'

Then before he could reply, she ran upstairs, grabbed the envelope from her drawer and slipped it into her handbag.

69

The first part of the day felt like a reunion, as Eddie, Tyler and Spencer, Zahida and Naomi all gathered together for the first time since they'd been in Evan's villa in France.

They had met at Giles's uncle's house, having been given free rein for the entire day, as the man himself was in South Africa. Giles, however, was very much present, and constantly rushing from room to room, constantly checking that Jamie was happy with everything – whether Jamie wanted him to or not.

'You and Evan look perfect together,' Zahida said, as she hugged Holly tightly. 'Such a gorgeous couple. And I hear he's been living with you.'

Holly winced at the words. 'It's just a temporary accommodation situation.'

'I'm sure it will become permanent soon enough. You both look smitten.'

'And I can't believe that Giles is here either!' Naomi added, joining in the conversation. 'Jamie said he organised almost everything.'

'He did,' Holly said.

She looked through the large bay windows. Outside, Giles was currently waving his hands irately to the small group of waitstaff he'd hired for cocktails after the ceremony, while simultaneously barking instructions at the florist. She didn't think she'd ever seen him look so flustered before.

'I thought the bride and groom weren't meant to see each other before the ceremony on the big day,' Naomi said, with a nod towards the doorway where Jamie and Fin were locked in a tight embrace.

'You can't possibly think the normal rules apply to those two,' Holly said. 'They did the hen and stag do together. They are going to want to be together for as much of their wedding day as possible.'

Holly scanned the scene. The high ceilings were decorated with gilded rosettes, while large oil portraits hung on the faded, rust-coloured wallpaper. At one end of the room was a large, marble fireplace, in front of which Ben and Michael were setting up a band. It wasn't what Jamie had envisioned, but somehow, Holly thought this might be better. All the guests had been told that anyone who could play an instrument was to bring it; that would be their music for the night. The cake was being made last minute by the bakery in the village and the chairs had been hired from the same village hall where Holly had held the charity fundraising night for the care home all those moons ago.

'Do you mind if I ask something?' Zahida said, bringing Holly back to the moment. 'You seem so sure about you and Evan, but surely you felt that way about Ben too? I mean, you had a child together. How do you know that this time is going to turn out any better?' As soon as she heard the words out of her mouth, Zahida looked horrified. 'I didn't mean... But you're not... That's not what I was saying at all.'

Holly smiled reassuringly. 'It's fine. I know what you mean. Honestly. I think the easiest way to explain it is, with Ben, I wanted to be the best version of myself. I wanted to show him I was a brilliant businesswoman, a fantastic cook, and a great person. Being around him made me want to be all those things, which is great, but it was exhausting. Being with Evan…' She looked across to where he was helping Ben set up the amp on speaker system. 'Evan helps me be the best version of myself. I don't have to try. He just brings it out in me. I could never get tired of that.'

'Wow, that's pretty deep,' Zahida said, eyes wide.

'Does it sound ridiculous?' Holly felt her cheeks colouring from embarrassment. After all, it felt like a pretty bold statement to make about someone she'd known for less than two months.

'No, no, not at all. That makes perfect sense. And I guess it's the same for him.'

It was a sweet thing to say, but doubt prickled in Holly's stomach.

'I really, really hope so.' She looked over to where Hope was currently with Caroline and the children playing. A sudden heat flooded over her.

'Sorry, I just need to head to the ladies' room. I won't be a minute.'

Without waiting for Zahida to reply, she walked away.

It took several moments until Holly found somewhere where she could be on her own, and even then it wasn't a bathroom, but a small drawing room. She didn't care. She just needed the quiet.

As she dropped onto the seat, she placed her handbag on her lap. The weight of the envelope within felt all the more present.

It didn't make sense to open it there. It didn't make sense to read Maud's final words to her on such a happy day, and forever taint it, but Holly knew she couldn't resist. Not until she had seen what the letter said. So, as carefully as she could, she pulled back the flap of the envelope, tugged out the piece of paper, and began to read.

70

'Where have you been? We're getting ready. People are starting to sit outside.'

Caroline bounded in with Hope in her arms, who immediately reached out for Holly.

'Are you okay?' Caroline asked, her face suddenly clouded by concern. 'You look... shellshocked.'

'I'm fine,' Holly said, forcing herself to smile.

'Hurry up!' Naomi's voice bellowed from the other room.

But while Holly rose to her feet, Caroline stayed exactly where she was.

'We ought to get going, as long as you're okay?' she said quietly.

'Yes, absolutely fine.'

Still, Caroline hovered just a second longer. 'It's not about Evan, is it? You two are okay, aren't you?'

'Yes. At least, I think so.'

'Phew, because I've got the sweepstake on a proposal before Christmas, and you know how I hate to lose to the others.'

At this, Holly had to laugh.

'You've got a sweepstake going on when he'll propose?'

'Yep. Come on, we'll talk about it later. Right now, we've got a wedding to attend.'

* * *

The ceremony was perfect. The sky was clear, and the vivid greens of the fields were even brighter than normal against a blazing blue sky that spanned out behind them. One of Fin's cousins, who happened to be a cellist, played while Jamie walked down the aisle, while a rock soundtrack accompanied them on the walk back.

And Jamie looked phenomenal.

Her white dress was the epitome of elegance and simplicity, while her hair was slicked back in an equally striking bun. Fin had opted for a dark-green suit that complemented the surroundings so well, it could have been as if they had chosen the venue from the start.

After the ceremony were drinks and canapés. And hugging, so much hugging, that Holly wished she had two working arms, because her right one was aching after only half an hour. At just before one, Wendy and Arthur came to pick up Hope, so that Holly could enjoy the meal with her friends.

But the whole time, the contents of the letter were burning away in the back of her mind.

Holly should've known it wouldn't be negative. Of course, Maud wouldn't have written anything in the slightest bit downbeat. That just wasn't who she was. And after reading her friend's final words, Holly hadn't been left feeling devastated or alone the way she had feared. Instead, it had left her with a sense of disbelief.

Despite Holly being seated next to Evan on the original seating plan for the day, the haphazard manner in which the event had come together meant that the table plan had gone entirely awry.

As Evan was best man, they decided it would be easier if he sat at the top table with Jamie's mum, while Holly found a place with Caroline and Michael, who had also passed their children on to the grandparents for the rest of the day.

As much fun as Holly had with her friends, her head was still lost in Maud's words. Trying to process what it all meant. In all the confusion, it was hard not to want to be with Evan. And to be solely with him. Still, Holly pushed thoughts of both Maud and Evan to the back of her mind. This was a day that came around once in a lifetime, and right now, Fin and Jamie needed him more than she did.

As such, it wasn't until Jamie and Fin had performed their first dance, and they invited other couples onto the dance floor to join them, that Holly finally had a chance to talk to Evan with some degree of privacy.

'I feel like I haven't seen you all day,' Evan said, as he wrapped his hands tightly around her.

'I know. I feel the same.'

For a second, Holly thought they were going to start dancing, but instead, a deep crease formed between Evan's brows.

'I know this probably isn't the best timing, but there's something I need to tell you. A couple of things, actually. Can we go outside? Talk properly?'

Around them, couples were holding each other close and swaying with the music – Ben and Georgia, Sandra and Eddie even. All looked completely lost in one another. And Holly wished she had that luxury, but Evan wasn't the only one who needed to say something. She had things of her own to say, too.

71

They headed outside, where the sun was sitting just above the horizon, casting the sky a pinkish hue. The chairs from the ceremony had all been packed away, but there were several hidden benches in the garden. Holly took a seat on one of those and, for a moment, she stared out at the rolling hills. Only when Evan cleared his throat did she turn to look at him.

He was looking unusually nervous.

'Okay, here goes,' he started, only for Holly to interrupt.

'I'm sorry. I know you want to talk to me, but I just want to let you know I've got something I need to talk to you about too,' she said, resting her hand on his knee. 'Something kind of important.'

Evan nodded as he bit down on his lip. 'Okay, the thing is, I know it's really ungentlemanly, but do you mind if I go first? Just I've been wanting to get this off my chest for quite a while. Although, if you need to tell me—'

Holly shook her head and smiled. 'It's fine. Mine can wait.'

With a passing look of relief, he momentarily closed his eyes and took a deep breath in.

'I've got a confession to make,' he started. 'A couple, actually.'

Fear flooded through Holly. Instantaneous and heated. Had he cheated on her? Was he already seeing someone else when they met? Had he just stayed with her until the wedding so he didn't ruin Jamie and Fin's big day? Those were the thoughts that rolled through her head until he finally spoke again.

'I don't like the fact that you live in your ex's house.'

'Oh,' Holly said, stunned by the unexpected route the conversation had taken. It took her a moment to find any more words. 'You know Giles isn't—'

'I know he's not technically your ex in a relationship sense,' Evan cut across her. 'And that you guys didn't date, but there was something there. Something that I think is still there for him. I mean, we know he didn't do all this for Jamie, did he?'

He paused as if he expected her to reply, but what could she say to that? Giles was her friend, one of her best friends. And she did love him as a friend, the same way she did with Caroline and Jamie. That was all it was. Still, as her pause lingered, Evan took her hand.

'And I know you don't feel the same way. I know you are all in with me. But that's how I feel. And it doesn't help that he's such a stand-up guy, too.'

Holly wanted to laugh. If she saw him later, she would have to tell Giles that Evan thought of him 'a stand-up guy'. He really was managing to shift his reputation.

'I get why you feel that way,' she said eventually. 'If it was the other way round, I probably wouldn't be too keen on the idea. In fact, I'd probably find it kind of crazy. But you know I said I wanted to talk to you—'

Once again, Evan interrupted her. This time with a hasty shaking of his head.

'Sorry, it's just you said I could speak first, and that was the first part. The mini confession before the big one.'

Holly's stomach lurched again. Being jealous of Giles didn't seem enough of a deal to warrant a serious talk outside.

'Okay, go on...' she said.

'You know the house we saw in Slaughter?' He looked at her expectantly, though Holly wasn't sure what he was talking about. After all, there were plenty of houses in Slaughter.

'Which house?'

'The one that was for sale?'

Holly's insides twisted. She was certain she knew where the conversation was going and she wasn't sure how she was supposed to react. Her jaw clenched involuntarily as Evan carried on talking. 'Well, it turns out it does have a bath. Two, actually. It's also got a big, walled garden, and the perfect view. Not to mention enough cupboards that we'd have room for my enormous shoes, and enormous suitcases, and everything else that I possess.'

'Evan, what did you do?' Holly said, nervousness filtering into her voice.

'I put an offer in on it.' His lips were twitching, as if he didn't know whether he should smile or grimace. 'I put an offer in and it was accepted. I wasn't sure it would be, but it was.'

Holly opened her mouth, though she didn't know what she intended to say. It didn't matter though; Evan hadn't stopped talking.

'I thought it was perfect for us. I still think it might be, but then I realised I was doing the same thing again. The same thing I always do when I get over-excited. I was making big gestures and not consulting you. I mean, it was a stupidly big gesture, right? Thinking I'd be able to choose a place where you'd want to live. And you'd hated Giles for doing almost exactly the same thing, so I realised what an idiot I'd been. So I pulled the offer.'

'You put an offer in on a house because you wanted us to live together and then withdrew it?' Holly said, trying to follow his babbling. 'Because you changed your mind? And that's what you wanted to tell me?'

'Yes. No! Sort of. I didn't know if I should tell you about the house, but I wanted to be honest with you. And I haven't changed my mind. Not about us living together. I still want that. If you do. But I went about it the wrong way and now I want to do it the right way. I want to get us a home. Somewhere here, in the Cotswolds or wherever you choose. I don't care, it's up to you. Whatever you want, you understand? So, what do you think to getting our forever home?'

His eyes were wide and unblinking, and only then did Holly realise how terrified he was. Terrified that this would be a step too far, that it would be the thing to send her running. She could see all that, and now it was her turn to take a deep breath in.

She wrapped her hand around his neck and looked into his eyes.

'I definitely do not want you to buy a house for us to live in, Evan,' she said.

72

Inside the manor, the music had kicked up a notch. The slow dances had obviously ended, and in its place, eighties rock music was filling the air.

But outside, Holly and Evan were surrounded by a deathly silence.

'No? No, no, of course not,' Evan said, pulling himself back into the moment. 'That makes sense. Of course, you wouldn't want to move in with me yet. I mean, that would be silly. It's just been temporary these last couple of weeks. And Hope needs more time to get used to me. It'll be fine. And I'm fine with you staying at Giles's place, really. It'll be fine.'

Holly pressed her lips tightly together, an internal chuckle escaping at the knowledge of how very sweet he was when he babbled. So sweet, her heart ached.

'Would you hold on a minute?' she said. 'It's my turn. I had something I wanted to talk to you about, remember?'

Swallowing visibly, Evan nodded.

'And what I want is for you to read something.'

From out of her bag, Holly pulled the letter and handed it to

Evan. He looked at her as she nodded encouragingly.

'Open it up, read what's inside.'

Slowly, as if it still might be some kind of trick, Evan pulled out the letter and unfolded it the same way Holly had, and read down the page. Just as Holly's had, his jaw fell open little by little.

Each passing moment made her heart beat faster and faster.

'Holly, this is...'

'Life changing?'

He nodded. 'I knew you two were close, but I didn't realise you were *this* close.'

The words were enough to churn up a knot of guilt within her.

'We used to be, for a long time. And then I drifted away. But I guess she and Agnes never forgot that.'

Evan looked again at the contents of the letter before turning to Holly.

'So what does this mean? What are you going to do?'

She pressed her lips tightly together. She hadn't really had that long to think about it, but she didn't need to. She knew from the moment she saw those words on the page, and the number written beneath, what she was going to do.

'I know I could pay off the mortgage on the sweet shop. There's more than enough to do that. It's probably the sensible thing to do, and it's definitely what Maud thought I'd do. But the sweet shop is doing so well that it'll sort itself out, and I've rather liked how I've stopped doing sensible things lately.'

'So, what does that mean?'

Holly reached out and took Evan's hand, wishing she could use both of hers to grasp his properly, but she couldn't, so she just had to make do as she looked up into his eyes.

'What you asked me a minute ago, I said no—'

'I know, because I rush things—'

'No, will you stop interrupting? I said no because that's not the way I want to do it. I don't want you to buy a house for us to live in and grow as a family. Whether I help choose it or not. That's not what I want. I want us to buy it together.'

Evan's eyes widened. 'You mean...'

'I mean, you need to ring your estate agent, or however it was you sorted out the house, and tell them we'll take a look at it together. And some others, while we're at it. And when we find the one we want, there are going to be two names on the deed.'

'Did I mention that I love you?' Evan said, before he planted his lips against hers.

Holly could have stayed there all night, kissing him until the stars filled the sky, and yet it felt like she had only just started when someone shouted at them.

'Hey, you two, what are you doing out here – secretly snogging?' Jamie was holding the train for her dress up so that you could see the trainers she was wearing beneath it. 'This is my wedding. You need to get inside and dance! Now!'

With a grin that stretched so wide, Holly's entire face ached, she looked back to Evan.

'I guess we'd better get inside then,' she said.

EPILOGUE

Growing up, Holly had believed there was an order to life. A way you were supposed to do things. Get a job, find a man, buy a house, get married, have a family. That was the route to happily ever after. Or so she'd thought.

So far, her route had gone nothing like that at all.

She'd had a job and left it. She'd taken over a business, had a baby, then found a man, and now, assuming everything went through the way she hoped it would, she was buying a house.

'So, what do you think?' Evan said, as they finished touring the cottage in Slaughter. The estate agent had been desperate to point out all the period features, from the fireplace to the original tiles. There was no denying it was beautiful. A perfect blend of modern and traditional, with a sleek, white kitchen and rolltop bath, combined with low ceilings and wooden beams throughout. It was the type of house she could imagine seeing in a double page feature spread of *Country Life* magazine. But was it the type of place where she could see herself baking away in the kitchen or painting with Hope on the dining room table?

'It feels like a show home,' Holly replied to Evan's question.

'Why do I get the feeling that's not a good thing?' he said.

She shrugged. 'I know it would be different when we've got all our things in here, but I feel like I'd be worried about messing things up. Scratching the worktops. Breaking the tiles. And I can only imagine the stress if Hope spilled something on the floor.'

'So we keep looking,' Evan said. 'This is our home we're talking about, and we're not going to buy something unless it's perfect.'

It was a tall order. *The perfect home*, but Holly then considered, she'd already got the perfect job, daughter, man, and – as cheesy as it sounded – the perfect life in general.

Evan was right; one day, they would have it all and she couldn't wait.

ACKNOWLEDGEMENTS

Holly Berry has come a long way since those early days starting over in Bourton-on-the-Water and I have loved taking her on this journey. However, even more than that, I have loved taking readers on the journey with us and am so grateful for all of you that are still here, seeing Holly finally get the love and life she deserves.

Of course, I am not alone in creating Holly's world and there are several people I would like to thank.

My heartfelt thanks go to Nina, who is the very reason this story exists. If she had not taken a chance on a young schoolgirl, trying to secure her first holiday job, then I would never have had all those wonderful years, bagging up sweets, laughing with customers, and falling in love with the sweet shop over and over again. There are not enough words to express the gratitude.

To Emily, my editor. This last year working with you has been an absolute dream. You bring out the best in all my stories and I'm so grateful for everything you've done to make me a better writer. The entire team at Boldwood is such a fantastic and supportive group of people and I feel so lucky to be with you.

To my family and friends who support me constantly, thank you. John, Ana, Magdalen, Lucy, Kath. Your belief in me is one of the reasons I am here. In that same vein, I would definitely not be here without Jake. My writing career has always been a team effort and he works tirelessly behind the scenes. Thank you for all you do.

Lastly, to my readers. I would not be able to keep writing these books if not for you, and am eternally grateful for all the support you offer me. Thank you.

ABOUT THE AUTHOR

Hannah Lynn is the author of over twenty books spanning several genres. As well as signing a new romantic fiction series, Boldwood is republishing her bestselling Sweet Shop series inspired by her Cotswolds childhood.

Sign up to Hannah Lynn's mailing list here for news, competitions and updates on future books.

Visit Hannah's website: www.hannahlynnauthor.com

Follow Hannah on social media:

facebook.com/hannahlynnauthor
instagram.com/hannahlynnwrites
tiktok.com/@hannah.lynn.romcoms
bookbub.com/authors/hannah-lynn

ALSO BY HANNAH LYNN

The Holly Berry Sweet Shop Series

Second Chances at the Cotswold Candy Store

Love Blooms at the Cotswold Candy Store

Family Ties at the Cotswolds Candy Store

High Hopes at the Cotswolds Candy Store

Sunny Days at the Cotswolds Candy Store

A Summer Wedding at the Cotswolds Candy Store

The Wildflower Lock Series

New Beginnings at Wildflower Lock

Coffee and Cake at Wildflower Lock

www.ingramcontent.com/pod-product-compliance
Ingram Content Group UK Ltd.
Pitfield, Milton Keynes, MK11 3LW, UK
UKHW012250290726
14090UKWH00016B/573

9 781836 031673